W9-CZW-090

THE CONSTELLATIONS

THE CONSTELLATIONS

A NOVEL

JAMES FINNEY BOYLAN

RANDOM HOUSE

NEW YORK

Library of Congress Cataloging-in-Publication Data
Boylan, James.
The constellations / James Finney Boylan.
p. cm.
ISBN 0-679-43021-0
1. City and town life—Pennsylvania—Centralia—Fiction. 2. Mine
fires—Pennsylvania—Centralia—Fiction. 3. Centralia (Pa.)—Fiction. I. Title.
PS3552.0914C66 1994
813′.54—dc20 94-10180

Design by Tanya M. Pérez

Manufactured in the United States of America
2 4 6 8 9 7 5 3
First Edition

for my mother, who never vanished

They have no doubt wondered, time and again, about the decades-old story often repeated in Centralia, the one about the priest and the roving labor gang called the Molly Maguires. Legend has it that the priest once denounced the Mollys from his pulpit. Later, as he prayed in the cemetery, the angry Mollys returned and beat him. The priest managed to stagger back to the church, where he summoned all his parishioners by ringing the church bell. When they arrived, he told them this: From that day forth, there would be a curse on the town of Centralia.

The little mining town, founded on a bed of coal, would burn forever.

—Renée Jacobs,
Slow Burn

CONTENTS

*

SUMMER STARS

THE VIRGIN

The Virgin is most easily spotted just after sunset.
Her chief star is the bluish, heart-shaped Spica,
which is often obscured.

After her father's unfortunate second marriage, Phoebe Harrison moved out of his house in Valley Forge and set up camp with her unsound Uncle Pat. He claimed to suffer from something he called "sour stomach," but there was a lot more to it than heartburn. On occasion the acid inside of him encouraged Uncle Pat to see the vague outlines of things that would have been better off invisible. Sometimes men in tuxedos came to visit him, for instance, asking him to go away with them and conduct their orchestras. They showed him staffs of music written not in notes but in the stars of the summer sky.

On Valentine's Day, a six-foot-long falling icicle had punctured the roof of the Coal Country Motel, on the outskirts of what had once been the town of Centralia, surprising the motel's owners as well as a couple named Feeney, who were not married, at least not to each other. Then the skies began to rain, and continued to rain, off and on, for weeks. In Columbia County, great gushing floods swelled the lakes and streams with brown water. The Catawissa River overflowed its banks, washing away a bakery and the Mister Formal Shop.

Uncle Pat, from the depths of his indigestion, looked out the window and saw the tuxedos and the cake tins floating downstream.

"You see?" he said sadly. "Jesus. There's no way I can get married now."

This last statement came as a kind of an insult to Phoebe's Aunt Clara, who was, in fact, already married to Uncle Pat, not that she was particularly happy about it. They had met six years ago, in the hospital, back when Aunt Clara had been Pat's nurse. Whatever affection had been between them, however, had cooled. Clara only seemed to like Pat when he was on his back, licking applesauce from a tiny Tony-the-Tiger spoon.

"That's your problem," she said to her husband. "There's more to marriage than cake. A lot."

A few months later, Phoebe went to her room and put on clothes the color of night, then lied to her uncle about her destination. By the time the stars came out, Phoebe and her evil friend, Dominique Bolero-Jones, were riding around in some guy's car, heading toward a tattoo parlor.

It was late June, and ninth grade was just a memory now. Tenth grade was still too far away to worry about. It wouldn't be that bad. About the worst thing they could do to Phoebe was to force her to calculate the circumference of trapezoids and rhombuses. Geometry wasn't the kind of thing that would keep you awake nights, at least not on a night like this, when the fireflies were out, darting through the smoke from the mine fire, approaching Centralia.

"I know what I'm gonna get," said the young man behind the wheel, driving on the wrong side of the road. "You want to know what I'm gonna get. I can tell you."

"What, Duard?" Dominique said, turning around to roll her eyes at Phoebe, who was sitting in the backseat.

"I'm gonna get me one a them aardwolf deals. You think I won't? You're wrong."

Dominique reached into her leopard-skin purse and pulled out a bottle of Southern Comfort. She bit down on the cap and spun the bottle around with one hand, then spat the top at Duard's face with a noise that sounded like *phuh*. The cap bounced off Duard's nose and fell onto his cigarette, which then plummeted onto his pants and lay there, burning, in his lap. Duard did not seem to be particularly affected by the fact that he was now aflame.

"Out of *control!*" he said.

Dominique looked back at Phoebe again and smiled with an affectionate expression that said, *He's a lot like an orangutan isn't he,* which was kind of a funny thing to think about the person who was supposed to be your boyfriend. Dominique's smile was missing several of its teeth, on account of Dominique having used her incisors to open a can of motor oil when she was eleven.

"Yo, Phoebe," Dominique said, handing the bottle in her direction. "Ya want a swig or what?"

Phoebe took the bottle and kicked back a good snort of Southern Comfort, which tasted like medicine for some benevolent but terminal disease. It made her whole body vibrate, as if she were an oversized gong that had just been rung with a mallet. Outside Phoebe watched the houses of Buchanan fading away. Soon they would be in Centralia, where she had lived until she was fourteen. By now there wasn't much left there, except for the cranes and bulldozers belonging to the Department of the Interior. Thirty years after the fact, they were still trying to put out the mine fire that had started in 1962. At this point, Phoebe didn't think it mattered much whether the fire in the coal mines of Centralia was extinguished or not. The small, pretty town she'd grown up in had already ceased to exist years ago.

Smoke from the mine fire surrounded the car, enveloping Phoebe and Dominique and Duard in a dense white mist.

"You smell something?" Duard said, as his pants burned slowly.
"I smell something."

Dominique shook her head. "You're on fire, Duard," she said.

Duard smiled. "Yeah, right," he said. "Very funny."

"You are," Dominique said. "I'm not kidding."

"Shut up," Duard said.

"Hey, Duard?" Phoebe said.

"What? Did you ask me something? You did."

"What's an aardwolf?"

"You mean you don't know?" Duard said. He looked over at
Dominique. "She don't know," he said, incredulous.

"You really are on fire," Dominique said. "I'm not kidding, asshole. You are. Go on. Look."

"Shut up," Duard said. He looked into the rearview mirror at
Phoebe, who he thought was a lot cuter than his actual girlfriend. She
was twisted halfway around in her seat, looking out the back window
at Centralia. Phoebe had big hair, same as Dominique. They had
spent almost forty-five minutes in the bathroom together coating it
with gel and hair spray to make it that big. The sides were all feathered out, and the top curled upward with a shameless antigravity.
Phoebe had a few freckles on her nose and her cheeks, and a pair of
emerald earrings. The earrings had been given to her by Uncle Pat
and Aunt Clara, who were rumored to have a million dollars hidden
inside a suit of armor in their basement. Uncle Pat owned a restaurant equipment business that sold all the meat slicers and walk-in re-
frigerators to the casinos in Atlantic City.

"I seen it on this poster. It's like a hyena that eats bacon and
toast. If I owned one, what would I name it? Bitey, probably. Either
Bitey or Waffles. Does it have fangs? I hope so. It's awesome. You
think it isn't? You're wrong."

"I didn't say it wasn't."

"Yeah, well good." He picked his nose. "Out of control!"

"Duard," Dominique said. "Your pants are on fire. I'm not goddamn kidding. Would you look at your pants? Your cigarette fell in your lap. That's what's making the car smell like burnt goddamn plastic."

Duard shook his head again. "Nice try, Dominique," he said. He reached toward Phoebe and took the Southern Comfort from her.

"My pants aren't plastic," he said, conclusively.

"Phoebe, will you tell him his pants are on fire?"

"They are," Phoebe said, knowing he would not be convinced. Duard would keep burning for years now, probably. In a way he was like the Centralia mine fire, only with more hair.

"You guys," said Duard, whose name rhymed with *Seward*. He blew his horn at an elderly woman riding a unicycle near the curb. He shook his head. "Goddamn old bitch," he said. "What does she, own the road? I don't think so!"

If you thought about it, Dominique was an unlikely person for Phoebe to have as a friend. She was two years older than everyone else in their class, on account of some still-unspecified scandal. Dominique did not appear to have spent her time off in an especially productive manner. She had a broken heart tattooed on her left breast, and underneath it her name: DOMYNYQUE. Dominique also liked to wear panty hose that were so ripped up there was more rip to them than hose. She wore a black leather jacket with the name of a motorcycle gang on the back of it: THE VISIGOTHS. Dominique did not have a motorcycle, but for the moment at any rate she had Duard, who owned this 1975 Dodge Swinger. Dominique had lost her license two years ago, when she drove her father's car into the loading dock of the Stroehmann's pretzel warehouse.

Until recently Phoebe had been an A student. She had only started being better friends with Dominique this spring, a year after she'd moved out of her father's house and into Uncle Pat's. In March, Phoebe even had her hair done like Dominique's, and in the final marking period her grades had started to drop, although Phoebe didn't think that was solely on account of hair spray. If anyone was to blame it was her father, Wedley, who ought to have thought twice before he moved to the Main Line and married Vicki Ambrasino, who weighed ninety-nine pounds and owned a little dog named Schnoodle, who liked to eat human hair. Once, eight years ago, Vicki had been the lover of Duard's older brother, Dwayne, back when Phoebe and her family lived next door, in Centralia. Things hadn't worked out.

Phoebe wasn't quite sure what she was going to do once they got to the studio, other than not get a tattoo. She had kind of been forced into this situation by Dominique, who said she was going to get another tat tonight, and wasn't it time Phoebe finally got her first one? "I mean after all," Dominique had said. "You wanna be a virgin your whole life?" Phoebe had been telling Dominique for some time how cool she thought the broken heart on Dominique's breast was. And in fact, she did think it looked cool, but that was because it was on Dominique's breast and not her own. Now, though, Dominique had raised the ante: if Phoebe were really as evil as she had been pretending to be for the last several months, she was going to have to get her breast tattooed. It had been impossible to say no to her. Now Phoebe was en route to the tattoo parlor, trapped in the backseat of the Swinger, as Duard drove down the wrong side of the street with his pants on fire.

The problem was that there wasn't any alternative to having Dominique as a friend unless Phoebe wanted to take a giant step back in time and hang out with Elaine Voron again, which in the world of New Buchanan High would have been equivalent to drinking molten lava. Elaine had been Phoebe's best friend until eighth grade; they used to go horseback riding together. Now, though, the only people that hung out with Elaine were the terminal cases like Kathy Glurtz, who had to wear a night brace on her teeth during the daytime. Puberty had, for some unknown reason, passed those girls by. They were fifteen years old now, but they still brought their lunches to school in little plastic lunch boxes with pictures of Barbies and ponies on the

outside. It was eerie. The cool girls, of whom Dominique was unques-
tionably the Czarina, spent most of their lunches trying to invent
methods of torturing them. The easiest way was to simply do something to their thermoses, like put liverwurst in them when they
weren't looking, which was most of the time. You could divert their
attention with as little effort as it took to say, *Look over there, I think
that's Madonna in the chocolate-milk line. Wonder what she's doing here.
Needs some chocolate milk I guess.*

There was another annoying aspect to Elaine, a weird predisposi-
tion to static electricity that had started when her parents got divorced. Whenever she was depressed, Elaine got huge shocks from
things, and not just metal either. Phoebe had seen Elaine get tremendous, unexpected jolts of current from chocolate cake. It was irritat-
ing. Just being in the same room with Elaine made Phoebe feel as if
she had left this world and entered another, some loveless universe
where even little dogs and cats weighed seven hundred tons.

When she hung out with Elaine, Phoebe's nickname had been
Icky. It was short for Ichabod, as in Ichabod Crane. They had called
Phoebe that because she was ridiculously tall and skinny for a ninth
grader. She already towered over all the other girls in her class, and
most of the boys. That was another reason she had started hanging
out with Dominique. Ever since she started having big hair and wearing leather and torn-up stockings, no one called her Icky anymore.

"Yaaaaahhhh!" Duard yelled suddenly. He jammed on the
brakes and the Swinger skidded to a halt. He opened his door and
leaped out onto the road, still yelling. Duard quickly grabbed his belt
buckle and his fly and pulled his pants down and started hopping all
over the sidewalk. Dominique turned around to Phoebe, handed her
the Southern Comfort, and said, "So: what do you think of him?"

Phoebe looked out the window. Duard was now lying on his back,
pulling his pants off over his shoes. Gray smoke was puffing from his
clothes.

"He's cute," Phoebe said.

"Do you think so?" Dominique said. "Really?"

"Yeah," Phoebe said. "He's awesome."

"I think he's funny," Dominique said.

"You're right," Phoebe said. "He is."

Dominique rolled down the window. "Hey come on, Duard. Stop messing around."

"Yow!" Duard said. "Yo, bitch, like my pants are fucking on *fire*. Why didn't you say something?"

"I did, shithead," Dominique said. "You weren't listening."

"Hand me the Comfort, would ya?"

"The what?"

"The 'Fort," Duard said. "Hurry."

Dominique looked at Phoebe, then shrugged. She took the bottle of Southern Comfort, then opened the car door and walked over to him. Phoebe opened her door and watched Duard billow. She wondered if she could maybe make a run for it while Duard and Dominique were distracted. But they had stopped the car in front of the Odd Fellows' graveyard, and Phoebe did not like the looks of it. Creepy bent trees surrounded the perimeter, as well as a broken-down iron fence. It was in a garbage dump right at the corner of this cemetery that the Centralia fire had first begun.

Duard reached for the bottle of Southern Comfort and poured it onto the burning part of his pants. There was a damp, sugary sizzle.

Phoebe looked up into a sky filled with stars. There was something about them that filled her with a sense of wonder and pity. It wasn't fair for things that distant to be impossible.

"Hey," Dominique said, gazing toward the street. "What the hell is that?"

Duard and Phoebe followed her gaze. "What?" Duard said.

"There. In the drain. What is that?"

A lumpy, crenellated blob sat by the curb. Its gray, ovoid surface was twisted with soft, unexpected wrinkles.

"Duh," Duard said. "Like, maybe it's somebody's brains. President Kennedy maybe. Did you ever hear that thing how they stole Kennedy's brains out of this safe or something where they had it frozen? Maybe like the guy that swiped it finally got grossed out and like, threw it out the window of his car. Do you think that's possible? I do. I mean like, if it was me who still had it after all this time I wouldn't want it. Am I the one that has it, though? Fuck no. I'm just saying."

"Shut up," Dominique said. "Don't say shit like that. Just don't."

They walked closer to the curb, and gathered around the blob. The three of them stood there for a moment, looking at it, as the stars glowed over their heads.

"Whoa," Duard said. "Like, it *is* somebody's brain."

"It's fake," said Phoebe.

"What's it doing here?" Dominique said. She sounded upset. Phoebe looked at her, and saw tears gathering in Dominique's eyes. Dominique raised both hands to her mouth as if to stifle a scream.

"It's not President Kennedy's," Duard said, trying to sound scientific. "You can tell that much." His voice took on an air of sadness. "Anyway it would have a hole in it."

"Maybe it's that Eisenhower's brain. Or Reagan."

"Naw," Duard said. "No one froze theirs."

"You don't know."

"Yuh-huh."

"Nuh-uh."

"Yuh-huh."

"How did it get loose?" Dominique said, in anguish. "Why would someone just leave their brain lying around, at *random*?"

"Maybe they're hiding it," Duard said. "Maybe they wanted not to have a brain for a while and so like they left it here and they'll come back."

"This is so wrong!" Dominique said.

Duard bent over to pick it up. "I bet it *is* plastic."

"Don't touch it!" Dominique screamed. "Jesus, Duard! What is wrong with you! I mean, gross me out raw!"

At the top of the hill, a pair of headlights stabbed through the smoke and mist. A cop car drove toward them, and slowed.

"Shit," Dominique said. "Shit, shit, shit. We are screwed!"

"Why are we screwed?" Phoebe said. "It's not our brain. We don't have anything to do with it!"

"It's plastic," Duard said. "You think it isn't? You're wrong."

"Oh, yeah, like they're going to believe it's not our brain," Dominique said. "We just happened to pull over and find it here. I am so sure!"

The cop car stopped behind the Swinger. Officer Calcagno rolled down his window and shone a flashlight on the teenagers.

Duard, Dominique, and Phoebe turned toward him, hands at their sides, forming a kind of human wall between Calcagno and the brain. Duard wasn't wearing any pants.

"Hey, you kids," Calcagno said. "What's going on here?"

"Nothing," Dominique said.

"Nothing?" Calcagno said. He flashed his light from face to face.

"My pants caught on fire," Duard said. "That's why I'm not wearing any."

Phoebe suddenly found a laugh building in her throat. It was terrible, but there was no way to suppress it. She struggled to keep herself from smiling idiotically.

"Hey, you, you think that's funny?" Calcagno said, shining his light on her. "Do you?"

Phoebe shook her head. Now that he had his light in her face, it wasn't funny anymore. "No, sir."

"That's Phoebe Harrison," Calcagno said. "Isn't it?"

"Yes, sir," Phoebe said. She knew Officer Calcagno from way back. He had once attempted to rescue Phoebe and her father, Wedley, in 1984, when this guy who called himself the Outcast had held them hostage in an abandoned high school. He hadn't succeeded.

Calcagno looked at her for some time, shining his light on her, not saying anything. Finally, he said, in a different voice, "What'd you

do to your hair? You look like that woman. What's her name, the one
I mean?"

"I don't know."

"Sure you do. That vampire girl who sells beer and junk."

"I'm not her," Phoebe explained.

"Yeah, well, I know that, you think I don't know that? The difference between you and somebody else?"

Officer Calcagno let out a long sigh, wiped some sweat from his
forehead. "Jeez, Phoebe, I remember when you were only this tall."
Since he had his flashlight in her face, Phoebe couldn't see how big
she had been when he remembered. "Your uncle know you're out
here by the side of the road with this fella who doesn't have any
pants?"

"No, sir," Phoebe said.

"Well, does he?" Calcagno said again. This was annoying, as
Phoebe had just answered his stupid question.

"They caught on fire," Duard explained, creeping over to the
place where his pants were, and stepping into them slowly. "That's
why I stopped. I was afraid I was going to get burned. How much
longer could I have kept them on? Not much."

"I don't know," Calcagno said, snapping off his light. He opened
up the door of his car and put his hat on. "I think I want to see some
IDs on the rest of yuz. And some registration and maybe a driver's
license and all the paperwork on your jalopy here. This thing's a men-
ace, you know that? Which one a you is driving?"

Duard, still hopping around with one leg in his pants, cleared his
throat. A large portion of the crotch of his pants was missing, and the
area around it was damp with Southern Comfort. All things considered it was a good thing Duard was wearing underpants, even if they
were covered with pictures of the Flintstones.

"I am," Duard said.

At that moment, something swooped down over their heads.
There was a large winged creature with grasping, handlike talons cir-

cling above them. The claws looked yellow in the starlight. Phoebe remembered a creature they had learned about in school—the griffin, which was half lion and half eagle. The only problem was that it was mythological, which was pretty much the problem with everything.

"Son of a bitch," Calcagno said, in wonder. "Will you look at that." He took off his hat and held it at his hip. With his other hand he pulled a handkerchief out of his pocket, mopped some sweat off his brow. "What is that, an owl?"

All four of them stared at the thing that soared above them. Hey you, Phoebe suddenly thought. Swoop down and take me. That would be so fine, if only the huge soaring thing would carry me off. Why should that have to be so impossible? Why is it so unthinkable that I could ever leave the ground?

The thing shuddered, screamed, and ascended into the stars.

"Wait," Calcagno said softly. "Elizabeth. I'm still here."

There was a long pause as Calcagno realized, to his humiliation, that he had spoken out loud. Phoebe thought to herself: Who's Elizabeth? An ex-lover? His mother? It was hard to be sure. Was it possible that Calcagno was on personal terms with an owl? How could you tell if an owl was a woman, anyway?

Calcagno cleared this throat. "Someone I used to know," he said, softly. The three teenagers were still staring at the night sky above them.

The officer put his hat back on. Something had happened. Now it looked as if he was going to let them go. The shared brush with the inscrutable that the swooping thing had provided was enough for Calcagno. Anyway, he didn't want these kids to go tearing around town telling their beatnik friends that a member of the police force talked to owls, or that he spoke to them with a soft voice full of sorrow and regret. For better or worse, Calcagno, Phoebe, Dominique, and Duard were all now members of the same unpleasant society.

"Well now listen," he said. "You kids be careful. I don't want any horsing around. Especially you, Phoebe Harrison. You get into any *fizzamuhtenten,* your uncle's going to hear about it. Understand?''

Phoebe nodded her head yes, even though she wasn't sure what *fizzamuhtenten* was. It was stuff Officer Calcagno wanted to keep you away from, was the important thing.

"All right," Calcagno said, and drove off. They watched the red taillights of the cruiser move down the hill toward Ashland.

Dominique, Phoebe, and Duard stood there for some time, until the lights had vanished. Then they looked at each other.

"You look like that woman, Phoebe Harrison," Dominique said, imitating Officer Calcagno. "What's her name, the one that sells beer and shit?"

"Elizabeth," Duard said. "Come back! Like he talked to that thing like it was his friend! Do I understand it? No way!"

They all started laughing. Adults were never so hilarious as when they were attempting to be serious. Calcagno's display of mercy had been all the more hysterical since Duard didn't actually have any registration or insurance for the Swinger. Dominique and Duard and Phoebe laughed uproariously, tears rolling out of their eyes. Duard clutched onto the side of the Swinger to steady himself. They laughed and laughed and laughed and then they each slowly remembered about the brain they had found and then they stopped laughing and looked nervously at the curb. Dominique sighed loudly. Duard cleared his throat. It was still there.

The three teenagers stood around the brain, crestfallen.

"Maybe we should have told Calcagno about it," Phoebe said.

"Oh yeah, right," Dominique said. "They'd slap me back in Skagville so fast it'd make your head spin."

Skagville was the name of a penitentiary north of Mt. Carmel. They had a large juvenile unit, where they sent you if you were too good for prison but not bad enough for high school.

Phoebe looked at Dominique. "I didn't know you were in Skagville, Dominique," she said.

Dominique blushed. Phoebe saw that she hadn't meant to admit it. This was what Dominique had been up to in the time she had "taken off" from school.

"Yeah, well," Dominique said. "There's a lot people don't know."

Duard was scratching his head. "There's no reason you should have to go back to jail," he said. "It's not *your* fuckin' brain!"

"Oh, yeah, like anybody's going to believe me," Dominique said. "I am so sure!"

"I don't mind," Phoebe said. "It doesn't make any difference to me that you were there, Dominique. In Skagville."

"Well," Dominique said. "It should." Phoebe looked hard at her friend. Beneath all that makeup and the radiance of her enormous hair, Dominique looked ashamed. For the first time Phoebe thought she looked like her real age, like a teenager. Only five years ago she had looked pretty much like Elaine Voron, sitting there in the lunch-room pouring chocolate milk out of a plaid thermos, eating peanut butter and grape jelly sandwiches in which the jelly had seeped through the bread. It wasn't really that big a leap from there to here.

"It was when I smashed my father's car," Dominique said, blushing. "They said I was aiming it, at old Grandpa Stroehmann. Like I could care if he lives or dies, I mean, really!"

"Let's get out of here," Phoebe said. "Let's go home."

Duard squatted down and picked up a stick. "Wait a minute. Lemme poke this brain first."

"Leave it *alone*, Duard," Dominique snapped.

"All I'm gonna do is poke it," he said.

"Jesus! I'm so tired of hearing about this goddamn *brain* all the time!"

"I want to poke it," Duard said, poking it.

"I'm not kidding!" Dominique said. "I'm getting sick and tired of it! I mean, it's like all anybody can goddamn talk about! There's more important stuff than that brain in life!"

"Hey," Duard said. He bent over and picked it up.

Dominique screamed. "Put it down!" she yelled.

Duard raised it to his nose.

"What are you doing?" Phoebe said. "Duard?"

Duard sniffed. "Chocolate," he said.

"Chocolate?" Phoebe and Dominique said. "It's like, a chocolate brain?"

He licked it.

Everything was very quiet. There was a soft lapping sound as Duard's tongue ticked against the brain's crenellations.

"Uh-oh," Duard said, lowering the brain.

"What do you mean?" Dominique said, looking at Duard, then looking at the brain, then looking at Duard again. "What's 'uh-oh'?"

Duard looked sad. He shook his head. A long time seemed to pass.

"Duard," Dominique said again. "Please. Tell me."

"Tell you what?" Duard whispered. "Tell you what, Dominique?"

"Duard," Dominique whispered back, urgently. "What's 'uh-oh'?"

Duard shrugged mournfully. "It's not chocolate," he said.

From overhead there came a vicious *hooooo*. There in the night sky was the silhouette of those beating wings, the grasping talons. Phoebe stared at the distant stars.

"Duard," Dominique whispered. "What is it? If it's not chocolate?"

"I don't know," Duard said. "What am I? Some scientist?"

"Is it marble? Plaster of Paris?"

Duard shrugged. "Naw."

"Plastic?"

"Naw."

"Rubber?"

"Latex," Duard said. He held the brain up for the girls to see. "Somebody made it."

"Somebody made it?" Phoebe said. "Then left it here?"

Dominique was still looking at Duard, and the brain, with great regret. "Go on," Phoebe said. "Don't you want to touch it?"

"I—I don't know," Dominique said. "I'm not sure."

"Here," Duard said, handing it to her. "It's yours. I want you to have it."

Dominique put her hands out to accept the brain, and Duard placed it gently in her palms. The brain looked strange with Dominique's long black fingernails around it. "But, Duard," she said. "It doesn't belong to us."

"Sure it does, Dominique," he said. "Now it's yours."

Dominique stood there holding the brain for some time. Then she seemed to soften. Phoebe thought she saw tears in her eyes.

"Oh, Duard," she said. "This is the nicest thing anybody ever gave to me."

"Aw, Dominique," Duard said.

"Aw, Duard," Dominique said.

They wrapped their arms around each other, Dominique still holding the brain in one hand.

"Domineeky," said Duard. "Neeky, Neeky, Neeky."

"Duard," Dominique said. "My only Duard."

Phoebe leaned against the side of the car. This was going to take longer than she thought.

As she waited for Duard and Dominique to stop sucking each other's faces, she tried once more to devise a scheme for avoiding the impending tattoo. Again and again she saw the face of Uncle Pat, filled with disappointment. She did not want to hurt her uncle, who was not a happy man in the first place. The last couple of days had been particularly rough on Pat because he had had to put up with a couple of Aunt Clara's friends, a former professor of hers named Quentin Smuggs and his strange daughter, Isabelle. The Smuggses had come up to stay for what Phoebe thought was only going to be a couple of hours on Thursday afternoon, but here it was Friday and they still showed no signs of leaving. You could tell Pat hated Quentin Smuggs. Every time the man entered the room, Uncle Pat assumed this pained, diseased look, which was reminiscent of his expression during his long periods of indigestion. Phoebe didn't blame him. There was something about Professor Smuggs, who taught something called *postcontemporary narratology*, that gave her a pretty good idea what "sour stomach" was like.

Phoebe looked out across the dark Odd Fellows' Cemetery. On a hill somewhere in this graveyard were the bones of her grandparents Rebecca and James Flinch. When they died the family had bought an enormous plot and put up a stone with everyone's name on it, even Phoebe's. On a large marble slab were the names of her grandparents, her father, her mother, her sister, herself, followed by the dates of their births. Phoebe wondered if the dates of their deaths would ever be inscribed here. At this point it didn't seem as if anyone would ever return to Centralia, even to get buried. Her father, Wedley, had moved to the Main Line, near Philadelphia, with Vicki. And her mother and sister hadn't been heard of in years. Phoebe's mother had left the family when her daughter was only six years old; Phoebe's older sister, Demmie, had disappeared eight years ago, in 1984, driving off in her father's Datsun. She would be twenty-five years old by now, wherever she was.

Phoebe frequently wondered about her missing mother and sister, imagining the lives they might be living. Sometimes Phoebe pictured them living together somewhere, maybe in a great white hotel by the ocean. They slept late and ordered waffles from room service and ate breakfast on a tall balcony, overlooking the sea. In the afternoon they got rubdowns from men who spoke Belgian. The men looked like that guy who was famous for posing on the front cover of romance novels. Fabritzio, his name was, like a kind of dancing midget from Iceland. The capital, Reykjavik, was where Reagan and

Gorbachev almost decided to completely destroy all the nuclear weapons in the universe, but then at the last moment they thought about it a second time and said, *Nah. Let's keep 'em.*

But what about me?, Phoebe thought, still looking out through the tombs and headstones. That's all great that you get to eat your waffles and hang out with your Fabritzio, but how come I'm the one who's left behind, stuck with Dominique and Duard, in Centralia? Even her father, Wedley, had managed to start over from scratch in a new town, with a new wife. It's not fair, Phoebe thought. Everyone gets a second chance but me.

"Yo, Phoebs," said Dominique, carrying the brain in one hand. "The needle's waitin'."

She turned to Dominique, who was sitting on the hood of Duard's car while he peed on a gravestone. She was a vision in black: extravagantly ripped black hose twisting around her calves and thighs, black leather miniskirt, and her enormous black hair spiraling up toward the moon. Phoebe could just see the green edge of the tattooed broken heart on Dominique's breast, peeking out of her shirt.

"I'm coming," Phoebe said, and walked toward her friend. I guess at this point it doesn't make any difference, she thought. I guess Dominique is pretty much what I deserve. Being me has turned out to be a total washout. I may as well be her.

Duard zipped his fly and got back in the car. Dominique put the brain on the floor under her seat. As Duard turned the ignition, Dominique skootched over next to him so she could rest her head on his shoulder. For a moment Phoebe felt a sad jealousy. *How come I'm never the one the boys give their brains to?* Dominique tried screwing around with the radio for a while, even though all three of them knew it was broken. Weird static drifted in and out of the speakers.

"Hey, Phoebe," Duard said. "You ever think about running away?"

"What, you mean like running away from home?" Phoebe said. "Is that what you mean?"

"Yeah," Duard said. "Is that what I mean exactly!"

"I don't know, Duard," Phoebe said, annoyed. "Do you think I should?"

"Hell yeah," Duard said. "That's what I'd do, if I were you. Not that I am you, or anything. I'm just saying. We're two completely different people, you and me. I mean, if I were you I'd have like bosoms and junk!" He swallowed. "Out of control!"

"What do you think it's like, Duard," Dominique said. "Having bosoms?"

Duard's face turned red. He seemed deep in thought.

Then he spoke, softly, as if to himself.

"Bouncy," he said. "I guess."

A distant voice crackled onto the radio. "This is Ed Sullivan, ladies and gentlemen, and welcome back to the show. Once again, will you welcome these fine boys from Liverpool, the fab four, the Beatles!" There was the sound of screaming and applause, then a rock and roll band playing.

Again the radio went dead. "Shit," said Dominique.

"Hey, what was that?" Duard said.

"Beatles," Phoebe said. "Live on Ed Sullivan."

"It's not live, it's some recording," Dominique said. "That happened like fifty years ago. All those guys are dead now anyway."

"I don't know," Duard said cautiously. "This radio is something else. Sometimes it gets really weird shit, like radio waves that bounce off Mars and stuff and come back still alive."

"Right, Duard," said Dominique. "Sure."

"Am I serious? I'd better be. It's not a recording, that's what I'm saying. It's actually happening live, *somewhere else*. Some other dimension where they haven't caught up to us yet. Do you ever envy those people, the ones twenty years behind us? I do. Jeez, back there, I'm not even born yet!"

"Shut up, Duard," Dominique said. "You are so mental when you try to talk."

"You think this is mental," Duard said, shaking his head. "This isn't nothing. When I get mental I haven't even started yet!"

The car proceeded through town. Up ahead, near the old elementary school, they passed some kids their own age dressed up in costumes. A girl Phoebe did not especially like, Arlene Bellows, was having a costume party this evening to which Phoebe, Duard, and Dominique had not been invited. Later on they were thinking of spying on it.

Two girls and a boy, encumbered by their disguises, were trudging down the sidewalk. There was a Little Bo Peep and a Furball. One of the girls was Elaine Voron herself, disguised as Peggy Fleming. She was having a hard time walking on the sidewalk in her figure skates. There was the distinct clattering sound of her blades scraping against the concrete.

As they drove past, Elaine's face suddenly opened up into an expression of longing. She waved at her classmates and called out. "Hi, Phoebe," she said. "It's me."

Phoebe was embarrassed. Sitting there in Duard's car with her big hair and ripped-up shirt, she had not felt that she was recognizable.

Duard honked the horn, and passed these strangers by.

Phoebe looked out the window at her ex-friend and Centralia, now disappearing in smoke behind them. They passed through the covered bridge that spanned the Catawissa River. Since the spring she had been typing out letters to her mother and sister, sealing them in envelopes, and throwing the envelopes into the Catawissa, which flowed out of the coal country toward the Allegheny. It was Dominique's idea. The ritual was supposed to be good for your unconscious, that is, if you had one. With any luck the envelopes might wash up somewhere, maybe Arkansas or Harvard. Phoebe pictured strangers standing around, people with Irish accents trying to decipher

her handwriting. Maybe someone would run for a detective, or a magnifying glass. *Catch me Lucky Charms. They're magically delicious.*

Before Phoebe's mother took off, she had given her daughter a necklace. It was on Phoebe's sixth birthday, back when they lived in Centralia and Dwayne lived next door. The necklace was a bluish heart-shaped crystal on a silver chain, which Emily said had magic powers. Until recently, Phoebe had worn it, occasionally looking through it to see the world divided into its crystalline chambers, or to make a wish on the thing. The wishes almost uniformly malfunctioned, however, and as a result, Phoebe had taken the necklace off and left it in her jewelry box, along with the gold earrings she got from her grandmother and a blank fortune which she once got inside a fortune cookie. Something about the necklace angered Phoebe, as if its failure as a good-luck charm were typical of her mother's absence in the first place. Thanks a lot, Ma, Phoebe thought. The one time she had wished for anything important, which was for Duard to call her up and ask her out on a date, he had called up Dominique instead. Maybe it was the tattoo on Dominique's breast that he had found irresistible. Boys had this thing about breasts, were convinced that they were interesting.

So she had abandoned her mother's necklace as a means of finding luck and adopted this new ritual, which Dominique had invented. You typed up a letter on a piece of paper, sealed it in an envelope, and threw it into the ocean. Since they didn't have an ocean, they used the Catawissa instead. This afternoon, before they went around driving in Duard's car, Phoebe had typed out a letter to her mother which consisted of the sentence: *I wish you wanted me.* She had gone downstairs to stuff it in an envelope, but then she got sidetracked when she discovered that, as usual, the washing machine was walking around the house by itself. By the time she got it anchored again her mind had moved on, and she forgot all about her secret envelope and its accompanying cleansing ritual. With humiliation Phoebe now remembered that she had left the piece of paper in the kitchen, on the table near the dryer. Aunt Clara was probably going to find the letter and would use it as evidence to prove her ongoing theory that Phoebe was emotionally disturbed and in need of hard-core psychotherapy. The next thing you knew Phoebe was going to have to start deciphering a bunch of inkblots. If it came to that, though, she had a pretty good idea how she'd handle the shrinks. Every time they asked her what the inkblots looked like, she'd just shrug and say: *I don't know. Penis, I guess.*

They pulled up in front of Rusty's Tattoo Studio, which was a trailer up on cinder blocks. There was a neon sign in one window. Duard turned off the engine and slammed his door, leaving the keys dangling in the ignition. "Out of control," he said, bounding toward the front door. "Aardwolf time!"

Phoebe lagged behind in the car, and Dominique paused halfway to the parlor to look back at her. "C'man, Phoeb," she said. "What are you waitin' for? Time ta pop yer cherry!"

"I'm not feeling so hot," Phoebe said. Dominique looked at her with a suspicious expression. "Really I'm not."

Dominique's face darkened. "Don't tell me you're chickening out," she said. "I don't even want to hear this."

"I am not," Phoebe said.

"Then what's the deal? Come on! I thought you wanted one just like mine."

"I don't know," Phoebe said. "I'm just a little scared maybe. I'm afraid it's going to hurt."

"Well of course it hurts. A little. But if you're not willing to go through with it, I mean, that's that. I just thought you were my friend, that's all. I guess maybe I was mistaken."

"Dominique, of course I'm your goddamned friend," Phoebe said. "Why are you being so mean to me? I'm trying to tell you I'm afraid, and you're being all mean."

"Phoebe, babe," Dominique said, going over to her. She kneeled down in the driveway in front of the open door of the Swinger. "I didn't mean that. I know we're friends. We're better than friends. That's what this is all about.''

"What all what is about? You being mean to me?''

"No, no,'' Dominique said. She reached forward and stroked Phoebe on the back. "I mean us.''

For a moment they sat there in the parking lot. Dominique seemed deep in thought.

"What about us?'' Phoebe said.

"You know,'' Dominique said. "I mean like, we done a lot of shit together this last year. 'Member when we put that oil on the road and watched everybody skid into the ditch?'' Dominique smiled her smile with the teeth missing. "That was excellent!''

Phoebe smiled, too. "Yeah, that was pretty funny.''

"So you know what I mean,'' Dominique said. "We done a lot of stuff together. I've never had a friend like you before, Phoebe. Fuck, I've never had a friend at all. I mean, you know what I'm like: I'm a *vedge*.''

"I'm just afraid it's going to hurt,'' Phoebe said. "That's all I'm saying. All those needles.''

"It doesn't hurt,'' Dominique said. "Not as much as some other stuff, anyway.''

They sat there in silence for some time. In the distance crickets chirped in the sewer. A dog was barking somewhere far off, and Phoebe thought of her own dog, Buddy, who was twenty-three years old now. The dalmatian was so old and senile he could barely move and spent most of his time asleep in the basement sitting next to the tank for the hot-water heater. Buddy's only known interest at this point was in eating his own legs. The dog was constantly gnawing at his knees and shins, opening up repulsive welts and sores that ran with unpleasant juices. Phoebe wondered if Buddy's obsession with self-consumption wasn't the dog's own inefficient way of committing suicide. It was hard work, eating yourself. You had to save your mouth for last.

"Do you think anyone likes me?" Phoebe said softly.

"What?" Dominique said. "Of course anyone likes you. What are you talking about?"

"I don't mean anyone," Phoebe said, irritated. "You know. . . . I mean *guys.*"

"Well jeez, Phoebe," Dominique said. "Are you kidding? Lots of guys like you."

"Nuh-uh," Phoebe said.

"Yuh-huh," Dominique said. "You're crazy. They're nuts about you. Most of the guys I know I think are really just hanging out with me so they can get to know you 'cause they know you and me are friends. Look at Duard. If he had the chance he'd dump me for you in two seconds. Not that I'm going to let him, or anything. But there are lots of guys like that."

"Then why don't any of them ever *do* anything about it?" Phoebe said. Phoebe hadn't really gone out with anyone since February, when she had this fiasco of a date with Lloyd Borker. He drove her to Centralia in his van and they had sex in the back, where he had this mattress and a stereo, and the whole thing took like five minutes. Afterward they went to the Ashland House of Pizza and right in the middle of everything he inhaled one of the dried hot peppers he'd shaken on his slice, and it went straight into his nostril and burned a hole in his sinuses. He wept and cried for like a half hour, and after that he just took Phoebe home and that was the end of it. At the time she figured he'd cried on account of the pepper, but now she wasn't so sure. If it was the pepper that did it you'd think he would have at least called her up and said something like *Listen, Phoebe. It was just that pepper.*

"Phoebe," Dominique said. "Are you jealous? Of me and Duard? Is that it?"

"I don't know," Phoebe said. "Everything's just so messed up, that's all."

"Messed up?" Dominique said. "What do you mean, messed up?"

"I mean everything," Phoebe said. She was practically yelling now, and again she felt the tears trying to work their way forward. "You want to know how I feel, Dominique, *alone,* that's how I feel. I feel like I'm the only person in the entire universe and everything else is just some stupid movie!" Phoebe choked on her words. She had to either stop talking or start crying.

The two girls sat there again, not talking. Again Phoebe heard the creaking of crickets, and she thought of her family's now-abandoned house at the crest of the hill in what used to be Centralia.

"Am I a movie, Phoeb?" Dominique said. She stood up. She had gotten dirt in the knees of her torn-up stockings. "Is that what you're saying?"

"No," Phoebe said. "No. You're not a movie."

"Damn right, Phoeb," Dominique said. "I'm your blood sister. It's just you and me against everybody. That's why you should get a tattoo that matches mine. To make it official."

Phoebe looked up. She couldn't really see Dominique very well. Half of Dominique's face was lit up in yellow and purple light from the tattoo parlor's neon sign.

"I'm just a little afraid, okay," Phoebe said. "Like, what if I get to be thirty years old or something someday, and I don't like it? What if I think it's ugly?"

"Ugly?" Dominique said. She seemed really hurt. For a moment Phoebe thought she was going to cry. "Ugly?" she said again.

"You know what I mean," Phoebe said.

"I don't," Dominique said. Her voice quavered. She unbuttoned one button on her shirt and pulled her bra back just enough to expose the tattoo. There was the heart with its tear down the middle, and the wavering green letters that spelled DOMYNYQUE. It looked especially bizarre in the flickering light from the neon sign.

"You think it's ugly?" Dominique said.

"No," Phoebe said. "No. It's pretty. Really it is."

"You think so?"

"Yeah."

Dominique relaxed and smiled. "I'm so glad you think so." She stood. "C'man. Let's go get you one. Then you and me will be *identical.*"

"But—"

"Come *on.*"

As Dominique pulled Phoebe up the stairs into the parlor, she finally understood. Dominique didn't want Phoebe to get a tattoo for Phoebe's sake. She wanted Phoebe to get a tattoo for *Dominique's* sake. It was like one of those science fiction movies where they put someone else's soul in your body, and your soul wound up in theirs. Once Phoebe got a tattooed breast, everyone would act like Phoebe was as much as a slimeball as Dominique; Dominique, meanwhile, would henceforward be treated like a good girl, like Phoebe used to be. Dominique was going to wind up living with Uncle Pat and Aunt Clara, spending all the millions from the restaurant equipment business, while Phoebe was going to have to live with Dominique's stepdad, Bert Meyers, who used to run a kennel for dalmatian dogs out near the Centralia airfield and drank grain alcohol and played xylophone in a 1940s big band. On the other hand, maybe she'd get to go out with Duard, who, even though he asked himself questions and then answered them, was still basically kind-hearted. From what she heard around school, he was supposed to be really good in bed, for reasons that no one would specify but which were supposed to have something to do with his unusual physiology. All Dominique would say was, *Listen, Phoebe. There's worse things than being slow.*

Duard lived with his brother, Dwayne, in Centralia. Theirs was one of the few houses still standing. Duard and his little sister, Dwenda, had moved back in after their mother died in a seaplane. Now Duard and Dwayne were raising their little sister, who was only six years old. Phoebe respected them for this, but she still worried about poor Dwenda. How was the girl going to turn out, being brought up by Duard and Dwayne? It reminded her of the story of Romulus and Remus, who were raised by she-wolves and wound up starting the Roman Empire by accident. Italy was the country that was shaped like someone's boot, but that wasn't the kind of thing you wanted to say in front of people that lived there.

Dominique tugged on Phoebe's wrist and pulled her through the front door of the tattoo studio. The walls of the parlor were covered with hundreds of intricate designs. Duard was standing in front of a huge and intricate arabesque of Satan. One of his cloven, hooflike hands clasped a burning bow and arrow. He had skulls for teeth and flames encircling his brow. Satan that is, not Duard. Duard had teeth like anybody else, except maybe a little more rotten.

"Evening, girls." A large man in a blue muscle shirt stood behind the counter, his arms crossed in front of him. The moment she looked at him, Phoebe thought, *Good god. It's Mr. Clean.* His head was shaved bald, and he had an earring in one ear. A large handlebar mustache fulminated from his nostrils. His skin was covered with ornate and complex tattoos, full of strange and varied patterns and colors.

The man just smiled at them and flexed his enormous muscles. There was a leopard on his biceps surrounded by black winged bats. The bats gave way to a jungle scene, and a beautiful and mysterious tiger lay in the midst of his inner elbow, waiting to pounce. An exotic, cartoonish woman with enormous, exposed breasts sprawled beneath that, although her eyes were little green and blue planets floating in a black universe. Stars and moons twinkled down the rest of his arm all the way to his wrist.

When he blinked, for a moment you could see a pair of other eyes, tattooed on his eyelids.

"All right, girls," he said, as if he had caught them doing something they shouldn't. "I'm Rusty."

"Hi, Rusty," Dominique said.

"Hey, Neeky!" Rusty's eyes twinkled as he recognized her. "What do you know! How's life on the outside treating ya?"

"Bitchin'," Dominique said. "This here's my friend Phoebe. She wants a tat, identical to mine."

"Excellent," Rusty said. "You gals know each other from Skagville?" He squinted at Phoebe for a moment, scrutinizing her.

There was an embarrassed silence for a moment, then Phoebe shook her head. For some reason she could not find her voice.

"Nah," Dominique said. "Phoebe's a good girl."

"Well," Rusty said, taking a towel off a chair. "Not anymore!"

"Rusty's a real character," Dominique said, somewhat critically.

"Hey," Rusty said. "You remind me of somebody. Who is it?"

"I don't know," Phoebe said.

There was a shattering sound from the back of the store. Duard had kicked over an empty can of paint.

"Am I sorry?" he said.

"Jesus, watch what you're doing," Rusty said, shaking his head. "I heard he's your boyfriend now?" he said to Dominique. "Sheesh."

"He's got his points," Dominique said.

"Hey, what's so great about me!" Duard said, looking up at them. He smiled at the others, swinging his arms, then resumed looking at the stencils on display at the back of the store. He had paused in front of a very large one of a coiled cobra colored red, white, and blue. Beneath it was the phrase THESE COLORS DON'T RUN.

Rusty ran his large palm over the surface of his smooth head. Phoebe thought about the fact that Rusty had to shave his head every day to achieve this effect. She sometimes saw Uncle Pat shaving in his bathroom, his chin covered in lather. Did this Rusty have to cover his whole head in foam each day? He'd look a little like a marshmallow.

He looked at Phoebe again. "I know who it is. That Scabbaxx. You ever seen her? You look a little like her."

"Scabbaxx?" Phoebe said. "I don't know who that is."

"Lead singer," Rusty said. "Poison Squirrels. I know you've heard a them."

"I thought they broke up," Dominique said.

"They did." Rusty put his hands in his pockets. Even with his arms hanging loosely, Phoebe could see his tremendous muscles bulging around his upper arms and chest. It was amazing to see a man so well developed. There was a small part of her that found him not disgusting. "You know why they're called the Poison Squirrels? 'Cause the bass player used to watch *Romper Room.* He thought Miss Suzy started off each program by saying, 'Good morning, poison squirrels!' " Rusty slapped his palm on his stomach and laughed. His deep laughter echoed throughout the dim parlor.

"Anyway," he said, finally, "whyn't you have a seat, Phoebe."

Phoebe felt the blood rushing to her head. She was trapped.

"Tell her what you were in for," Dominique said. "Phoebe will like this."

"Aw, nothing," Rusty said. "Kidnapping, I guess."

"You hear that?" Dominique said. "Kidnapping!"

He shrugged. "Somethin' to do."

"Rusty would hang out in front of the bus station, pick up kids that had run away from home," Dominique explained.

"Yeah, that was a great scam," Rusty said. "At least until I got caught. How was I supposed to know that Santa was wearin' a wire?"

Dominique shrugged.

"You know," Rusty continued, "I miss it sometimes. It's satisfying, kidnapping people, you know what I mean? My men's group says it's an important ritual. Whenever you grab some kid, stuff 'em in a sack, you're really connecting to your ancestors. But I don't know. Maybe you can't relate to that. It's kind of a guy thing." He put on a pair of rubber gloves. "Okay," he said. "So you want one just like Dominique's?"

Phoebe didn't say anything. She looked at a poster on the wall that said: YES IT HURTS. Another sign said: YOU MUST BE OVER EIGH-

TEEN AND SOBER. Would it make any difference if she told him she was only fifteen, and that she had been swigging Southern Comfort on the way over? Phoebe had the suspicion that nothing she could say would make any difference now.

He started hooking one of the machines together. He had an instrument that looked like a combination of a fountain pen and an electric drill. The ink itself was held in place on a kind of spindle. Several bolts and screws held the rest of the needle together, and a long electric cord trailed toward the foot switch on the floor.

"You'll need to take your shirt off," he said.

"I will?" Phoebe said. She had a strange feeling, as if she were slowly leaving her body, looking down on the situation from a great distance.

"Hey, I can't do it through your shirt now, can I?" Rusty laughed. "Hell no."

"Go on, Phoebe," Dominique said. "Do what he says."

Phoebe didn't really want to take her shirt off in front of this Rusty. The only man that had ever seen her with her shirt off was Lloyd Borker, and the lights in his van had been out at the time. Still, this wasn't like that; she supposed it was more like being at the doctor's. Dominique was standing right behind her. There was no way she could back out now.

As Phoebe pulled off her white T-shirt, Dominique turned to Duard. "You stay back there, Duard," she said. "We need a little privacy up here."

Dominique took Phoebe's shirt, then her bra. Phoebe felt cold. Rusty started rubbing the top of her left breast with a cloth dipped in rubbing alcohol. It smelled like the hospital.

"Okay now, lean this way a little bit," Rusty said.

Please don't let this happen to me, Phoebe thought. Even now she wondered how she could escape this terrible situation. She looked down at her own breast, thinking, This is the last time in my life I'll ever look at myself without seeing that ugly green heart. This is the last time I'll ever be clear.

On the wall in front of her was a poster of a woman with a tattoo that seemed to cover her entire body. A Lucifer surrounded with flames was engraved on her stomach; he was shooting burning arrows toward her shoulder blades. From neck to waist the woman was consumed with tattooed fire.

"Yo, Rusty," Phoebe heard Duard's voice saying, from miles away. "Like, whatever happened to those things? Do I see them? No, I don't."

"What things?" Rusty said, not looking at him.

Duard sounded kind of embarrassed. "The little aardwolves," he whispered. "They used to be right here."

"What?" Rusty said. He sounded annoyed. "What are you talking about? I don't know nothing about no aardwolf."

"You used to have a whole sheet full of 'em! There was one coming out of a top hat. I saw it."

"Well, if it used to be there, it's still there," Rusty said. "Nothing around here disappears without permission."

For a moment, Duard thought about this. He looked at Phoebe with an odd expression of regret.

Then, all at once, the motor started and Phoebe felt the needle cut beneath her skin. The thing sounded like a sewing machine. She cried out for a moment, then bit her lip. The needle moved around on her breast. It stung. It didn't feel exactly like a razor digging into her skin; it felt more like alcohol or something stinging in a cut. It wasn't what Phoebe had expected, but it still hurt. It felt like she was bleeding.

The earring in Rusty's ear swung back and forth as he operated the needle. His jaw was set tightly, and Phoebe could see the muscles in his neck clenching. It was as if he were using every muscle in his body to keep his hands steady.

Phoebe was determined to remain sophisticated and aloof during the proceedings. But then she felt herself shaking, and hot teardrops poured out of her eyes and down her cheeks. She was crying uncontrollably now, and she did not give a damn. Let them see her cry, if it came to that. Was that some federal crime, that she was crying? Everything hurt. From miles away she heard Rusty whistling to himself. It sounded like some Doors song. "Riders on the Storm."

"Looking good, Phoeb," Dominique said.

She saw it forming, even as she felt the pigment shooting beneath her skin. The outline of the heart, and the jagged tear down its center. The letters of her own name.

"He's finished the heart," Dominique said, squeezing Phoebe's hand. "Now he's filling it in."

In her mind's eye Phoebe saw her mother and her sister in their hotel suite. The door to the balcony was open, and the ocean breeze was blowing back the long white curtains. Sunlight filled the room. "Hey, lamebrain," Demmie said, looking up at her sister through the shafts of bright light. "Where ya been all these years?"

Phoebe's mother lay on the bed, reading Italian *Vogue*. Demmie stood on the balcony, looking out over the ocean, her long hair whipping around in the wind. Jeez, Phoebe thought, staring at Demmie. After all these years she doesn't even look anything like me. The needle cut again into her soft breast, and she could feel the ink of the heart seeping into her. The waves crashed on the beach.

"It's okay, Phoebe," Dominique said. "We're sisters now, just like we wanted."

But Phoebe was flying far from here, grasping onto a pair of yellow talons. She could feel the wind around her as the wings beat through the air. On the horizon she saw the remains of Centralia, enveloped in drifting smoke. *You see, Phoebe,* Demmie said. *Now you're one of us.*

Phoebe just looked at Demmie as one would look at a stranger. This woman obviously had her mixed up with someone else.

I'm sorry, miss, she said. *I'm sisters with somebody else now.*

"All done," said Rusty, standing back from his work. Phoebe's eyes were clamped shut.

"Can I see?" said Duard. "Can I see?"

"Hey, we told you to make yourself scarce," said Dominique.

"How does it look?" Phoebe said.

"Awesome!" Dominique said. "Outrageous!"

"Is that how you spell 'Phoebe'?" Duard said. "That doesn't look right."

"What?" Phoebe said. "How did you spell it?"

"Just like it sounds," Rusty said. "F-E-E-B-Y. Ain't that right?"

"No!" said Phoebe. "That's totally wrong!"

"It's all right," Dominique said. "That can be your biker name!"

"But I don't want a biker name!" Phoebe wailed. "I don't want one!"

She opened her eyes and looked down at her own breast. There was the twisted green heart with the tear through its center, and the misspelled letters of her name.

"Well," Dominique said. "Ya got one."

There was a soft groan from Duard. His jaw was moving up and down as if he were trying to form the words of a private language. He was looking at the tattoo on Phoebe's breast, then glancing up at Dominique, who was smiling with a look of malformed satisfaction.

With a sudden moan he lurched forward, grabbed Dominique's hand, and bit it.

"Goddammit, Duard," Dominique said, trying to get her hand out of his mouth. "That hurts."

There was a soft crunching sound as Duard bit down harder on Dominique's knuckles.

"All right, you kids," Rusty said. "Stop horsing around." He looked at Dominique, annoyed. "Come on, Dominique. Get your hand out of his mouth."

"What do you think I'm trying to do?" Dominique yelled. "Ow, goddammit!"

"I'm not kidding," Rusty said.

"What should you do, Phoebe?" Duard said. Since Dominique's hand was in his mouth, the words were somewhat muffled. "You better hurry. Before I forget why I'm doing this."

"Jesus Christ, Duard!" Dominique yelled. "I'm serious!"

Duard looked up at the wall where the poster of the aardwolves was missing. "I was going to call mine Bitey," he whispered, sadly. "Or Waffles maybe."

"Why *are* you doing this?" Dominique said, still trying to get her hand out of Duard's mouth. "Goddammit, let me go!"

There was a long pause. Duard looked at Phoebe with longing.

"I forget," he said.

Phoebe understood. He was trying to set her free.

She turned, grabbed her T-shirt, and ran. The door of Rusty's slapped closed behind her.

Outside the Swinger was still sitting there, bathed in the neon light of the parlor. The keys dangled from the ignition. It wasn't hard to get the car started. Phoebe had seen this done before.

In a few moments she was soaring down the big hill through Centralia. Driving a car was easier than it looked, although the Swinger did have the annoying tendency to veer from one side of the road to the other without warning. You had to keep turning the wheel around.

Her breast ached where the needle had been. She turned on the radio. Somebody sang:

> *For the benefit of Mister Kite*
> *There will be a show tonight*
> *On trampoline.*

Trampoline, Phoebe thought. *Yeah, right. That'll be the day.* She drove past the old graveyard. A bright moon illuminated the cemetery with a soft blue light. For a moment she thought about pulling in, parking the car, and looking for the tombstone with her name on it, with the names of her mother and sister. But that would have been stupid. They weren't even dead.

She glanced down at her T-shirt. A heart-shaped ring of blood had seeped into it, along with the misspelled letters of her name.

Phoebe gave the car some more gas and climbed the hill that led out of town. She passed through a cloud of drifting smoke. Maybe I'll never see any of this ever again, she thought. If I could drive far away enough, I might wind up someplace I actually belong. In the place where she wanted to go they didn't have the need for mine fires. There would be the ocean, and the high balcony overlooking the sand, and the sound of the waves thundering on the beach. The sun set in crimson mist, hanging above the Atlantic. Phoebe and her mother and Demmie laughed at a joke known only to themselves, and raised their wineglasses to the sea.

Sure, Phoebe thought. I could get there from here. She passed an orange Department of the Interior sign that read: NOW LEAVING CENTRALIA MINE FIRE IMPACT ZONE.

A few minutes later she passed Elaine Voron, still wearing her party costume, walking home now in her figure skates. Phoebe honked the horn and waved, to let Elaine know that at last she was on her own.

But this time Elaine didn't recognize her, and shielded her eyes from the oncoming car as if it were driven by someone she did not know.

SKUNKS

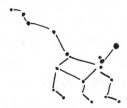

The Skunks are divided into the Greater Skunk—
Viverra Putorius Major—
and the Lesser Skunk—Viverra Putorius Minor.
On occasion they are occluded by Succi Hirnea
(the can of tomato juice).

Phoebe's uncle, Patrick Flinch, stood in the kitchen, reading the note over and over again: *I wish you wanted me.* It could only have come from one person, young Isabelle Smuggs, one of his house-guests. He had been gnashing his teeth over her since the moment that they first met. Still, he had thought that an affair right under his wife's nose would be immoral, not to mention difficult to pull off without detection. But there it was: a letter to him, typed by the young woman, left right there in the kitchen where Pat would be sure to find it. Okay, so she wants you, Patrick thought to himself. Now what happens?

He looked through the glass doors which led into the living room. Isabelle Smuggs was lying, apparently asleep, in a large easy chair by the fireplace. Her father and Patrick's wife, Clara, were out of the house, jogging. Surely this was a moment in which some benevolent form of evil might be perpetrated. But how should he proceed?

Was he just supposed to waltz into the living room and wake the woman up and say, *Excuse me. Got your note.* Was that the way these things were done?

It could honestly be stated that Patrick Flinch did not like Isabelle's father, Professor Quentin T. Smuggs, Ph.D. "A disease," he once said, carefully considering the man's various attributes. "Rat vomit. Ejectamenta." Clara held a differing opinion. "He's a genius," she gushed irritably, as if this should be self-evident. "A prophet." Smuggs had been Clara's professor at the University of Pennsylvania in the 1970s, when he taught a course called "Reinventing Beinghood." After years of hearing about it, Patrick still wasn't sure what had gone on in the class. Apparently in some sessions the students had coated themselves with oil and yanked on their own hair and spanked themselves in order to experience their own births, which was fine except that Clara had had to deliver herself by cesarean section and they charged extra.

Since graduation, Professor Smuggs and Clara Flinch regularly sent each other letters. At Christmas, the Flinches got a picture of Smuggs standing in front of a tepee he'd built out of Cream of Wheat. The card said, *Happy Winter Solstice with love, Two Rocks.* Two Rocks was the name Smuggs had been given when he lived with the Iroquois for a semester. Patrick wasn't sure, but he didn't think Two Rocks was the kind of name the Iroquois gave to people they liked.

The Smuggses had arrived over thirty-six hours ago, on Thursday. Apparently in one of her recent letters Clara had said, Come on up sometime when you're in the mood we'd love to see you, meaning this in a general, abstract sense, and Smuggs had replied, Hey, we're on the way. The night before the professor and his daughter arrived, Pat suggested that his wife call the Smuggses up and say that this wasn't a convenient time. Clara said she didn't see how she could rescind her offer at this point. Patrick said it was easy; you just called him up and explained you were busy. Sorry. Other plans. She could write him a letter, even. But Clara said it wasn't that simple. Sure it's that simple, Patrick said. Here. He picked up a sheet of writing paper and began to scribble. *Dear Quentin. We're going out of town. Catch you another time maybe.* Clara had stomped her foot and asked if he was deliberately trying to "piss her off."

"Maybe you should just take off for a few days," Clara suggested. "And let me see my friends alone."

"Alone?" Patrick asked. "I can't have that. I won't have your friends thinking I hate them."

"But you do hate them," Clara said. "You despise my friends!"

"How can I hate a man I've never met?" Patrick said.

"I don't know, bub," Clara said. "You tell me."

Patrick Flinch did not like being seen as intemperate and cranky. In spite of his abundant volume (two hundred fifty pounds) and his high altitude (six feet six), he thought of himself as sensitive and decent. He had a great belief in the power of cans of beer to solve problems between people. When Quentin Smuggs arrived, Pat had intended to drink a Bud with him. He hoped that would soften him up.

Now, however, Pat knew better. Professor Smuggs didn't like beer. He said the bubbles could make you foamy.

On Thursday, as they'd unpacked what seemed like an unusually large number of bags out of their car, Pat had said something along the lines of "So, Quentin, how long do you think you can stay for? Just wondering!"

Professor Smuggs just smiled and said, "I don't know, man. We don't have to put a time limit on it."

"We don't?" Pat said.

"Naw. I don't believe in that shit anyway."

"What shit?" Pat said. "Time?"

Clara took the professor's bags and cleared her throat. "Darling," she said, meaning it as a kind of threat. "Why don't you help Isabelle with her bags?"

What he really had wanted to do at that moment was to vigorously rub some steel wool cleansing pads across the professor's tongue, but instead he had just nodded, and turned to help the professor's daughter. That was when he had laid eyes upon Isabelle Smuggs for the first time. She was a robust, bright-eyed young woman who, best of all, reeked with an unmistakable contempt for her own father. Patrick had liked her immediately. As it turned out, there was more to admire about Isabelle Smuggs than her physical beauty and her awareness of her father's putrefaction. She was a sculptress of some renown in Philadelphia, and had gained an unusual reputation for making large replicas of things that were not people.

That first night, Professor Smuggs had managed to get Pat to drive them all to some restaurant called Farmer MacGregor's Kountry Kitchen, which had been written up, apparently, in *The Philadelphia Inquirer*'s Sunday magazine. The professor was very excited about experiencing "New Amish Cuisine," which mainly consisted of incredibly small servings of potato pancakes and corn. The dinner conversation mostly concerned itself with how people who acted more or less like Pat here were wrecking the world, and how people who acted more or less like Quentin Smuggs, on the other hand, were helping to save it. The only good thing about the meal was the presence of Isabelle. She kept looking at Pat every time her father made one of his idiotic pronouncements, letting a wave of intimacy, based on hatred, pass between them.

Pat recalled that there had been something memorable and sad about their waitress that night, as if, even as she recited the grim list of the daily specials (which included scrapple and chicken à la king), her mind was on some tragedy miles away. Quentin Smuggs made everyone order the duck flambé with the Farmer's Special Mayonnaise. Apparently this mayonnaise was revered for miles around. It was all anyone could talk about. Patrick kept trying to steer the conversation in a different direction, first by describing the beauty of one of the nearby lakes, then by asking Isabelle about her sculpture. Still, no matter what he said, the conversation kept coming back to Dan

MacGregor's special mayonnaise. Eventually Patrick gave up and let the mayonnaise take center stage.

"It's good!" Clara said.

"I knew you'd like it," Dr. Smuggs said. "It's made by pain-free chickens."

"Pain-free?" Patrick asked.

"Yes," Dr. Smuggs explained. "These chickens aren't kept in a coop. They're free to fly off if they want. But they don't. They stay! Why? Because they *want* to make the mayonnaise."

On their way out the door, the sad waitress gave everyone a little card, advertising the fact that the local Cub Scout troop was giving a kind of charity jamboree that weekend. The scouts and their den mothers were all dressing up as the four basic food groups. The thing was called the Pork Chop Festival. Apparently it had been going on every June for years. The waitress grimaced. "I'm going to be a ham," she said. "My sister's like some giant pie."

For the next several hours, Patrick felt somewhat out of sorts, riding the oceanic waves of his sour stomach. He was a little embarrassed by his nausea, because he feared it made him look like the kind of person who liked mayonnaise better when it came from chickens who weren't happy in their work. He had had to work the next day, Friday, and by the time he got home, his wife and her former teacher had gone out to dinner again, heading, apparently, back to Farmer MacGregor's for a second helping of the very mayonnaise that had turned his stomach in the first place. Isabelle, for her part, had had to drive down to the police station. While everyone was out of the house, someone had broken into her car and stolen her repulsive artwork. The police suspected some local kids.

Pat had gone to sleep, hoping that the entire mayonnaise nightmare would be over in the morning. He slept until eleven Saturday, got a shower, and came downstairs to find his house quiet, his wife and the professor absent. Pheobe wasn't around, either. Isabelle had left the note for him on the table: *I wish you wanted me.*

He stood there, reading and rereading the single line over and over again. Through the glass doors lay the sleeping form of the sculptress. Patrick Flinch was not sure what would happen next. He did not have an answer to her question.

Isabelle Smuggs lay in the easy chair, listening to the sounds of Patrick Flinch standing there in the kitchen. What was going through his head? What could possibly have motivated him to leave such a brazen missive right out there in the open where anyone could find it? She did not quite know how to respond to his query and decided that the best strategy, until she formulated a reply, might be to lie there pretending to be asleep. But does he know I'm pretending?, she wondered. Can't he see right through me? Isabelle Smuggs had spent most of her life plagued by what she thought of as her own pathological transparency.

Slut, she thought to herself. *Harlot.* It was bad enough for this Patrick Flinch to leave her a love letter, but she had already spent the last two days trying to tell herself that the attraction she felt for the man was childish, unreasonable, and stupid. For Christ's sakes, when on earth am I going to outgrow these monster crushes on total strangers? When I'm a hundred, maybe? She pictured herself in a retirement home, totally gaga over some drooling old goat. You got it, Isabelle thought. That's exactly where you're headed.

She had never had a relationship yet that had not led to total fiasco. Throwing pots and pans at men, breaking sculptures on their heads. Sobbing her lungs out into pillows and ripping their love letters into tiny bits. She had been in love dozens of times in twenty-four years, and every affair was terminated for more maddening and arcane reasons. Jonathan needed more time alone, and Andrew wanted more time together. William decided to go back to his wife. Buzz wanted to marry her. Samuel said he loved the person he was when he was with her but this person was not himself and so in order to go back to being himself they had to break up even though he liked the person who was not himself better than the person who he actually was. Eliot spent all the time talking to her, complaining, for the most part, about how they never talked anymore. Spanky died of cancer. Raul was the leader of a cult of people whose main object of worship, near as Isabelle could figure it, was Raul himself. Graham was old enough to be her father, and kept showing her off to his corporate partners like she was some kind of prize racehorse. Wendell said he needed more time to devote to his bodybuilding. Arthur had joined Alcoholics Anonymous and one day got to Step Nine, Kill Your Girlfriend. Sidney left his underwear all over the furniture. Ricky wanted to spend the entire weekend watching professional sports on cable. George wouldn't ever let her have the remote control for the television. Thomas said he was afraid of her breasts.

"My goodness, they're just so big," he said, looking at them. "It's intimidating."

Thomas was an idiot, but he was right about one thing. Her breasts were excessive. Everywhere she went men acted like she was the centerpiece of some ticker-tape parade, like she was a victorious and conquering astronaut. In every public pavilion she was the lucky recipient of an endless series of slathering glares, guys in bars elbowing each other in the ribs and looking at her and whispering phrases in each other's ears that ended with the interjection *hey-hey-hey*. Other women, total strangers sometimes, came up to her in the fitness center and struck up conversations, telling her she was the "luckiest woman in tarnation." Some women, on other occasions, were just as likely to come up to her and say, with an almost inexplicable anger, *Hey you. I think you're disgusting.*

From the kitchen came the sound of Patrick Flinch putting the letter back down on the table. How much time did they have? For how many minutes longer would Clara and her father stay outside, jogging down the country roads? She felt her heart pounding. Please let them come back soon, she thought. Before I let myself make another mistake.

Tell me this, then, Isabelle thought, trying to maintain the illusion of sleep, if I hate men so much, why am I constantly falling in love with them? It was an annoying contradiction. What's the deal? Is going out with men and having these terrible relationships my way of paying them back?

Isabelle made some sounds that gave the impression she was dreaming. No, that's impossible. I can't have reached that degree of self-loathing yet. If that were true I'd have to think that going out with me is some kind of punishment. Which it's not. I'm smart, artistic, funny. What's so wrong with me that every guy I go out with turns out to be impossible?

When she was little, her mother used to give her directions on how to attract a man. She had saved this article from the *Farmer's Almanac* that was full of really stupid romantic superstitions. *"If you want to fall in love, you should sleep with your head at the foot of the bed."* Or: *"If you want your love to last forever, throw your left shoe at the moon."* And finally, definitively: *"If you want to get married, you should at all costs avoid shaving your legs with a razor owned by a dead woman."*

Isabelle's mother had taken her own life when she was eight. Hanged herself in the bedroom and left a suicide note in her daughter's book bag. *It all just makes me tired,* she wrote. Within the year Isabelle's father had gotten remarried, this time to one of his students, Marybeth Backup, who analyzed people's colors for a living. Two years after that, Quentin Smuggs was divorced again, shortly after Marybeth proclaimed him a "winter," tending toward blacks, grays, and whites. "Can you believe the nerve of her?" Quentin said to his new girlfriend, another, albeit younger, ex-student named Lavender. "Me, a winter! Whoa!"

It's probably all Dad's fault, Isabelle thought. That's what Freud would say. I'm trying to get back at my father by having all these awful relationships. If he weren't so putrid I'd be perfectly well adjusted.

Still, I don't really believe in that. When I go out with someone, it's not for some secret whacked-out reason. It's because I like them and I like the way I feel when I'm with them. You can get all hot and bothered if you want coming up with complicated reasons for why things don't work out, but in the end it's probably just because I've been unlucky. It's as simple as that. One of these days my luck will change, and I'll see how all these bad relationships were simply the road I had to travel to the one good one that will last.

Maybe the one that would last would be one with this Patrick Flinch, she thought, feeling something spinning inside her like a reeling gyroscope. She heard the sounds of him coming closer, sitting down on a couch next to her. What was he going to do? There was obviously something passing between us at dinner; every time Dad made one of his stupid pronouncements, Patrick looked at me and we knew. That was one good thing about Dad, in a way. He was kind of like a test you could administer to prospective lovers. Any man that found her father annoying was likely to be someone Isabelle could get along with.

Still, Barton Sumac had disliked her father, and look where that wound up. Another bloodbath. Last January, she had finally gotten introduced to the famous avant-garde painter at a party in Philadelphia. She had felt that old throbbing in her ribs within moments, and, miraculously, Sumac had called her the next day. It was like some lovely dream. Within no time they were going out and he was promising to promote her career as a sculptress. She had just begun a new series at the time, a series she felt that with the right kind of guidance might be her breakthrough. It had started when she sculpted this human brain out of latex. *Brain,* she called it. Barton Sumac saw it and asked her if she would allow him to paint her, and to this she agreed, thrilled and stunned at her good fortune. So she

modeled for him, nude, every day for several months, in his tastefully
horrible studio in Wynnewood. She had had to sit on a piece of cold
marble holding a piece of chicken in one hand.

After three months, Barton Sumac said he was done. He poured
her a glass of white wine and unveiled his work. There, centered on a
canvas six feet high by eight feet across, were her breasts, and not
much else.

"Voilà!" Barton Sumac said. *"It is you!"*

What she should have done was throw her wine in his face and
storm out of there. That would have shown him. What she did instead
was to stand there trying to look pleased, hoping that this painting
might somehow still help her career. Soon, though, tears were coming to her eyes, and the next thing she knew she was sobbing and
Barton Sumac was holding her in his arms. There she was being com-
forted by the very bastard who had humiliated her. If he wanted to
comfort her, for God's sakes, maybe it might have occurred to him to
paint something other than her tits. Was that so wrong, that she expected him to paint her face? Did it never even occur to him that she
might be self-conscious about her body? Why had he made her hold
that piece of chicken, anyway? When they broke the embrace, she
discovered that his smock had been covered with small blobs of still-
wet oil paint, blobs which were now smeared onto her white Laura
Ashley dress. She took her latest work, the stomach from her Innards
series, and smashed it on Sumac's head. Then she stomped out, still
crying, and that was it. Sumac never even called her back. The showing of her work he had promised, of course, never came to pass. The
forty-eight square feet of her bust, meanwhile, was snapped up by the
Barnes Foundation in Merion, and was tastefully framed and bathed
in spotlights and accompanied by a small bronze plaque: *Isabelle.*

That was a month and a half ago. The rest of the sculptures from
the Innards series rode around in the hatch of her Chevrolet Vega, or
at least they had until yesterday evening, when someone had appar-

ently pried open the back of her car and made off with the brain and the nose. Her father had responded to the news of the robbery with his maddening carelessness: "Don't worry, Izzy. They're just *things.*"

Isabelle's father was nothing if not sensitive.

Over the years, in fact, Isabelle's father had demonstrated such an abundance of sensitivity that he had slept with almost two dozen of his own students, and that was only counting the ones Isabelle knew about because they stayed overnight at the Smuggses' house in Bryn Mawr. She had spent all of high school sharing breakfast with the girls her father referred to as his "lab assistants." They always looked at Isabelle with the same expression in the morning, as if she were the one who was somehow intruding. They smoked cigarettes and blew the smoke in Isabelle's face and smacked on their Pop-Tarts in a manner seemingly calculated to get Isabelle to leave the house as quickly as possible, which she did.

But Quentin Smuggs finally got caught in 1986, after the incident with Ophelia Low. Ophelia was house-sitting for a couple called the Tattas, who taught Latin and had taken a year's sabbatical to spend some time in ancient Rome. It wasn't the fact that Dr. Smuggs was caught red-handed with Ophelia Low that was really the worst part of the scandal, or even the fact that the persons doing the catching were the Tattas themselves, who had returned from Italy a month early after they accidentally guillotined some statue. No, what did it was the fact that when Quentin and Ophelia were apprehended by the embarrassed Tattas, Dr. Smuggs was wearing only a pink baby bib and an enormous diaper and insisted that his girlfriend refer to him as *Skipper.* There was a quick meeting with the dean of faculty the following week, and pretty soon Dr. Smuggs wasn't teaching "Reinventing Beinghood" anymore.

Isabelle had been fortunate, in that she was out of the country when her father lost his job. Even now she was not sure she could have consoled him. In a way it was good that Quentin had been thrown out of the academy; it was not a good thing for higher education to have some smarty-pants rolling around in a baby bib. Still, the years since his dismissal had been hard on Isabelle's father. He had been unable to get any work for a while, until at last, in the late eighties, he became a book reviewer. This paid the Smuggses' bills, but somehow it lacked the charm of symbolically delivering each of your newborn students into a new world and spanking them for extra credit.

At the time of the scandal, Isabelle had been finishing her degree at the Cotswold School of Sculpture and Design in London. When she finally got back to the country, she hadn't been able to find work, had barely been able to afford studio space. It was only now, years later, that things were finally beginning to work out. Even the unpleasantness with Barton Sumac had only made Isabelle tougher. If you wanted to make art in this society you had to want it with a passion so all-consuming that even the constant discouragement from goons and jerks didn't dissuade you from your goal.

It was with this sense of purpose that she had managed to finish most of the Innards series, with the exception of the stomach, which she had, of course, smashed on Sumac's head. This week, when her father asked her to come with him to visit his old student, Mrs. Flinch, up here in Buchanan, she accepted, because the Reading Museum had expressed some interest in her work, and she figured she might use the trip to show them what she had on hand. She was not going to be showing the Reading Museum anything now, though. Her work was probably in some linen sack, halfway to a pawnshop.

If only they hadn't stolen that brain, Isabelle thought. That was my best one. The nose I know I can duplicate, but that brain is a separate matter. Of course, the fact that a work of art created with Isabelle's own toil and imagination had been stolen out of the back of her Vega should not have been a surprise. There was very little that Isabelle had created in this life that had not been filched, ignored, or misconstrued by ignoramuses.

Isabelle lay there in the easy chair, feeling like it was her own organs that had been stolen. I'm empty, she thought, feeling Patrick Flinch watching her. If I could actually fall in love with somebody then maybe all my guts wouldn't keep getting stolen. Like what right do I have to have a bunch of guts in my car when I haven't even got any guts in my guts? Jesus, I must be outta my goddamned gourd. How is it possible for any person to create a lasting work of art as long as you yourself keep feeling like a botched-up work in progress?

Isabelle suddenly wondered what she looked like, lying there with her eyes shut. He probably thinks I'm a complete idiot, she thought. She wished she had remembered to shave her legs that morning, a task which she continually postponed as long as possible, at least in part because she had to do it in the shower with her mother's old safety razor.

You see. Isabelle heard the voice of her mother's ghost, whispering in her heart. *Your legs. That stubble. I warned you.*

You should never use the razor of a dead woman if you want to be in love.

Patrick Flinch sat on the couch, holding a pair of books. To his left, Isabelle Smuggs sighed. "Oh please," she whispered from some dream. "Oh please, please, please."

He turned away from her, embarrassed at hearing this unconscious plea. Pat looked at the parlor of his lavish house for a moment, at the piano and the archway and the grand staircase in the front hallway. He had been born in this house over four decades ago, and had grown up here with Emily. He still remembered his sister's debutante party, held in this very room. A three-piece accordion band playing in the corner. *Sunrise, sunset.* A champagne fountain. It was odd to think of him being the only Flinch left, now that his parents were dead, his sister invisible. Someday he would give it to Phoebe, probably, unless the impossible happened and he had children of his own, with Clara.

Pat looked up at the staircase, and did not remember hearing any sounds of his niece. The more he thought about it, the more he realized he hadn't seen her since she'd gone out for a drive with her friends on Thursday night. Duard, and that terrible girl Dominique, the one who was such a bad influence. Phoebe'd even started to act like her now. He wondered what had ever happened to the little girl he had known before Emily left. Where was Phoebe now? Was she ever coming home?

There was a painting of Emily on the second-floor landing, staring down at him with her sarcastic beauty. How he longed, sometimes, to be free of this place, to be relieved of the dead and their unreasonable expectations.

In the chair next to Patrick, Isabelle Smuggs sighed again. "Oh please," she whispered. "Please."

Yeah, right, Pat thought. See, this was what always happened when he thought too long about his sister. He left this world a little bit and entered the outskirts of his sister's universe, a place where it did not seem impossible to imagine the dreams of strangers.

Pat cleared his throat and opened his two books. Clara and the professor would be back soon. He had just begun a simultaneous reading of the collected John Cheever and *In Watermelon Sugar* by Richard Brautigan. They formed a kind of diptych for him. He loved Cheever but after a time grew tired of the man's assumption that the world was a giant suburb. At this point he'd switch over to the Brautigan, and enter that writer's exuberant prose-poetry, full of the sarcastic optimism of the sixties. He could stand just so much of it before having to run back to the Cheever again, to restore the order of the world. The two books made up a single work for him, satisfying both sides of the brain. *In Watermelon Suburb.*

He had not read the Cheever for some time, however, and it was with great satisfaction that he opened the collection toward the back. There was something irregular to the volume, though—pressed between the pages was an envelope with his name on it. It was an old love letter, from years ago. It was from Julie Zacks. The actress.

Dear Moron, the letter began. *Never in my life have I known anyone so selfish. I mean I have known a lot of jerks in my time but you really take the cake. What did you mean by mailing me that letter? Were you trying to hurt me intentionally or does inconsideration just come naturally for you? You are the most insufferable, egotistical maniac I have ever met. With all the hate in the world it seems amazing to me that anyone could go out of his way to make someone so unhappy.*

The letter continued on in this way for six or seven pages. Patrick read it with amazement. He remembered those days, years and years ago, before he had returned to Pennsylvania, before his sister had run away. Julie Zacks had had a run-down studio on 113th Street, in a building with a doorman who had enormous, vacant eyes. There was a fake health food store on the ground floor that sold marijuana. Thinking about it now, the relationship seemed to have taken place in a foreign country, in another time, between two other people. That building had long since gone co-op, and the pot store was a French restaurant. He hadn't thought about it, or Julie Zacks, for years.

He looked over to see if Isabelle Smuggs had sensed his guilt and apprehension, but she just kept snoozing. The woman's mouth was wide open. He tried to be quiet. This letter was not something he wanted to draw attention to. Could the presence of a guilty conscience nearby wake someone from sleep? It wasn't usual, but with this Isabelle, who knew? She was sensitive to things.

He had loved Julie Zacks at one time, though, during what he now referred to as his "lost years." In his early twenties his only ambition had been to get as far away from the house in Buchanan as he could. He had lived on 103rd Street in Manhattan and taken odd jobs and gone out with Julie Zacks and stayed up late into the nights, closing down bars with her. The affair he had had with her had been fiery and passionate, and had ended suddenly, as a result of this furious letter. She had told him never to bother her again, and suddenly dropped out of his life. By then Emily had long since married Wedley, and his parents had died. Soon he was living in his ancestral mansion again, and the life he had lived in those lost New York years, and the person he had been then, had irretrievably vanished.

It was remarkable, though, to find this testament to some wrong Julie Zacks thought he had done her years ago. What was it he had done to her to get her so mad, anyway? He could not recall having given Julie any justification for such vitriol.

He read the letter three times, all the way through. There was something haunted, something pathetic about it. He imagined Julie Zacks sitting there, writing by her kitchen table, pouring out her heart to him, immortalizing her grief in writing. And now, years later, that same letter falling out of a book, and him reading it, in the midst of his sad marriage. Where was Julie Zacks now? What could have become of her?

Had he been a better person then? He had always thought of himself as a gentle person, with a good sense of humor, who could get along with strangers. In fact, that had been his chief strength, he used to think: the ability to get along. Since he'd married Clara, though, he seemed to spend most of his time fighting. At first he had found the contentiousness of his relationship exciting and energizing. You never really knew what you thought about things until someone challenged your most basic beliefs. But later, the charm of fighting and negotiating all things seemed to pale. Everything with Clara was a battle, even things that seemed to have only one aspect to them, like mailing a letter. But Clara would fuss over what size envelope to use, and how to address the recipient, and what kind of stamp suggested the message she intended. If they talked about it, she wound up tearing most of her letters up into small pieces, called people on the phone.

Ultimately, Patrick thought, there were only two kinds of couples. The ones who agree on everything (who are essentially boring), and the ones who fight about everything (who get divorced).

Outside the wind blew the limbs of a maple, the leaves in full flourish. There was a large blue jay sitting on the feeder. It was very quiet. Patrick sat in his chair, looking out toward the green trees, holding the letter Julie Zacks had written almost two decades ago.

Isabelle Smuggs sighed softly in dream.

He remembered that there was something about the way she had made love, something joyful and funny, something that at least one time had made him start laughing. It was summer, her room lit by a single candle, and she was playing Ornette Coleman on the stereo. She slept on a mattress on a wooden floor; there were tapestries hanging from the walls and ceiling. The windows were wide open, and on the streets there were the sounds of firecrackers and people standing on corners drinking beer and shouting. And she had done something that had started him laughing so hard that he rolled off her mattress onto the floor.

And was it the next morning—or was it weeks later?—when he had woken at dawn on a Sunday to see a great orange glow over the skyline of Harlem, and Julie sitting in a chair, wearing only her underwear, watching the city? He had only seen her for a moment before closing his eyes and going back to sleep, but there she had been, wearing a blue bra, and that picture of her stayed with him. He had woken hours later to find her still in the same position, and he put his glasses on and he saw that that orange glow was a tower of flame ripping through the roof of a church four blocks away. He heard the horns and sirens. Had they broken up that morning? Was that the prelude to an argument that had separated them? Or had they just drifted apart, the way people do? For what reason had she written him that furious and passionate letter, the one that began *Dear Moron?*

Patrick looked over at the sleeping Isabelle Smuggs. Julie had been the exact same age then as Isabelle was now: twenty-four. He would like to have written a letter to her, a letter that put things in perspective. But how could this be done with grace? Should he say that he was sitting by a sleeping girl in Buchanan, Pennsylvania, on a perfect June day, and he had found a letter of hers and it got him to thinking about old times and that he wished the best for her? Could he write such a letter and send it off? What would she think? He could see her standing by her house near the La Brea Tar Pits, finding his letter in her box, and bursting into tears, tearing it up, the tiny pieces of torn paper flying in the wind through the streets of Los Angeles. Did he have that kind of effect on people? Why shouldn't Julie have matured, just as he had? She'd take out the letter and read it to her new husband, and she'd tell him about the early days, about the lost years. The seventies were a time people had forgotten. Wouldn't Julie's husband like to be reminded?

Patrick realized that the main deterrent from writing such a letter was not some imaginary Mr. Zacks; it was Clara. What would she think of him writing to Julie, pouring out his soul? She would think he was still in love with her. Which he wasn't. That was the whole point. But how could he explain it in a way she would understand?

It was not likely that she would understand. Still, it was not fair to discard the memories of that fruitless time. His curiosity about his other life would keep him awake at night, as he considered and re-considered the life he might be leading now were it not for a few misremembered and random decisions. He'd wonder, whatever hap-pened to that Julie Zacks? Did she ever star in a movie? What was that thing she had done that had made him laugh? How had that sweet young love gone sour? It would be pleasant to write to her, to describe himself as he had become: *I'm sitting here in Buchanan, and I thought of you.* That would be all that would be necessary to get her to write back. He could use the address at work so Clara wouldn't find out. That was important, for otherwise she might open the letter, or at least watch him while he was reading, and she'd ask: Who's that from? And then he'd have to explain, and then there would be a fight.

But Clara, along with Quentin Smuggs, was out huffing and puff-ing up the road to Buchanan Mountain. There was no reason why he couldn't just write Julie a letter. No one would ever know. Patrick could get some paper and a pen and write the letter and mail it when he went to work on Monday. He suddenly wanted to do this thing with a great passion. It would be a good thing for his soul, Patrick thought. It would be like taking stock of things, explaining his life to her.

Patrick Flinch looked around for something to write with; he rooted through the drawers of his kitchen and living room, taking care to move in silence, to keep Isabelle from awakening. But there was nothing to write with; as usual it was next to impossible to find a pen when he needed one. He found only an abundance of lobster paraphernalia—bibs, crackers, tweezers, picks—and apparatus for roasting a chicken vertically. There were keys to bicycle locks and insect repellent and dish towels and sunblock, but no paper, and no pencil. He hunted around the ground floor a bit more, then went upstairs. He looked in the guest room, halfheartedly scanning the luggage of Quentin Smuggs, but even the man's suitcase filled Pat with distaste. There was a book called *Genre as Trope: Deconstructing the General Significance of Things.* Hoo boy, Pat thought. Now I'm sorry.

Pat walked across the hallway to the wood-paneled study. On the walls were paintings of his grandfathers and great-grandfathers. A set of stairs led back down to the kitchen. Dust drifted in the sunlight cast through an open window. No, Pat thought. This is not the room I want.

He went over to the other guest room, where Isabelle was staying. It was a sunny room, filled with plants, the room Clara had called "the nursery" when she first moved in. Sometime in the last few years, though, she had stopped calling it that and started referring to it as "the second guest room."

Isabelle seemed to be in the habit of throwing her clothes on the floor. T-shirts and bras and socks were strewn in every direction. He opened up the top drawer of the guest room dresser and found a maze of socks and scarves and berets. Wrong drawer. He checked the time. Eleven-thirty. They might be coming back soon. Who knew how long they would be gone? He had to work quickly. He had a fading vision of Julie Zacks checking her mailbox and finding it empty, walking back to her front porch alone.

He opened another drawer, and came face to face with two tubes of birth-control jelly, one almost empty, and a small case for Isabelle's diaphragm. Jesus, what was it the woman was expecting to find in Buchanan? Civility required for him to close the drawer, perhaps even to leave the room and abandon his quest for pen and paper at this point, but civility had been left behind. If he were civil, he wouldn't have broken Julie Zacks's heart in the first place, causing her, one afternoon in the seventies, to write a letter that began *Dear Moron*. He had lost his chance to be civil long ago.

He picked up the almost-empty tube of contraceptive jelly. It had been rolled up from the bottom, like a tube of toothpaste, rather than squeezed at random.

Patrick felt his heart beating wildly in his chest. What are you doing? he asked himself. You aren't looking for a pen anymore, is that it? Now you're spying on Quentin Smuggs's daughter? He saw Julie Zacks's eyes, twinkling and shining as she removed her diaphragm from its case, the music from 103rd Street coming through the window. Bottles breaking on the pavement. Kids shouting. Will you always love me? she asked. Not just now, while we're young, but forever?

He felt a sudden sense of shame, and checked the clock. Eleven-thirty-two. What if Isabelle were to come upstairs now, Patrick thought, and she were to find me here holding her diaphragm case? At that moment he saw the tip of the pen, sticking out from beneath the pile of clothes on the bed. He still wanted to write that letter. Julie Zacks. That was who he was looking for, not this Isabelle. There was still time to undo this ancient wrong. He picked up the socks and the panties and the bra and pushed them to one side. He paused for a moment, then thought: *what the hell?* He picked up Isabelle's brassiere and examined the tag on its side. *38-DD*, it read. *Do Not Bleach*.

Patrick gritted his teeth. Yikes, he thought, then put her bra back on top of the other clothes. He thought for a second, then moved on. The pen lay between the leaves of a book with flowers on the cover and an inscription: *My Diary.*

She had been writing that morning. She had very artistic, expressive handwriting, really rather beautiful if you paused to consider it. *It's all a dream,* she had written. *Can't seem to get any sleep. So glad it's the weekend at last. Still, nothing I do seems to be able to lift this weight off of my shoulders. If only I could meet someone I could mean something to. Still afraid that even if I do fall in love again I'll just wind up thinking about stupid Barton Sumac. Sometimes I think I'll never be free of him.*

We're up here in Buchanan staying with some friends of Daddy's. They're kind of strange. Their niece who lives with them is this heavy metal chick. Her aunt, Clara, used to be a student of Daddy's but she's a bitch and a half. The husband, Patrick, is huge—like six eight and well over two hundred fifty pounds. You'd think that someone that large would be disgusting but he's not. He's almost cute in some oversized fashion. In a weird way he reminds me of me. I wish there was some way to get him.

"What are you doing?" Isabelle said suddenly. She was standing in the doorway, looking at him.

Patrick yelled, dropping the diary onto the floor and throwing up his hands. "Jesus!" he said. "Don't do that to people!"

"Do what?" she said.

"Sneak up behind them," he said. "I could have hit the roof."

"Sorry," Isabelle said. "I would hate that. You hitting the roof, I mean."

"Me too," Pat said.

The two of them fell into silence for a moment. They both stared at the diary, lying faceup on the floor.

"So," Isabelle said.

"So," said Patrick. He suddenly caught the whiff of a mysterious odor. It seemed to be coming from all over. The smell was familiar, haunting, repulsive, and yet he couldn't find a name for it.

"That smell," Pat said. "You smell that?"

"Yeah," she said. She moved toward him, sniffing. Isabelle looked out the bedroom window at the bright sunshine. Wind shook the branches of the trees.

"So what do you think," she said. "Do you want to go someplace?"

For a few moments he just stood there, looking at her, her words reverberating in his mind.

"Go?" Pat said finally, his heart beating rapidly. "Go where?"

"We could take a bike ride. Maybe a swim at that place you mentioned at dinner. Isn't it beautiful at this time of day? So quiet."

Pat sniffed the air again.

"That smell," he said. "Jesus! What is that?"

"I think it's some skunks," she said. "It's mating season."

"Mating season?" Pat said.

"Yeah," Isabelle said. He could feel her breath on his neck. "For skunks. You know how it is."

"Skunks," Pat said, swallowing. "Well." He could see the dramatic outline of her nipples against the soft cotton of her T-shirt. "I guess they're making the best of things."

"Yup," Isabelle said. "You gotta admire that. They got courage. Even though they're like, you know. Skunks, and all that."

"Uh-huh," Pat said. The house seemed very quiet now.

"So what do you think?" Isabelle said. She touched the cotton sleeves of his shirt with her fingertips. "Do you want to take a ride?"

"I'm not sure," Pat said. "I'm afraid."

"Oh, don't be," Isabelle said. "We can wear bathing suits if you're scared."

"Well," Pat said. "I guess that's all right then. Sure it is."

"All right then," Isabelle said. "Let's go." She looked downstairs for a minute. "But hurry. They might be back any second."

Pat followed her down the steps. That smell in the house seemed to be growing overwhelming now. What was it she had said about wearing bathing suits? He had missed something. At what point had anyone suggested they not wear them in the first place?

A few minutes later, Pat and Isabelle were riding bicycles down a gravel path, birds singing all around them, sunlight pouring through the deep woods. Isabelle rode in front of him. She was wearing the top half of a yellow bikini and European-style biking shorts. The bikini top in particular seemed to be doing only a marginal job of withholding the woman's considerable bust. Good god, Pat thought, riding behind her. What lovely and terrible story awaits me down this road? They passed by a bush full of yellow flowers, and Pat thought of the book his sister Emily had once said she wished to write. She called it *Goldenrod.*

Pat and Isabelle parked their bicycles at the end of the path, and walked onward into the lush green marsh. "We better take off our shoes," she said. "It's getting pretty muddy." They took off their shoes and socks and squashed on into the muck. Pat heard the rushing of the Catawissa River. Before them was a green clearing with a small tree in its midst. A rope hung from a branch that reached out above a small pond formed by a bend in the river.

"Hey," Isabelle said, looking at the Catawissa. "It's pretty."

"Yes," Pat said. "It is."

Isabelle smiled. "Ready?" she said, then peeled off her top and threw it at him. "Are you coming?" she said. She stepped out of her shorts and her underwear and kicked them toward Pat with one foot. "Wa-hoo!" she said, and dove into the river.

For an instant she was gone completely, then she surfaced, laughing and gasping for breath. Again she spread her arms overhead.

"What are you waiting for?" she said. He did not have an answer.

He took off his things and rolled them into a ball and placed them underneath a honeysuckle bush. Isabelle smiled. "Come on, Pat," she said. "What do you think, lightning's going to strike us? Really, it's okay. It's the most wonderful thing there is."

Patrick Flinch dove in and swam underwater toward her. The undersea world was cool and blue. When he resurfaced, he saw that Isabelle had swum back to land to grab the rope swing. She grasped the rope and swung through space toward him. She let go of the rope almost directly over his head. Isabelle Smuggs flew through the air, weightless, in splendor.

She crashed into the water and disappeared, then resurfaced with her cheeks inflated. She splashed over toward him and spat water into his face, then submerged again.

"Hey," he said, "come back here."

She resurfaced with another mouthful of water. She squirted it into his face. "Hey," he said. "Stop it."

"Make me," she said.

He reached out and encircled her with his arms and they held each other in a long embrace. Isabelle, her eyes closed, let her head fall back. Pat kissed her and held her tighter. He felt her palms on his shoulder blades, moving in a soft spiral.

Isabelle sighed softly. "Well dee well," she said. "Oh my goodness gracious."

They stood there, waist deep in the clear water, kissing, for a long time. Pat moved his mouth down her neck to her breasts. "Goddamn," Isabelle said, and he gently kissed her nipples. A shiver seemed to run through her. Reaching down now he threaded his hand beneath her knees and let Isabelle float there in his arms. She put her arms around his neck and kissed him again. Her hair drifted loosely in the clear water.

Slowly Pat carried Isabelle back to the far bank and lay her down beneath a pine tree in a soft moss-covered place. Again he kissed her pink nipples, puckering now from the cold water. His kisses moved further and further down her body. "Goddamn," Isabelle cried again, more softly now. Small drops of water glistened like dew in her pubic hair, Pat noticed, and she sighed as he kissed her there. Each cool drop tasted like sweet briny nectar.

"Wait," Isabelle whispered. She sat up.

"What?" Pat said. "Is something wrong?"

She dove back into the water and swam across the Catawissa to the opposite shore, where her bike was. She reached into the pack beneath the seat and removed something, then got back in the water and swam over to him.

"Here you go, cowboy," she said, handing him a condom. "Saddle up."

Jesus, Pat thought. She thinks of everything.

Pat was aware of at least three selves as he and Isabelle Smuggs gently made love. The first was his immediate, sexual self, an almost unconscious, swooning being. He felt like the lowest note on a double bass as a bow is drawn across it. The second self, a bit more removed, observed his first self's actions with a boyish wonder and joy. *You're really doing it,* the second self said. *Yes sir. You're really doing it.* To which the first self replied: *Shut up. I'm busy.* There was a third self there, too, one that stood at an even greater remove, its arms folded, its foot tapping. *You're a weasel,* it said. *A slimeball. You're betraying your wife.* At this point the first self turned to the second and said: *Tell your friend to get lost.*

Isabelle clutched the moist moss beneath her ass, sighing softly into the summer morning light.

They lay there sometime later, her head resting on his chest, looking up at the sky.

"Hey. Patrick Flinch," she said. "You like the stars?"

"What? The stars? I don't know. The Big Dipper's all right, I guess."

"You should know the stars, Pat. Tonight maybe I'll teach you." She exhaled. "Maybe that's all it would take. Maybe that's the one good thing I can do in life, is teach you the stars."

"What are you talking about?" he said. "What one good thing?"

"It's a kind of bet I have with myself," she said. "If I can do one good thing in the world for somebody then I won't be such a jerk.

Maybe I'll be able to stay with one person for more than twenty seconds."

"Isabelle," Pat said. "You can do more than just one good thing. You're a good person."

"Oh, you don't even know me!" Isabelle said. "I'm not a good person. Believe me. I'm not, the way I never finish anything! But if I do this one thing maybe then I will be. Have you ever gone stargazing, Pat? I mean for real?"

"When I was a kid a couple of times," Pat said. "But I could never see what I was supposed to see. It made me feel stupid."

"You want to hear a story? One time I was in school, maybe sixth or seventh grade, and the teacher, Miss Bolgin, was going around the room, asking, 'What street is this? What city is this? What state is this?' on and on like that, until at last she said, 'What country is this?' and Jimmy Hoffman said, 'America.' Next she turns to me, and she says, 'Very good, and Isabelle, what planet is this?' So guess what: I freeze, the way kids do sometimes. I couldn't think of the answer. So she says, very sarcastically, 'Well, is it Mars?' And I nodded my head, yeah. It's Mars. Next thing you know all the kids are laughing their heads off, like I really didn't know the difference between my own hometown and Mars. You want to talk about feeling stupid, I got lots of stories, Pat."

Pat laughed, then leaned over and kissed her again. "You're not stupid," he said.

"I know," Isabelle said. "But the world sure makes you feel stupid sometimes. No one ever explains anything."

He looked at her, then leaned over and kissed Isabelle on the cheek. "I love your body," he said.

She squinched up her nose. "You're nice," she said, but looked sad.

"What?" he said. "You don't like it?"

Isabelle just shook her head. She blushed.

"But you're beautiful," he said. "Really."

Isabelle cupped her breasts in her hands, then let them fall. "I don't know. I just wish there wasn't so much of it," she said.

"I like that there's a lot of you," he said.

"Thank you," Isabelle said, still blushing. "You're a kind person, Pat." It didn't sound like she was convinced.

He ran his fingers through her wet hair. "You know I never knew an Isabelle before."

"You like it? I hate it. My name I mean. My friends call me Izzy."

"I like it," he said. "I'm so glad you wrote that note."

"Note?" Isabelle said. "What note?"

"The one you left in the kitchen. You know."

"What, the one that says you wish I wanted you? I thought you wrote that."

"I didn't write it. You're saying you didn't write it?"

"What, and just leave my feelings out there on a piece of paper in your kitchen, where someone could just come along and *read* them?"

"Wait a minute. If you didn't write that note, and I didn't write it, then who did?"

"Izzy," said a male voice, calling through the woods. "Izzy?"

Isabelle Smuggs and Patrick Flinch looked at each other for a moment in fear. Jesus Christ, Pat thought. Here comes one of her friends.

"Oh my God," Isabelle said. "Quick. Hide."

"Who is it?" Pat said. "What's going on?"

"It's my father," she said. "Oh my god. Hurry. Hide. Here, behind this bush. Hurry up."

Pat jumped behind the bush, even as he heard the sound of Quentin Smuggs and Clara coming down the path. He saw their bodies crashing through the ferns on the other side of the brook. Clara practically stepped on the honeysuckle bush where her husband's clothes lay hidden.

Good god, Pat thought. Now I'm in for it.

Isabelle jumped into the water. "Hey, you guys," she said, surfacing, keeping all but her head and neck underwater. "What are you doing?"

Clara Flinch and Quentin Smuggs, their arms wrapped around each other, started laughing and laughing. They had never heard a question funnier than the one Isabelle had just asked. "What *are* we doing, anyway?" Clara said, shaking her head. "That's a good one."

"Daddy, turn your head while I get dressed."

"I don't mind your being naked," Quentin Smuggs said. "I can relate to it, I mean, that is, in my own non-naked way. Hey, did you know clothes were invented by the Egyptians? It's true."

"Daddy, I said turn your head. Jesus."

"How did you ever find this place?" Clara said. "I thought that Pat and I were the only ones who knew about it."

Isabelle strapped herself back into her bikini top. "I don't know," she said. "I just followed the path."

"Have you seen Pat?" Clara said. She looked at Quentin Smuggs nervously. "We aren't going back to the house."

"No," Isabelle said. "I haven't seen him. What do you mean you aren't going back to the house?"

"It's good we ran into you," Clara said. "You may as well know."

"Know?" Isabelle said. "Know what?"

"Like we're getting married," the professor said. "Out west maybe. Maybe by some Elvis or something."

"What are you talking about?" Isabelle said.

"We're lovers," Clara said. "We've been lovers for years."

Across the river, Pat bit the inside of his mouth.

"Oh my god," Isabelle said.

"Clara's very special," Quentin Smuggs said. He reached forward with one finger and poked her in the bosom.

"Don't tell Pat," Clara said. "We'll let him know in a couple of weeks. Maybe we'll call him from Vegas."

"You can't do this," Isabelle said. "It's insane."

"It is," Clara said.

"Hey," said the professor. "Not as insane as we're gonna be!"

"Isabelle," Clara said. "I know this is hard. You don't have to call me Mommy right away. Only when you're ready."

"I'm not going to call you Mommy," Isabelle said. "Don't be ridiculous. That's disgusting. I'm not calling you Mommy, all right?"

"You should," Quentin Smuggs said. "That's what I call her!"

"Jesus Christ," Isabelle said, getting on her bicycle. "You two are sick, you know that? Sick." She turned her head and pedaled down the path.

Quentin Smuggs and Clara Flinch stood there watching her go. Patrick crouched behind his bush across the stream.

"Gee," Clara said. "She didn't take it very well."

"She'll adjust," the professor said. "This whole world is just a process of adjusting."

"Oh, Quentin," Clara said. "That's so true."

Quentin Smuggs unbuttoned his running shorts and stepped out of them. He wasn't wearing any underwear. Even from his vantage point on the other side of the Catawissa River, Patrick Flinch could see that the professor had a remarkably large penis. He did not like being the kind of person to notice such things, but in this situation it was impossible to ignore. Smuggs's awful thing swung down almost halfway to his knees. *Son of a bitch,* Pat thought, cowering and shivering behind his bush. *It's a goddamn liverwurst.*

"I don't know what's bothering her," Quentin Smuggs said. "Maybe she's just not a morning person."

Pat's wife pulled off her running clothes, then her brassiere and her panties. She turned to Professor Smuggs, naked as a statue. "Well, I am," she said. "I simply love the morning."

"So do I," Professor Smuggs said. "I love the morning that is you."

They moved toward each other and embraced.

"Am I really like the morning?" Clara said. "Tell me how I'm like the morning."

"I will tell you, Clara," Professor Smuggs said, placing his tongue on her nose.

"Oh tell me," Clara said, falling into his arms. "Tell me, tell me, tell me."

"I will, I will, I will," Professor Smuggs said. He yanked on her hair.

"Yowch," Clara said.

Crouching there behind the bush, on the opposite bank of the Catawissa, the naked Patrick Flinch could not quite decide on the movement that represented the best reaction to his present situation. On the one hand, he wanted to burst out of hiding, jump into the river, and catch the two of them in the act, demanding justice. On the other hand, it would be hard to seem morally superior to them as long as he didn't have any clothes on. They would figure out the situation pretty quickly, too, remembering Isabelle's hasty exit, and quite reasonably ask him what made their transgression so much more ethically reprehensible than his own. They'd have him there.

Pat's other option, then, was to turn in the other direction and try to make his way home. It wouldn't be so bad if it were possible to get his clothes back, but these, unfortunately, were stuffed under the bush on the other side of the river, next to the trysting couple. The forest around him was dark and swampy.

The professor reached up and started slapping on Pat's wife's rear end with his flat, open palms. The sound was similar to that of horses' hooves galloping across the plain. "Wee-ha," Clara said more determinedly, as Smuggs's palms smacked against her bottom. *Whacketa whacketa whacketa.*

All right, Pat thought. That's enough. He turned his back on the couple and made his way into the dark forest before him, wanting to hear and see no more. He would have to find his way back to the house on his own. Mosquitoes and dragonflies buzzed around his head.

Gingerly, timidly, nakedly, Patrick Flinch moved through the woods. The sounds of his wife's passion faded gently behind him. The sun moved higher in the sky.

Pat felt tears in his eyes. Jesus, what a sap! What was it he was crying for? he wondered. The untimely interruption of his *petit mort?* His unfinished conversation with Isabelle? His wife's betrayal? Or was it the unbearable economy of Quentin Smuggs's atrociousness? "Goddammit," Pat said, moving forward. He let the tears roll down his face.

Something moved down by his feet, curling around the green vines. A long black snake lay in the ferns, with a yellow underbelly and orange diamonds on its back. The forked tongue flickered. Well, Pat thought, there it is, exactly: the lizard Smuggs incarnate. And yet, as he walked past the snake, climbing over a fallen pine tree, he wondered again: what was the difference between his wife's tryst and his own? What made hers so much more condemnable? Well, Pat thought, I can explain that. It's because the two of them have been planning this for years, probably. They might have even been making love behind his back since college. What Smuggs was doing was adultery. What had passed between himself and Isabelle was an accident, a happy, serendipitous accident. There was a big difference between collision and collusion. Still, Pat thought, what would Clara have concluded about his interlude with Isabelle, if she had watched it from across the water? Would it have been obvious to her that his heart was still pure? He swatted a mosquito, and a small drop of blood spattered against his shoulder. It was hopeless: there was no logic to condemn his wife's affair that did not condemn himself as well.

Twigs and pine needles snapped gently beneath his feet.

Patrick kept assuming the woods were just about to thin out, leaving him in a spot somewhat near his home. Still, a long time seemed to go by, and the forest just grew deeper. Any moment now I'm going to stumble on a little gingerbread house, Pat thought. *That witch is in for a real surprise.* Time passed, however, and the shadows of the surrounding trees grew longer; light was slowly draining out of the dense, primeval woods. *Look at this shadowy paradise,* he thought. *I could be the first man, walking around like this, fleeing from Eden.*

If I ever get out of here, there's no reason I couldn't just keep moving. Assuming I ever find a pair of pants again. I could stick my thumb out and try to start life over, in a new city, far from that entombing family mansion. Was it so impossible to think of him traveling all the way across the country, traversing the deserts and crossing the mountains, sleeping under bridges, eating at soup kitchens, until at last, months from now, he arrived at the home of Julie Zacks herself? She would be glad to see him after all these years. *Hello, Moron,* she'd say. *I have known a lot of jerks in my time, but you really take the cake.* He pictured her looking at him in his stolen pants, then softening, laughing. Julie opened her arms wide. *Patrick,* she said. *At last.*

Patrick Flinch, aggravated and confused, charged onward through the forest in his pink and warlike nudity.

CANIS MINOR

•————.

Canis Minor is also known as the little dog,
although it doesn't look much like a dog, actually.
Some observers think this is unfair.

Isabelle Smuggs had already decided to get the hell out of Buchanan even before she got back to the Flinches' house. There
was no form of love that did not lead to bedlam. She parked the bike
near the back stairs and walked inside. It was disturbingly quiet in the
old house, full of its antique and dusty aroma. Patrick's ancestors
looked down at her, accusingly, from their darkening oils. Because of
you, they seemed to say, this house is now empty. Because of you we
have to hang here in silence. Jesus, Isabelle thought. As if I had anything to do with it. All I wanted was for him to kiss me.

"Pat?" she whispered, but there was no reply. The paintings of
the ancient Flinches stared down at her in contempt. He won't be
back, not for years. Thanks a lot, you *slut*.

Isabelle walked into Pat's bedroom. The drawers of his bureau
were open. Was it possible he had flung his things into a suitcase and
taken off? On his bed were two books: the collected John Cheever

and *In Watermelon Sugar*. It didn't look like he was going to finish either one of them.

She had a feeling of creepiness and dread, which reminded her of the way she had felt when she saw the underwater pictures of the *Titanic* on television. Some guys from Woods Hole had drowned a little robot and forced it to take photographs on the bottom of the ocean. There was the bow of the mighty ship, looming out of the hideous ocean, surrounded by darkness and rust. The robot went inside and found the grand staircase that led into the ballroom. The man on television said there wasn't much chance they'd find any bodies down there, not now. The pressure of the water would have crushed them years ago.

All right, she thought. Time for me to head out of town. She quickly packed her things and went downstairs again. For a moment she considered leaving him a note, but there on the kitchen table was the note she had seen that morning. She did not wish to be redundant. *I wish you wanted me.* Well, so maybe he did, she thought. But that didn't solve anything. She remembered the note her mother had left her, so long ago. *Everything just makes me tired.*

She got into her car and drove away without her brain.

Back in the house, the two burglars who had been hiding behind the drapes in the living room slowly crept out into the light. They were a man and a woman, both wearing panty hose on their heads. "All right," the woman said. "The coast is clear."

She looked at her companion. The legs of the panty hose hung down around his shoulders like the drooping ears of an enormous rabbit. *"Don't try to understand 'em,"* he sang softly. *"Just rope 'em up at random."*

"You got the sack?" the woman said.

"Yeah," he said. "I got the sack. Where's the dog? In the basement?"

"Yeah," the woman said. "I heard him barking. Tell you what. I'll give him the steak, you get him in the sack."

The man didn't say anything for a moment, then muttered, softly, "How come you always get to give them the steak?"

The woman was about to explain, but then she paused. "Hey, wait a minute," she said, looking more carefully at her surroundings. "Hey, wait."

"What," said the man. "What is it?"

"This place," she said, the terrible truth dawning on her. "I've been here before."

★

Isabelle Smuggs was almost a mile away by this time. Through the window to her left she overlooked what had once been the town of Centralia. She could see Route 61 snaking through the mountains, rolling down toward Ashland at the bottom of the hill. There was a small hollow in the mountains where smoke and steam hung in the air. Beneath this great gray cloud were a few streets, organized in blocks, but there weren't any houses on the blocks anymore. They had all been taken away.

Near what had formerly been the center of town a graveyard stood behind a fence. What looked like a kind of municipal building sat across the street from that, near what had probably been a school before the fire. The steeple of an abandoned church poked through the smoke toward heaven.

Isabelle looked down upon Centralia, feeling her heart pound in her breast. Jesus Christ, she thought. It's all been erased.

There was a sudden, stunning *thunk* from her right front tire. She had been looking at Centralia instead of the road, and as a result had driven into an absolutely huge pothole. Her car swerved out of control. There was a sound of something metal rolling around loose. Isabelle hit the brakes. The car screeched to a halt by the side of the road, only four feet away from the cliff that overlooked Centralia. Smoke was billowing out of the ground next to her car.

In front of her, rolling down the road, was one of her hubcaps.

Shit, she said, and jumped out of the car. Her front right tire was flat, and there was a considerable dent in the rim. Leaving this aside for the moment, Isabelle ran down the road after her hubcap. It was rolling toward the edge of the cliff.

She had almost caught up with it when the earth began to give way around her. As she rolled down the hillside, she had a tumbling half memory of her father explaining about the subsidences and sinkholes that the mine fire had created. Her nose filled with the smell of sulfur.

Below her loomed a small polluted pond, the color of copper piping. In another moment, Isabelle splashed into it. There was a great smacking sound, and then she looked up to find herself stationary, on earth.

There was another loud splash next to her. She looked over and saw her hubcap sinking in the brown water. There were other unexplained chunks of unknown and disgusting origin floating in the water. One large piece of matter vaguely resembled a slice of pizza. Another looked like a kind of buoyant roast beef.

A strange, mournful wailing filled the air. Isabelle was confused for a moment until she realized that she was crying. Apparently the trip through space had caused something inside her to come unmoored.

Isabelle Smuggs sat there in the waist-deep slime, and raised her palms to her face, sobbing her heart out. Oh, I'm a failure, she thought. This is the end of the line. Sitting in some pool of polluted guck in a ghost town.

"Hey, you," said a voice. A car was idling on a road nearby. "Hey."

Isabelle looked up. A woman of about thirty years was leaning out the window. She was holding a glass of milk in one hand.

"Yes?" Isabelle said. She tried to hide the fact that her personality had pretty much dissolved.

"What's the matter with you?" the woman said.

"Matter?" Isabelle said. "With me?"

"Yeah," she said. "You know what you look like, sitting there, crying your eyes out. Pathetic, if you ask me."

"Yeah, well," Isabelle said. "You don't know what's happened."

"Well that's true," the woman said. "Still, there's no reason to sit there crying. You deserve better. Believe me, we all do. Come on, stand up, let me give you a ride somewhere."

"I'm fine," Isabelle said.

"No you're not," the woman said. "You're falling to pieces. I can't even bear to look at it. Please. Let me help you. Stand up."

Isabelle was embarrassed to have been caught red-handed in the midst of her unbearable jag. She stood.

"Now get over here."

Isabelle walked over to the car, dripping wet.

"Get in," the woman said.

"Where are you taking me?"

"Wherever you say. Back to your home."

"I don't have a home."

The woman drank a sip of her milk. Now she had a creamy milk mustache. "Well," she said. "Maybe we can get you one."

Isabelle climbed into the car. "I'm wet," she said.

"Yeah, well there's a reason for that. You been in water."

"That's right."

The woman put the car back in gear and drove down the road. "I'm Wendy Walisko," she said.

"I'm Isabelle."

"I'm not trying to intrude. Really I'm not. I know what it's like to come all to pieces, believe me. You want some milk?"

Isabelle took the glass from her. "Thank you." Isabelle sipped some. Now both women had creamy milk mustaches.

"All I know is that nobody deserves to sit in a pool of industrial waste and cry their brains out. Am I right? Of course I am."

Wendy pulled her car into a driveway and stopped the engine. "This is where I live," she said. Her house was the only one on the street, although the remaining sidewalks and driveways suggested that at one time this had been a neighborhood full of houses and people. Isabelle tried to imagine this Centralian street the way it had been. Families going about their lives, people being born here and growing up and getting married. It was hard to imagine the immensity of all the things that had vanished.

Isabelle looked off into the distance, thinking.

"Well, come on in," Wendy said. "You want some dry clothes and a towel and stuff, don't you? Of course you do."

Isabelle wiped the top of her lip off with the back of her wrist and nodded. She did want a towel and stuff.

Wendy unlocked the front door. It had four different locks, which seemed a little funny in a town that only had about five houses in it. Wendy winked at Isabelle. "It's for protection," she said. She nodded in the direction of the vacant lot next door. There was a brown patch in the middle of the lawn where a house used to be. "Jacobsons used to live there, back before the mine fire. Their son Binny couldn't even move, just blinked one time for yes and twice for no, at least that's what they told everybody. Turned out later, guess what: only fooling." Wendy shook her head. "That kid was nothing but a big fraud," she said. She opened the door, and Isabelle walked into the house. Wendy redid the locks behind her.

The house was in a state of disarray. Open bags of potato chips and plates of cheese rested on almost every horizontal surface; several dozen brassieres were hanging from the lampshades and draped across the backs of chairs. On the mantelpiece was a small aquarium. Tiny little blobs were moving around inside.

"Sea-Monkeys," Wendy said, defensively. "It's a hobby I have, okay? That doesn't make me insane."

"They're nice," said Isabelle. "I didn't say you were insane."

"You're right, you didn't! I call it Insta-Life! Isn't it fabulous? Insta-Life I say! All you do is add water and they *materialize*! It's so inspiring!" Wendy brightened.

"I remember these things from comic books when I was a kid," Isabelle said. "They're really brine shrimp, aren't they?"

Wendy's face fell.

She didn't say anything for a moment. Then she said, softly, "I call it Insta-Life."

"Uh-huh."

"I say you just add water and they materialize."

"Well," Isabelle said. "Like I said, they're nice."

"All you do is add water," said Wendy.

"They're nice."

"You're about a size twelve, aren't you," said Wendy. She was looking Isabelle up and down. "My, what large breasts you have!"

Isabelle felt herself blushing. She looked back at the door with all the locks on it. It would be hard to make a sudden run for it, without this Wendy's detection.

"Yeah," Isabelle said, gritting her teeth.

"Oh, don't be embarrassed," Wendy said. "I'm just saying!"

"You know, if you'll just give me a towel, I think I can just dry off and get out of your hair," Isabelle said.

"Oh, but you've only just arrived," Wendy said. "And I have so much to show you! You know my house has an upstairs, *and* a down!"

Isabelle swallowed, but she did feel somewhat guilty about dripping on the woman's floor.

"Here, why don't you put this on," Wendy said, handing Isabelle a crumpled-up dress. She turned her back and walked into the kitchen.

Isabelle looked at the dress Wendy had given her and had a bad feeling about it. It was stained with a substance the color and consistency of guacamole.

Wendy came back with two glasses of milk. "Here," she said. "Let's get you on the mend." She looked at the dress, which Isabelle had not put on. "What, you don't like it?" A look of terrible rejection came to Wendy's eyes.

"It's fine," Isabelle said. "I just think I'll wait a little bit."

"You want to be wet? That's what you're saying?"

"I'm not that wet."

"But you're a little wet. And the stuff in that pool isn't even water. Trust me, I know." She leaned forward to whisper. "I've had it tested."

"Really, I'm fine," Isabelle said, looking at all the locks on the front door.

Wendy sipped her milk. "You know milk acts as a binding agent."

"A what?"

"A binding agent, I say. Creates mucus!"

Isabelle looked over at the Sea-Monkey aquarium.

"Women need mucus," Wendy said, kind of sadly. "But it's hard to get enough." Her face turned suddenly bitter, and her eyes seemed to focus on something that was not in the room.

"Have you lived here a long time?" Isabelle asked.

"Oh for-*ever*," Wendy replied distantly. "I keep meaning to move, to go somewhere. But where? Where can you go?"

"I don't know," Isabelle said. "Don't you have any family? Anything like that?"

"Family, oh yeah, tell me about it." Wendy shook her head.

"What?" Isabelle said. "That doesn't sound so far-fetched to me, that you'd want to see your family."

"Oh, those people," Wendy said dismissively. "With their little minds! They don't understand a thing."

"What don't they understand?" said Isabelle.

"What? Oh, forget it. We aren't here to talk about me, we're here to talk about you! You're the one who's all messed up. We shouldn't forget that."

"I'll be all right. I just got into a situation." Isabelle was still clutching the dress with the stains on it.

"I hate that," Wendy said. "Situations." She looked across the room and stared at a bear trap hanging from the wall. "That's another reason I stay here. To avoid them."

"But is it safe?" Isabelle asked. "I thought it was dangerous now, in Centralia."

Wendy looked at Isabelle like she was crazy. "Dangerous?" she said. "Here?"

"Yes," Isabelle said. "That's what I heard."

"Well of course it's dangerous," Wendy said, waving her hand through the air. "But where isn't it dangerous! You name me a place!"

"I don't know," Isabelle said.

"There are places where people just jump out at you and make you give them your belongings. Other places where the ground shakes back and forth and the buildings can just fall over, like they were nothing. I know somebody who saw a picture of this mountain in Oregon they used to have. Guess what: *exploded*. No, I'll take my chances in Centralia, thank you."

"Well," Isabelle said. "As long as you're happy."

"I wish!" Wendy said. She finished her milk. "Listen, Isabelle, do you like to play games?" She smiled nervously. "I do."

"Games?" Isabelle said. "What kind of games?"

"I don't know," Wendy said. "Never mind. Are you feeling all right now? Are you recovered?"

"Yeah," Isabelle said. "I'm just wet, is all. I'll be all right."

"Why don't you put that dress on? The one I gave you? Is it the wrong style? Does it make the wrong statement? I know it isn't very up-to-date, but how often do I get out? I just told you: hardly ever. And if I did go out, where would I go? Buchanan? You know what kind of people live there? Sickos. You think I'm joking? I'm not. A lot of those people used to live in Centralia. When the government said we were all in danger here, supposedly, guess what: they just *moved*." Wendy shook her head in disbelief at the stupidity of persons like this.

"No, no," Isabelle said. "The dress is fine. It's just—it's got some stains on it." She showed Wendy the stains. "I don't know what this stuff is. Guacamole I think, maybe." On the back was a large hole; there were burn marks around its edges.

"Oh yeah," Wendy said, looking carefully. "I forgot. Well, that's definitely *not* guacamole." Wendy looked sad.

Isabelle put the dress down on the couch next to her and rubbed her fingers against each other, hoping she hadn't gotten any of this green whatever-it-was on her. "Well, I'll just drip-dry. I'm practically dried off already."

"That's nice," Wendy said. "When you have the kind of problem that just dries up like that. That's the best kind." She swallowed, looked back at her locked door. There was something hungry about the woman's eyes, as if she didn't get much sleep. Isabelle wondered about the carbon monoxide from the mine fire, and whether or not it leaked into the house through the basement. Carbon monoxide poisoning was supposed to turn your face cherry red, though. This Wendy was as pale as goat cheese.

"So like, do you have a boyfriend," Wendy stammered. "I was just wondering if you had one."

"I don't know," Isabelle said. "I thought I did. I mean, I almost did."

"I'm sorry," Wendy said. "I shouldn't have asked." She raised her fists to the sides of her temples as if she had committed an act of unforgivable rudeness. "Oh, I'm stupid, stupid, stupid!"

"It's all right," Isabelle said. "I don't mind talking about it. You're not stupid."

"Oh, but I am," Wendy said. "The things I believe!"

"Well," Isabelle said. "It's not what you believe that makes you stupid." She wanted to be reassuring, but wasn't sure exactly that this had come out right.

Wendy looked at the bear trap again and licked her lips. "Anyway, Isabelle," she said. "Tell me. What's it like?"

"What's what like?"

Wendy seemed to withdraw deep inside herself. It was as if she were looking out of her own eyes through distant telescopes.

"You know. Having a boyfriend."

Isabelle looked at the woman for a moment as if she were joking, then realized that she was serious.

"You've never had a boyfriend?" Isabelle said.

"Well, it's not like I haven't tried!" Wendy said, defensively. "But I never see anyone! Anyway, the men I meet, they don't like to play the games I do."

"What kinds of games do you mean?"

"I don't know," Wendy said. "Just the things I like to do."

"Do you work?" Isabelle said. "Do you meet people at your job?"

"Oh, I don't work anymore," Wendy said, smiling. "I get a disability. Everyone's happier if I stay home, really. I get into—you know. Situations. About all I do now is sell these vacuum cleaners door to door. But I don't really sell so many. They're junk."

"Well, maybe you should get out more," Isabelle said. "That might be good."

"I get out," Wendy said, irritated. "That's how I found you." She smiled. "You know I found a cat once and I kept it for nine whole months. I named it Kitty."

"What happened to it?" Isabelle said.

"Died."

"Oh. I'm sorry."

"Hey, it's not your fault. You weren't the one who dented it."

"That's right," Isabelle said. "I wasn't even here."

"Hey, you don't need a vacuum cleaner, do you?" Wendy said,

suddenly. "I mean, as long as you're here I could give you the whole demonstration."

"I thought you said they were junk."

"Yeah," Wendy said. "That's true."

"Well, I guess I'll pass," Isabelle said, hoping this did not sound rude. "I already have a vacuum anyway, to tell you the truth."

"So what's it like?" Wendy said. "Having a boyfriend? A real one, I mean."

"What do you mean, a real one?"

"Well, I mean, of course I've got the other kind. I've got a whole basement full of *those*. But they aren't the same. They only say the stuff I force them to. The things they say about me behind my back, goodness, I'd hit the roof if I knew about it!"

Isabelle felt her heart beating quickly. An awareness that she was in some kind of danger was becoming more and more insistent. Still, there was something about this Wendy that called to her. It was getting harder to leave.

"Well," Isabelle said. "I guess that's the first thing. Real men don't just say what you make them."

"Yeah," Wendy said. "I'm not sure I'd like that." She licked her lips. "But what about the kissing, and all that. The sex. I've read so much about it! Is it nice?"

Isabelle felt herself blushing. "Yes," she said. "It's nice. Most of the time, it's nice." Isabelle paused. "You'd like it."

"Yeah," Wendy said. "That's what I've heard." She looked at her empty glass of milk. "I hope I have sex someday. The real kind, I mean. I think it's really important, for a person to have sex, at least once. You know. Just so you can know what it's like."

"Well," Isabelle said. "You don't want to make love with someone unless you're sure about it."

"I think that's true," Wendy said. "That's why I'm being so careful! To make sure!" She thought of something. "Men aren't like women," she said, suspiciously.

"That's true," Isabelle said.

Wendy thought for what seemed like a long time.

"They're bigger," she said.

"That's right," Isabelle said.

"And they have, you know—penises and junk," Wendy said. "In the book I read they looked kind of like giblets, you know, like in a chicken. What's that thing that hangs off of a rooster's neck? Anyway, I've done lots of reading."

"You certainly seem well-informed."

Wendy looked across the room at the mantelpiece that stood over a bricked-up fireplace. There was a fake fireplace heater on the hearth. A long electric cord ran from the flames to a wall socket.

On top of the mantelpiece was a photograph of a soldier in a silver frame.

"Isn't it a shame?" Wendy said, absently. "That he died?"

"Who?"

"My husband," she said. Wendy walked over to the mantelpiece and removed the photograph, handed it to Isabelle. As Isabelle stared at it she noticed that the soldier was absolutely walleyed.

"You were married?" Isabelle said, trying not to sound surprised.

"Well, not actually. We were only engaged to be engaged, if you know what I mean. But we wrote lots of letters. I still have them."

"That's good. You'll want those someday."

"Yeah, maybe," Wendy said.

"What did he die of?" Isabelle asked.

"I don't know," Wendy said. "They didn't say. He was in some experiment. I don't really want to talk about it."

"I'm sorry."

"No, I started it. I just miss him sometimes. Does that seem crazy, to you, to miss someone you've never met?"

"You never met him?"

"We were *going* to meet. We used to talk about it all the time.

'Let's get together,' Herman used to say to me in that special way he had. 'I'll call you.' Isn't that something?''

Isabelle thought for a moment, looking at the photograph. It didn't seem crazy at all, to miss someone you'd never met. "Yes," she said. "That's something."

Wendy looked at Isabelle as if she had been hiding something from her. "Did your boyfriend put you in that pool of slime? Somebody did."

"No," Isabelle said. "Not directly. I fell in."

"Not directly, you say. So he had something to do with it. Maybe you were off someplace with him and you had to leave in a big hurry and you weren't looking where you were going, and the next thing you know, guess what: splash. Maybe he acted like a big jerk, not thinking about you, thinking only about himself! See, that's just typical! They aren't interested in you at all! You know, personally, I don't think men like women very much. I mean, why *would* they?''

"Because," Isabelle said. "They don't want to be alone."

"They don't?" Wendy said. "Why not? What's so bad about being alone?''

"Nothing," Isabelle said.

"Oh, I don't know if I agree with that," Wendy said. "It's got its problems."

The women sat in the room for a moment in silence. Then Wendy said, "Do you want to go downstairs, Isabelle? And meet the boys I've got?''

Isabelle's face must have shown some dismay, for Wendy quickly added, "Don't worry. They aren't real!"

Isabelle opened her mouth and heard herself say, "Yes, Wendy. I'd like that." She cast her eyes at the long series of locks on Wendy's front door. The Sea-Monkeys floated in their tank.

"Okay," Wendy said. She stood up. "But I better put on the Naked Music first."

"The what?"

Wendy hunted around in a stack of old records on the floor until she found a scratched-up album. She placed it on the turntable. Slowly, the second movement of Beethoven's Seventh Symphony began to swoon from the speakers.

"The *Naked Music*," Wendy said, pulling her shirt off over her head. She reached around her back to unhook her bra, which Isabelle now noticed was covered with a leopard-skin pattern. Wendy smiled as she dropped her panties to the floor. "I mean, you can't get naked without the music!" she said. "It wouldn't be kindly."

It was four o'clock when Patrick Flinch finally arrived back at his home. Onto the floor in the front hallway he dropped the cardboard box he had found to conceal his nudity. FARMER MACGREGOR'S KOUN-TRY KITCHEN, read the words printed on the box's side. SECRET MAYONNAISE: ONE CASE. Perspiration poured down the sides of his face. He was covered with mud and dirt; scratches from branches and thorns adorned his calves.

"Hello?" he called. "Is anybody here?"

His voice echoed in the empty house. The place was deserted.

"Goddammit," he said. "Goddammit to hell." All this time he had been thinking about murdering Quentin Smuggs, about the expression the professor's face might bear if he were unexpectedly strangled by accident. It seemed unfair that Pat should be denied this pleasure simply because the man was not at home. The least this Quentin Smuggs could have done, considering all the trouble he had caused, was to be where he was supposed to be when Pat finally showed up to asphyxiate him.

Large, pink, and naked, Patrick Flinch stormed toward the kitchen. The only known antidote to his current situation was beer. It had never failed him yet. If he sat at the kitchen table and drank a Bud then it was possible that something might occur to him, a way perhaps of murdering Quentin Smuggs by telepathy. *We know of no brand produced by any other brewer which costs so much to brew and age.* It said so right there on the can. Yeah, Pat thought, as he reached the refrigerator, but how hard were they looking?

He was about to pull out a can when he had another unpleasant premonition. He opened the basement door and looked down into the darkness of the cellar. "Buddy?" he said. "Buddy?"

There was an unnatural silence. Even for a dog that was almost dead, Buddy usually produced a certain volume. It took a certain amount of noise just for the dalmatian to breathe and fart. The basement, however, was soundless.

At the top of the steps, somebody had dropped a T-bone steak. A bite had been taken out of it. Pat looked at it for a long time.

Okay, he thought. Fine.

He returned to the refrigerator. For a moment he stood there at the open door, feeling the chilled air against his skin, looking at all of his failed meals. Cartons of Chinese food. Half-empty bottles of salad dressing. Tupperware containers full of the mysterious and unknown. Jesus, Pat thought. Who would ever eat this stuff? Can this actually be the junk that keeps me alive?

He removed a red and white can of Budweiser and cracked it open. Pat threw back his head and let the golden liquid glug down his throat. He belched, and felt no satisfaction. Somehow it tasted different now, kind of like the can it came in. Metallic.

The beer had failed to cheer him. Goddamn, he thought, maybe Quentin Smuggs was right. This stuff does make you foamy.

Still holding the cold can, Pat walked upstairs to his bedroom. The first thing a person needed in a situation like this was a pair of pants. He was still angry about his ordeal. In order to get the mayonnaise box in the first place he had had to cross a field full of angry dairy cows, some of whom gave chase to Patrick, lowering their horns and thundering after him with a kind of disgusted, fed-up lowing. When he finally got inside the barn he had discovered, to his horror, that he was in the basement of Farmer MacGregor's. From the restaurant upstairs had come the sounds of the Pork Chop Festival. The only thing he could find to wear was that beat-up cardboard box, and there was great difficulty getting that. He'd had to remove a dozen jars of secret mayonnaise just to empty it, and while he was doing this, a cow had come up behind him with its big wet nose and surprised him. A tag on a collar around its neck read: *Mrs. Cleaves.* He could tell just by her expression that this Mrs. Cleaves had fallen in love.

Pat reached his bedroom and thought about pants.

There on his bed were the unfinished books which had started the trouble, the Cheever and the Brautigan. *In suburbia the deeds were done and done again, as my life is done in watermelon sugar.* He remembered his earlier fugue concerning the fate of Julie Zacks. Do you know what you've done to me, he asked her. Do you? He thought about that morning he had seen her sitting in her chair in her blue bra, looking out on the burning church. Why hadn't she woken him? Was the fire something she had not intended to share?

And this was the moment at which he noticed that his wife's closet was empty. All of the drawers in her bureau had been cleaned out. Even her jewelry box was empty. Jesus. She hadn't been kidding. Even now she was probably halfway to Las Vegas, to get married to Quentin Smuggs by some artificial Elvis.

Goddamn, Pat thought. *This is some day I'm having.*

Patrick sat down on the bed, feeling as if he had been slain with a bow and arrow. His sour stomach gurgled with its acid.

With a rising panic he stood up and went across the hall to Phoebe's room. He looked at the calendar on the wall, on which the girl put a big slicing X through each day as it passed. She hadn't crossed off the last two days. He suddenly recalled the note he had found, the note which read, *I wish you wanted me.* At last, too late, he understood. Phoebe had left it for him on her way out of town. Dang it, Phoebe, he thought. I did want you.

He went over to her bureau. There next to a pair of earrings was the necklace that Emily had given her daughter, with its pale crystal jewel. It was supposed to have magical properties. Through the window he saw the banks of the Catawissa River, the water trickling softly toward the sea.

Patrick began to feel like a tremendous zeppelin, losing air, heading groundward. In a moment he was going to crash somewhere, burst into flames like the *Hindenburg*. That guy on the radio sobbing into his microphone. *It's crashing yes it's crashing, oh get out of the way ladies and gentlemen please.*

She didn't even take the necklace with her. Wherever she was going now, the girl had decided to leave her mother's charms behind.

Well, hell, Pat thought. Maybe she wouldn't need them.

AUTUMN STARS

ANDROMEDA

*Andromeda, the daughter of Cassiopeia and Cepheus, is
also known as the Girl in Chains. In her hair is the famous
Andromeda Nebula. It is said to be the most distant
object the human eye can see without narcotics.*

Three months later, on an afternoon in late September, Phoebe
Harrison jogged through the quiet streets that surrounded her
father's house, in Valley Forge. Today Phoebe was listening to this
new Bruce Springsteen tape, *Human Touch,* on her Walkman. Her
new friends at the Dillinger Academy for Girls didn't like Bruce very
much. They said he had sold out since he moved to Hollywood and
married his backup singer. There was a rumor that Bruce really
weighed like five hundred pounds now, didn't do anything but sit
around watching cable and eating tub after tub of ice cream with his
bare hands, but Phoebe didn't believe this was true. She had seen
him on MTV, and he was swinging his arms around playing "Human
Touch" with his shirt off and snarling. If he weighed five hundred
pounds now the video had to have been made with a bunch of special
effects to conceal it, and Phoebe didn't think that there was any effect

that could hide that much human fat, not even in Bruce's neighborhood.

Phoebe was wearing white running shorts, a pair of Nikes, and a black top. Her huge hair was withheld by a baseball cap that said PHILLIES, which she wore backwards, catcher-style. Sweat poured down the back of her neck as her feet slapped, one after the other, on the pavement. The leaves in the trees had just begun to change color; the air around her was crisp and cool.

Even with the baseball cap, a lot of her hair kept swinging into her face. Today was the last day that she would have this problem, however. As soon as she got back to the house, Phoebe was having her stepmother, Vicki, cut it all off and dye her hair blond. Her heavy metal days were over.

Phoebe thought about the impending haircut. It wasn't that she had enjoyed her hair any less here than she had in Centralia. But it was exhausting, standing out all the time, attracting attention. Once Vicki gave her the honey blond bob, she would look like everyone else, and at this point that would be a relief. Now if there was only some way she could lose four inches so she wouldn't tower over everyone else in tenth grade, that would really fix things. It was horrible being so tall. The boys at the Rutherford Academy, her school's male counterpart, were at least a head shorter than she was. Above all she dreaded her old Buchanan nickname arising in her new life. She was not sure she could endure it if someone started calling her Icky.

She ran south on Glouster Road, past the huge mansions and gardens and fields. Phoebe didn't understand how everyone on the Main Line could be so wealthy. What was there to do in Philadelphia that created all this money? You'd think that anyone with enough cash would move the hell out of there, head up to New York or something. Still, there they were: estate after estate surrounded by pools and tennis courts and greenhouses. People parked their cars out front, too, so you could see them: BMWs and Mercedeses and Jaguars. Phoebe didn't understand this either, figured that if you had the resources to own a car like that you'd have the sense to keep it in the garage.

Phoebe Harrison jogged onward, breathing, feeling the world recede, as if she were running in place on an elaborate treadmill while someone wheeled the scenery by. Bruce was singing in her ear: *You and me we were the pretenders/We let it all slip away/In the end what you don't surrender/Well the world just strips away.* Phoebe took a left on Barkley Street and jogged up the short hill toward the Valley Forge Elementary. On the right, behind a great black iron fence, was a tremendous mansion, with columns and gardens and fountains. It didn't appear that anyone was living there anymore. You saw this on the Main Line sometimes: the houses built back in the late 1870s were simply too huge for even the wealthy to support these days. Usually these places got divided up into condos or razed for the land, which was almost instantly covered with dozens of overpriced, shamelessly snooty minidwellings without any lawn. This one, though, was still standing. As Phoebe jogged past it, she wondered briefly about the people who had built the place, how long ago they had died. It was sad to see it all run-down, but sometimes this happened. On occasion people on the Main Line just got so fabulous that they popped like ticks.

All this money, and people's nonchalance about it, was a real shock after Centralia. Phoebe got the sense that the girls at Dillinger didn't really understand that they were among the wealthiest young women in the world. Most of them had their own cars, and their families went to places like Acapulco and Bimini for spring vacation. There was one girl whose name really was Muffy, and it wasn't a nickname either, her parents had *baptized* her Muffy. Her full name was Muffy Aurora Pennypacker, and she had a brother named Lyons and a sister named Willa. Everyone acted like Muffy was pretty normal, in spite of the fact that she wore white headbands and knee socks, even on the weekends. Muffy didn't talk to Phoebe, not least because Phoebe had big black hair and wore rock and roll buttons on her school tunic.

On Monday, though, when she showed up for classes, the stranger with the big, feathered, jet black hair would be gone. Instead they'd get a little honey blond girl with a short bob. By the end of the week Muffy and Willa were going to think they had known Phoebe all their lives. People liked you better the less you looked and acted like yourself.

It was a realization of the truth of this philosophy that had landed Phoebe back at her father's house in the first place. Even now, three months after the fact, Phoebe would wake up some nights, wondering where she was. For a moment she would imagine that she was asleep in the temple of her imagined destination, in the oceanside hotel with her mother and sister. But then she'd hear the old pipes clanking in Wedley's house and she'd remember how dramatically her attempt at finding them had failed. She had spent only one night as a runaway, driving west in Duard's car. At dawn the engine died on the outskirts of Hershey and the Swinger rolled to a stop. Rain was pouring down.

She had gotten out of the car and walked into a field in the downpour, letting the water soak into her blouse, feeling her hair spray dissolving and her hair falling down around her back and shoulders. The warm summer rain splattered off her forehead. Dim shoots of corn stood calf-high all around her, shaking in the breeze, raindrops ricocheting off the leaves. Tears had come to Phoebe's face and rolled down her cheeks. The tattoo ached on her breast.

From the distance came the sound of a dog barking. For a moment Phoebe was afraid, but then she thought of Buddy. It's okay, she thought. He's just doing his job, which is barking. That's what dogs are for.

As the light dawned around her, Phoebe thought about trying to survive on the road, as a runaway. Mist was rising off the field. The contents of her purse weren't really going to help her much. Already her giant hair had collapsed around her, and her mascara looked beaten up and raccoonish. I just don't have the courage to go out in the world alone, Phoebe thought. All I really want to do is go home.

Soon she was walking down a dirt road, following the course of the rolling hills into Hershey.

At last, in midmorning, she arrived at Phartley Park. A smell of gasoline and popcorn hung over the place, and Phoebe remembered having come here years ago, with Emily. Over the entrance was a statue of something called Thoraxx the Clown, who appeared to have had his eyes shot out with a BB gun. It cost Phoebe $7.50 to get in, which was a lot for a place that didn't even put any money into fixing its own clown. She walked through a turnstile, then got her hand stamped by a man who had pinkeye. "Welcome to Phartley," he said, wiping his runny nose on his plaid shirt cuff. "Make a nice day."

Yeah, right, Phoebe thought, and looked for a pay phone.

To the right was a long midway full of barkers trying to get fairgoers to attempt any of a series of unlikely feats, like busting balloons with darts or knocking over a pyramid of Coke bottles with a baseball. There was a steam calliope, a real one, playing from an antique carousel, and there was extremely loud heavy metal music blasting from a ride called the Matterhorn, which was kind of like a merry-go-round that spun around at a forty-five-degree angle. A siren went off in the Haunted Pirate Ship. Water guns were spraying into the mouths of cartoon characters on the midway; a giant wheel of fortune spun round, its notches clacking. At the far edge of the park was something called the Sky Master. Its prisoners screamed out their innocence as it wheeled them mercilessly into the heavens.

Phoebe found a pay phone next to a booth marked SMASH EM UP, in which one hurled baseballs at piles of milk bottles. It was three balls for a dollar. I could play that, she thought, using the fifty bucks I have left. I could go up to the guy and say, Here's fifty bucks, I want a hundred and fifty baseballs. With enough patience, and enough time, she could smash up the whole damn place.

"Hello, Wedley?" she said. "It's Phoebe. I want to come home."

An hour and a half later, Wedley had driven up and taken her away. Three months later she had entered a new school, in Bryn Mawr, where the girls were named Muffy and had their own telephones.

The Springsteen tape ended and Phoebe flipped the cassette. On the other side was a band called 10,000 Maniacs. They did a cover version of Cat Stevens's song "Peace Train." Cat Stevens was the musician from the sixties who had lost his mind and sat around now wearing a white dress, playing bongos. When the ayatollah came out with his edict of death on Salman Rushdie, Cat Stevens, whose new name now was something like Abdullah Wackamoley, said, *Hey, that's just fine. Kill eem.* Phoebe didn't understand the way the world worked. How was it possible that one minute this guy was singing "Peace Train" and the next second was discussing the list of people who ought to get their brains blown out? I guess I just don't understand religion, Phoebe thought.

She took a left on Xavier Road. On her right was a tremendous green field, several square miles of soft grass. At the top of a small hill was another swollen Main Line mansion, but this one had been sold several years ago to the Swenson Academy, which was a school for children who suffered from not having an "inner child." One of the kids who had lived there had recently decided to burn the place down, and as a result the mansion had stood for a year or two abandoned and gutted by a great fire. Then they sold the thing to a professional coin collector, who rebuilt the place from the ground up, and added a five-car garage. Again, Phoebe didn't understand how collecting coins and stamps could give anybody enough money to own a fifty-room mansion and a hundred acres of lawn, but as she kept reminding herself, this was not Centralia.

Everyone had agreed that her moving back in with Wedley had

been the best thing. By now Uncle Pat and Aunt Clara had split up for what looked like forever; Aunt Clara and Professor Smuggs had gone off on something called the Around-the-World-Cruise-to-Nowhere. Phoebe had returned to Valley Forge to find that her father's business had ballooned, with the result that Vicki and Wedley were wealthy, after a fashion. When he first married Vicki, he had still been sweeping chimneys for a living. In less than two years, though, Wedley had expanded this into his own chimney-sweeping/wood stove/hot tub maintenance business, and he had reached the stage now where he didn't even have to leave his office all day. He had a score of people working for him, contractors, handymen, even some chimney sweeps, who went out in a fleet of specially painted minivans that had a small picture of Wedley wearing a top hat painted on the side, and the name and phone of the business, Mister Chimney. Again, Phoebe didn't understand how her father could make any money out of this, but there it was: her father was a hit, even had his own little jingle on the radio:

Sweeping, sweeping sweeping, and we're feeling so fine.
The sky is blue for miles 'cause relaxation's on your mind.
You just called Mister Chimney and now everything's okay!
Hot tubs, wood stoves, fireplace,
Chimneys swept with style and grace!
Call Wedley!

The girls at Dillinger, meanwhile, had unveiled contempt for anyone whose father went around calling himself Mister Chimney. Some of them, inevitably, insisted on naming her Phoebe Chimney. It was better than Icky, but it was still embarrassing. It was hard not to feel ashamed among these girls, even though most of *their* fathers should have been riding around in vans engraved with the words *Mister Embezzlement,* or *Mister Insider Trading,* or *Mister Imitation Soybean Baby Food Formula.*

Phoebe crossed over Devon State Road, still listening to 10,000 Maniacs. She loved the sound of the drums. Phoebe wished sometimes that she could have been a musician, but whenever she wished this she thought about her sister, Demmie. That was what Demmie had wanted, too, and now she was gone.

A car approached Phoebe from behind. It slowed down as it got closer to her. The lyrics to "Peace Train" echoed in her head.

The car behind Phoebe trailed her slowly, and she got a sick, empty feeling in her stomach. This had better not be the jerk in the Miata again, she thought. There was this guy in a red Miata that sometimes trailed her in his car, just long enough for it to be creepy. The second she broke her stride and turned around to look at him, he hit the gas. It wasn't unusual for guys to yell stuff at you when you were out minding your own business, but the fact that the same person kept tailing her was really twisted. She already had his license memorized, but the one time she called the cops they told her there wasn't anything illegal about it unless the driver threatened her or tried to coax her into the car. This was pretty typical, Phoebe thought. This was what happened when you asked men for help. They just smirked and guffawed and pretended like doing anything decent was like asking them to send a chimpanzee to Mars.

The guy in the Miata drew up next to her and took a good, blatant slather. He was wearing a Panama hat and green sunglasses. Phoebe gave him the finger, and he hit the gas. With a great squealing of rubber the car patched off down the street toward Lancaster.

Phoebe jogged the rest of the way home without turning her tape player back on. The longer she ran, the angrier she got. Why wasn't there any law that prevented goons from slobbering all the hell over her? Was this part of becoming a woman, accepting the fact that for the rest of her life men she did not even know were going to look at her like she was a side of beef? She felt guilty about giving the stranger the finger, as if she had lost the encounter by allowing herself to get mad.

She got back to her father's house and walked through the kitchen. "Hello, honey," Wedley said. He was sitting at the table, reading *Newsweek*. Wedley looked different since his business had taken off. He had at last cut off his long ponytail and now had his salt-and-pepper hair combed neatly to one side. He still had big, powerful biceps, though, which he'd achieved from years and years of shoving brushes up and down people's chimneys. "So, how was your run?" he asked. Wedley Harrison looked at his daughter and smiled.

"Don't *talk* to me," Phoebe said, storming through the kitchen.

Through the archway to the "conservatory" Phoebe could see that Vicki had set up a chair for her haircut. She had covered the floor with newspaper and draped a large sheet over the chair. There was a small table full of combs soaking in blue liquid and gels and curlers and tipping caps. Vicki's little dog, Schnoodle, whose hair was tied up in ribbons, lay on the floor near the newspaper with one eye open, anticipating Phoebe's haircut. For some reason the dog loved to eat freshly clipped human hair. Schnoodle smacked on it like newly mown wheat.

"You get yourself all ready," Vicki said, standing there in her white apron, her curly, permed hair gathered at the top of her head in a kind of vertical ponytail. "You can't believe how long I've been waiting for this. Years."

Schnoodle licked his lips.

"I'll be right down," Phoebe said, and thought, *Idiot.*

She climbed the stairs toward the bathroom. Wedley's new house had a bathroom that was larger than her bedroom had been in Centralia. It had an ornate bathtub with brass claw-shaped feet on it, a separate shower stall in one corner, and a Jacuzzi built on a kind of platform near the center of the room. There was a wall of mirrors, a vanity table, and a sink that instead of a faucet had a brass fish that shot water out of its mouth. There was velvet wallpaper and an Oriental rug. And this was the *bathroom,* Phoebe kept thinking.

The phone rang suddenly, and Phoebe picked it up.

"Hello?" she said.

"Hello? Is this Phoebe?" a woman's voice said. It was not the voice of anyone she recognized. "Don't tell anyone I'm calling."

"Who is this?" Phoebe said. Her heart started beating quickly in her breast.

"Don't you know?" the woman said. "I mean, my voice doesn't mean anything to you?"

Phoebe listened to the voice, trying to figure out what was going on.

"No," Phoebe said. "I'm sorry. I don't know who this is."

The woman sighed. "Oh, I don't know what difference it makes. You hardly know me. My name is Isabelle, Isabelle Smuggs. I'm a friend of your uncle Pat's. I mean, I was."

Phoebe sat down on the bed, slightly irritated. She vaguely re-membered the woman from last summer. Isabelle's father and Phoebe's aunt Clara were lost at sea by now, halfway to nowhere.

"I remember you, I mean sort of," Phoebe said.

"Have you talked to your uncle recently?" Isabelle Smuggs said.

"What do you mean, recently? I mean, every couple of weeks or something, I don't know."

"Is he—I mean, is he—you know. All right?"

The woman sounded nervous. Phoebe couldn't figure out what the hell was going on. Why didn't this Isabelle just call him herself?

"I don't know," Phoebe said. "I mean, a lot of stuff has hap-pened to him. You know that. You were there."

"Yeah," Isabelle said. "I was there. I wish I hadn't been."

There was silence on the line.

"Does he—I mean, when you talk to him, does he ever say any-thing about me?"

"About you?" Phoebe said.

"Yes," Isabelle said. She sounded ashamed. "Me."

"No," Phoebe said. "But like I said. I don't talk to him much these days."

"Yeah, well, sometimes I wish I could apologize to him, your uncle I mean. To tell him I'm sorry."

"Well, why don't you call him already?" Phoebe said.

"I do," Isabelle said. "But he says he doesn't want to talk to me. He says I'm responsible for everything that happened. Like it's my fault he got stuck in some box of mayonnaise! I didn't do anything, besides maybe fall in love. Is that some capital crime, like now everybody has to go to prison for the rest of their lives?"

"I don't know," Phoebe said. "Listen, I'm not really on such good terms with Uncle Pat right now. He's sore I went back to living with my father."

"Well, he shouldn't be. That's where a girl belongs, is with her family."

"Aw, what do you know about it?"

"Nothing," Isabelle said. "You're right. I shouldn't have even called."

"I don't care if you call or not."

"Just do this one thing for me, will you, if you ever talk to him, will you tell him I'm sorry the way things turned out? It's been a hard couple of months."

"You're not kidding," Phoebe said. "You don't know the half of it."

After Isabelle hung up, Phoebe sat there holding the receiver in one hand, trying to recall what the woman had been like. All she could remember was that she had a bust that was so big you almost wanted to stare. She kind of felt sorry for Isabelle. Yeah well, I should talk, Phoebe thought, taking off her running clothes. Maybe it was better to have some enormous joke breasts than to have normal ones that had your own name misspelled on them in wiggly green letters. That Isabelle isn't the only one around here who deserves anybody's pity.

She put her clothes in the white wicker hamper and got in the shower. She thought with renewed sadness of the haircut she was about to endure. It wouldn't have been nearly so horrible had Phoebe not known one terrible truth about her stepmother, which was that the woman was having an affair behind her father's back. That wasn't the worst of it either. The thing that really turned Phoebe's stomach was the fact that the person Vicki was having an affair with was her old flame from Centralia, Dwayne. Dwayne was even more inarticulate than his little brother, Duard. When he opened his mouth to talk it was less like someone speaking to you than accidentally listening to a radio that was stuck between two stations.

Vicki and Dwayne used to live together in Centralia, when Phoebe's family lived next door. It made you wonder what Vicki thought of Wedley, if her most previous idea of a good date was Dwayne. Before Vicki, Dwayne had lived with a woman named Edith Schmertz, who jumped out of a plane one time and didn't pull the rip cord on her parachute, simply in order to make a point. You had to admit: Dwayne could really pick them.

Things had changed for Dwayne since Edith's swan dive. A few years later his parents had suddenly died, and Duard and his little sister, Dwenda, had had to move in with him. Dwayne was not a good authority figure for Duard, and the two of them together had had an even more dramatic effect on the development of little Dwenda, who, although she was only six years old, was already staring out at the world with big vacant eyes.

To support his siblings, Dwayne had started a company of his own. He named it Dwayne's Services. Basically it had two functions: landscaping and paving. Half the week Dwayne spent his time fixing up people's lawns and pruning shrubbery; the other half he tore lawns up with a bulldozer and covered them with cement. He'd even purchased his own cement mixer, which he parked in front of his house in Centralia. Sometimes, just to show everyone he was serious, he left the mixer on all night, the huge cylindrical drum rotating round and round in the smoke and steam from the mine fire.

Phoebe got out of the shower and dried off. She stood in front of the full-length mirror, looking at her long, curly hair. In the distance she recalled the sound of the Matterhorn, the gears groaning on the Sky Master. While she had been waiting for Wedley to come and get her that day, she had gone into the bathroom at the amusement park and fixed her hair with the hair spray she had in her purse. It had taken over a half hour, but it had been worth it. It had been like restoring order to the world, to make her hair big again. For once she felt as if she had power over something.

Well, Phoebe thought. Say good-bye to that Phoebe. There's another Phoebe waiting for me downstairs now and I guess I'd better not keep her waiting.

Phoebe slipped on a T-shirt dress and walked down the stairs, thinking about her future self, the little blond one, waiting for her at the bottom. *Jeez,* Phoebe thought, thinking about this person, this blond shy stranger. *I hope she likes me.*

Vicki stood in the conservatory downstairs, feeling nervous. The last time she had done Phoebe's hair the girl had moved out of the house. Wedley said that it wasn't her fault, but Vicki wasn't sure. She had been a novice then, and had turned Phoebe's hair slightly green by accident. It hadn't been that hard to fix, but Vicki would never forget the look in Phoebe's eyes when she caught a glimpse of that green hair in the mirror. *You bitch,* Phoebe had screamed, tears coming to her eyes. *You did it on purpose.* This was nonsense, of course. If she had wanted to send her stepdaughter a message she would have chosen a medium other than hair.

Phoebe came down the stairs wearing a long white T-shirt dress, sat on the chair, and folded her arms. Vicki tried to make eye contact with her. "Ready, honey?" Vicki said. Phoebe nodded her head yes. Vicki ran a comb through Phoebe's hair. It snagged a couple of times. "You have such nice hair," Vicki said. "I've always admired it."

"Just do it," Phoebe said.

Vicki could see this was not going to be easy. She cleared her throat. "Okay," she said. "Maybe you'd like to know a little about what we're going to be doing here today. Usually it's nice to know what's happening, isn't it."

"I said just do it."

"All right, we will," Vicki said. "First thing we're gonna do is cut the whole thing back, like a rough cut, so it's more or less the length you want it. Then we're gonna use a color stripper to get rid of this midnight black." Vicki held up a can of Metal-X. "This will strip out the old color and get rid of all that hair spray buildup. Honestly, Phoebe, you can't imagine the way that spray builds up on your hair; right now if you looked through a microscope you'd think your whole head was like *varnished,* ha-ha."

Phoebe didn't say anything.

"Then we'll wrap your head up in Saran Wrap and set you under the dryer. When that's all processed we'll wash out the stripper. After that I'll give you the real haircut, nice and careful. After that we'll put you under the dryer again, and that's when I'll mix up the bleach."

"Bleach?" Phoebe said. "I don't want to be some bleachhead."

"No no," Vicki said. "You won't be. But I've got to bleach it first so that there's a base for the color later. We'll give you a bleach, shampoo that out, condition it, then dry you off again. After that we'll do the actual coloring. I've got just the color for you, too, it's called Frivolous Fawn! Isn't that fantastic, Phoebe? You're going to be a Frivolous Fawn!"

"That's swell," Wedley said, listening from the next room. He was smoking a pipe. "Frivolous Fawn, Phoebe! How about that!"

Phoebe gritted her teeth. "Just get on with it," she said.

"Okay," Vicki said. She could tell Phoebe was getting mad, but it was better that she knew now what she was in for rather than getting impatient halfway through. This whole process could take three, maybe four hours, more even if things got complicated. It was hard to know what Phoebe's hair was like under all that midnight black.

Vicki wrapped a sheet around Phoebe's neck. She held a large pair of shears up to her head.

"Ready?" Vicki said.

Phoebe nodded.

Vicki held the long swaths of Phoebe's hair in her fingers and clipped off about eight inches. In less than fifteen seconds, all that huge black fluff was gone. Phoebe felt something gulp in her throat. She clamped down her teeth so she wouldn't cry.

"Boy," said Wedley, from the kitchen. "Look at my two girls! Sure wish I had a camera right now, maybe even some Super-8!"

"Some what?" Phoebe said.

"Oh, Wedley," Vicki said, clipping off the rest of Phoebe's long tresses. "Nobody uses Super-8 film anymore."

"Whatever," Wedley said. "These are Kodak memories, I'm telling you."

Phoebe shut her eyes, still fighting back the inevitable urge to cry at the loss of her beautiful long hair. Maybe if she could put herself into some kind of hypnotic trance for the next few hours this process would be less humiliating. Something on the floor started smacking. Phoebe opened one eye.

Schnoodle looked back at her. He had a long length of Phoebe's midnight black hair in his mouth. He lapped it up like a piece of spaghetti. Schnoodle licked his little chops.

"Isn't he just the cutest thing?" Vicki said.

"Adorable," Phoebe said.

"Okay, Phoebe," Vicki said. "Here comes the Metal-X."

She started slapping the stripper on Phoebe's head with a long plastic-handled paintbrush. Vicki piled Phoebe's hair into a single mass and mushed the creamy paste onto it. It took a while to get all of it evenly distributed. When Phoebe's head was completely consumed by the rich tan glop, Vicki started wrapping it with Saran Wrap. Phoebe didn't even want to ask why. She figured this was just par for the course. If you wanted to get by in a world of plastic androids you wrapped your skull with Saran Wrap. That wasn't so hard to figure out.

"Upsy-daisy," Vicki said, taking Phoebe by the hand.

"Where are we going?" Phoebe said. She had the sudden feeling that Vicki was going to lead her somewhere, like the two of them were about to go out and get in the car and drive around.

"Over here, silly," Vicki said, easing Phoebe into a metal chair. She had a kind of antique hair-drying apparatus set up on a table next to the chair; it looked like a plastic suitcase with someone's esophagus hanging out of it. At the end of the esophagus was a sort of bloated shower cap, which Vicki eased down over Phoebe's plastic head. Vicki hit a switch and the shower cap inflated. It was huge. Phoebe's head was now surrounded in a baking, blowing, blasting hurricane of heated air.

Something strange happened the moment the dryer went on. Phoebe felt that she was no longer in the room. Vicki went over to Wedley and talked to him for a little while. They held hands at the kitchen table. Phoebe couldn't hear a word anyone was saying, since her ears were full of the whine of the dryer's motor and the rush of the baking air. But she saw Wedley looking at Vicki with his sad, trusting eyes. Oh, Pa, she wanted to say. Can't you see what a liar she is? She's boofing old Dwayne, right under your own nose, right in your own house. And you want to take Super-8 movies of her. Phoebe suddenly remembered about the old Super-8 movie camera he had had when she and Demmie were kids. What had ever happened to that thing? There were little reels of film somewhere, maybe in the attic of the Centralia house, of Demmie and Phoebe and their mother playing in the surf at Rehoboth Beach.

After a while Wedley got up. He kissed Vicki on the cheek, then got his keys and left. Probably was headed over to the hardware store.

Wedley did this on Saturdays. He went down to the True Value and spent hours there in a kind of mystical dadlike trance, looking at drill bits and fertilizer and paint mixers. After a while he'd come home, his arms full of strange and mysterious things that he'd take down to the basement and leave on his workbench. Usually that was the last you'd see of this stuff, and Wedley would come upstairs a few hours later, ready for cocktails.

Vicki came back and stood by the conservatory door. She looked at Phoebe, sitting there melting under the dryer, with a strange expression. All right, she seemed to be saying. Now that it's just you and me let's cut out the shit.

She's got me, Phoebe thought. All this time Phoebe had been thinking that her knowledge of her stepmother's affair gave her power, but she was wrong. She was at the mercy of Vicki now, trapped under the dryer coated with Metal-X. And at this moment Phoebe knew that the last fiasco, the one in which Vicki had turned her green, had not been an accident. She had turned Phoebe's hair green with the express purpose of getting her out of the house so she could have her affair with Dwayne without anyone watching. Oh my god, Phoebe thought, what is she going to do to me now? The glop beneath the Saran Wrap on her head felt like it was boiling. Bits of it were starting to drip past the plastic and roll in steaming, gooey beads down her neck.

She's going to kill me, Phoebe thought. Vicki smiled with a look of malice. Oh my god, she's going to kill me.

Vicki did not like the way Phoebe was looking at her. She knows, Vicki thought. That's what she's telling me. From underneath all that Metal-X and plastic and the dryer cap, Phoebe is sending me a telepathic message. She's going to tell Wedley.

Vicki was so upset that she went into the kitchen for a moment and got herself a Tab. This whole thing was turning into a fiasco. Why in hell had she allowed Dwayne back in her life? It was the third time she had gotten wrapped up with him. There was the first occasion, back in high school, when they had both attended the Miniature United Nations together. Dwayne had been the Belgian Congo. Vicki got to be Sweden, which at the time had made her proud but which she found out years later was for all the wrong reasons. Anyway, they dated in high school, then they broke up, as people do. When she was twenty-five, she had unexpectedly started going out with Dwayne again. He had walked into the Wurlitzer showroom when she had been working there and played "Clair de Lune." They lived together for two years then, but Dwayne was always a little distracted. He was obsessed with his former girlfriend, Edith. When he found out she had jumped out of that plane on purpose, he blamed himself. Dwayne had become so morose that in the end she had had to leave him, which naturally hadn't cheered him up any, but it was the only way Vicki could save her own sanity. She'd started dating Wedley Harrison from next door, whom she found almost as morose as Dwayne at first, but who later seemed to find release from his sadness as a relationship with Vicki progressed. That was the thing that had attracted her to him, in fact; she had been able to bring to Wedley the very kind of self-confidence and joy that she had failed to bring Dwayne.

That should have been the end of it. They'd gotten married and moved to the Main Line and now Wedley was making some real money and the two of them had been able to leave Centralia behind. But she kept thinking about Dwayne, felt that she had abandoned him, felt guilty about his sadness. When he called her up last year, she had practically wept right there on the phone. Dwayne said he was doing fine now, that he was still living in Centralia, working construction, and that he'd love to see her sometime especially if she ever needed some heavy lifting done or maybe some work with a cement mixer. The next thing you knew Dwayne was standing in Wedley's front yard, planting shrubs with a posthole digger. Vicki came out and offered him some iced tea. They were kissing, deeply, before the ice cubes in the glass had melted, and Vicki could tell that Dwayne had broken out of his muddled, depressed spell in the interim, that he had at last gotten Edith out of his system. "Oh, Dwayne," she said to him. "My only Dwayne."

In the weeks to come, Wedley found, to his pleasure, that there was a lot of really intricate landscaping work being done on the property.

A timer went off, and Vicki looked up suddenly. She had finished her Tab without realizing it, had even chewed up the ice. She went back out to the conservatory, where Phoebe was sitting beneath the dryer, the brown stripper goozing all over her.

Vicki reached over and turned off the dryer.

"Okay," she said. "Rise and shine."

"Oh man," Phoebe said. "I feel like I'm covered in like, dough, or something."

"I know," Vicki said. "Here, let me towel you off."

She took off the cap and unwrapped the Saran Wrap. A big puddle of guck slid off Phoebe's hair and onto the newspaper on the floor.

"Follow me," she said, and walked Phoebe over to the sink. With a hose attached to the faucet, Vicki rinsed out the rest of the stripper. Again Vicki was glad that there was no mirror immediately available because Phoebe's hair was now tinted a whole array of odd and unpleasant shades, most of them variations on army green and brown. This was more or less what was supposed to happen, though. So far things were going pretty well.

She towel-dried Phoebe's hair and then escorted her back to the chair. Schnoodle was still sitting on the floor, looking up expectantly. The remains of Phoebe's previous hairstyle were lying in shards all around the base of the chair. Vicki combed out Phoebe's hair, trying to imagine her stepdaughter as a little blond preppy girl. It was hard to visualize.

"What side do you want to part it on?" Vicki asked.

"I don't care," Phoebe said. Her voice sounded like it was coming from a place many miles distant. "What side do most of them part their hair on?"

"Left," Vicki said. "Left if you're right-handed. You're right-handed, aren't you?"

"Yeah."

"Okay, left," Vicki said. She parted Phoebe's hair slightly to the left of center, then parted it into four sections, which she held in place with oversized clothespins. Starting in the back, Vicki made a horizontal part, closest to the collar, then bent Phoebe's head down. She started cutting a long series of inverted U-shapes.

This was not a hard haircut, as these things went. It was fortunate that Phoebe's hair had not been permed out before, because that would have made things really complex. Still, by the time they were done today, Phoebe's scalp was going to be like a toxic waste dump. The fact that she only wanted a simple bob cut was a blessing.

Vicki cut the sides, keeping the front of the bob a little bit longer than the back. She clipped the bangs straight across the face, just above Phoebe's eyebrows. She stood back to look at what she had done so far. It was a good cut.

"Okay," she said. "Now it's back under the dryer for you."

"Yes, master," Phoebe said sarcastically, but Vicki was glad that Phoebe was at least feeling good enough to make a little joke. She put the dryer cap back on Phoebe's head and turned it on. Phoebe's head expanded once more.

While Phoebe sat in the chair, Vicki mixed up the bleach. This was the tricky part. She reached down below the sink and grabbed a bottle of the 20 Volume peroxide and some Kool Blue bleach powder. She dumped them into a small bowl and mixed this with an oil conditioner. Whipping it around with a plastic spoon, Vicki waited until she had the consistency she wanted. She poured in the cream oil peroxide, and the stuff began to bubble. Boy oh boy, Vicki thought, I feel like Dr. Vicki Frankenstein here.

When Phoebe's hair was dry, Vicki got her back in the chair again. She looked at the clock. She'd been doing Phoebe's hair for an hour and a half now. Holding the bowl of bleach in one hand, she quickly applied it with a long paintbrush that had a black plastic handle.

"How's it going?"

"Good," Vicki said.

The phone started to ring, but Vicki did not want to answer it, not at this juncture. The bleach had to all go on at once, and go on quickly, or else some of it would start lightening part of Phoebe's head before the rest and she would get white spots, or something worse.

"Aren't you going to get that?" Phoebe said.

The answering machine in the kitchen clicked on. There was the sound of Dick Van Dyke singing "Chim Chim Cher-ee," over which Wedley's baritone voice boomed: "You've reached the home of Wedley, Victoria, and Phoebe Harrison. If you'd like to leave a message for us, or if you'd like to get in touch with Mister Chimney, you can do so at the sound of the beep."

The tone went off, and someone started breathing into the phone. Oh no, Phoebe thought. That creep in the Miata. He's got our number.

"Vicki," the voice said. There was a long, long pause.

It was the pause more than anything else that let Phoebe know that it was Dwayne calling. You could hear the gears turning around in his brain as he tried to think. Dwayne was wondering if he could say who was calling without giving away the fact that he was in love with her. He would be thinking about the way people's emotions are betrayed in their speech. He would be wondering if he ought not have called at all, and could even be already lamenting the impossibility of time travel, enabling him to go back a few seconds and hang up before he started talking.

"Maybe I'll just see who that is," Vicki said, running into the kitchen. She was afraid Dwayne was going to say something like I love you, Vicki, or I like your bosoms, Vicki, or I want to bite your tongue, Vicki, because these were all things that Dwayne had said, in fact, in previous messages, although he had had the good sense to leave these on the machine during the week instead of on a weekend. Vicki had warned him not to do it, but he couldn't or wouldn't seem to remember that. Sometimes it took a lot to get through to him.

"Hello?" Vicki said. There was a screech of feedback for a moment until the machine disconnected itself. "Who is this?"

Phoebe enjoyed listening to Vicki trying to pretend like she didn't know who Dwayne was. It was interesting to see how convincing people could be when you knew that they were liars.

"Vicki," Dwayne said.

"Yes," Vicki said.

"It's Dwayne," Dwayne said.

"I know," Vicki said. "Listen, I'm right in the middle of something. Can you call us back on Monday, please? Thank you."

"Vicki," Dwayne said.

"I'm really afraid we're busy right now," she said.

"I have to tell you something," Dwayne said. "It's important."

Vicki sighed. "What?" she said.

"It's about—" he said.

There was a long pause. Vicki waited for him to remember what he was saying.

"Yes, Dwayne?" she said. "What is it about?"

"It's about—" Dwayne said.

On Phoebe Harrison's scalp, the half of her hair that had the bleach painted onto it began to feel a little itchy.

"What?" Vicki said. She almost shouted.

"It's about the way I—"

Vicki waited again. Surely he would remember the way his sentence would conclude. The way he what? Drives? Thinks? Eats? Talks? For heaven's sakes, Dwayne, the way you what?

"The way I feel," Dwayne said. He breathed easier, as if greatly relieved.

"Dwayne, I seriously have to go," Vicki said.

"No," Dwayne said. "The way I feel," he said. "It's important. That's why I'm calling now. On Saturday. You have to know."

There was something of alarm in Dwayne's voice. Vicki's heart was beating rapidly. Something had happened. Did he not want to see her anymore? That was it. He had decided that the affair they were having simply had to come to an end, that the vows Vicki had made with Wedley were too solemn to be ignored. They were going to cause a whole series of people pain and anguish. All of this they had decided to risk, solely for the sake of their own pleasure? It was wrong, and Dwayne had at last realized the terrible truth.

"Yes, Dwayne," Vicki said. "Tell me how you feel."

"I feel—" he said. "Uh."

"I know," Vicki said. "You don't have to say it. I know."

"Good," he said. "I feel good."

"What?" Vicki said. "You say you feel good."

"Yeah," Dwayne said. He laughed a little. "Huh. Huh. I feel good, Vicki."

"Dwayne?" Vicki said. "Is that what you called up to tell me? That's what was so important?" She felt a sudden flash of anger at him.

"Yeah," Dwayne said, impervious. You could feel him beaming at her, all the way from Centralia. "I feel good, Vicki. 'Cause of you."

"Oh, Dwayne," she said. Her anger dissolved. "You're special."

"Yuh," Dwayne said. "You too. Special, Vicki."

Vicki turned around suddenly, and saw Phoebe looking at her. She had forgotten for a moment that her conversation was being listened to. And what about the bleach on Phoebe's head? "Oh my gosh, Dwayne, I have to go now. You call back on Monday about this matter, please?'' she said. ''Thank you.'' She hung up.

Vicki rushed back to Phoebe's head. How long had she been talking on the phone? It couldn't have been that long. Quickly she painted the bleach onto the rest of Phoebe's scalp and checked the time.

''It hurts,'' Phoebe said. A tear stood in the corner of one of her eyes, then fell onto the girl's cheek. ''Don't you know it's hurting me?''

''Oh my god, Phoebe,'' Vicki said. Another tear fell off her step-daughter's lid. It was like feeling a knife twisting around in her ribs. Again she felt the monumentous selfishness and evil of her affair. She had not meant to bring Wedley's daughter to tears.

''Can't you do anything about it?'' Phoebe said. ''It stings.''

''It's too late,'' Vicki said, shaking her head.

''Please?''

''I'm sorry,'' Vicki said. She wondered if she could explain things to Phoebe, woman-to-woman. The girl was almost sixteen now; she had to have some idea of the impossibility of dealing with men. But Vicki doubted that Phoebe would be open-minded when it came to Wedley, a man who had spent almost ten years alone, waiting, trying to be faithful to a wife who had never come home.

''It shouldn't be burning like this, should it?'' Phoebe said.

Vicki looked at Phoebe and did a double take. She wasn't talking about Dwayne at all. She was talking about the goddamn *bleach*.

''I'm afraid it does sting a little bit,'' Vicki said. ''That's part of the process.''

''The process,'' Phoebe said, vacantly, then looked at her again. ''Who was that on the phone?''

''That,'' Vicki said. ''Was the landscape man.''

''Oh,'' Phoebe said. ''What did he want?''

''He just wanted to say he was thinking about us. About our lawn.

He's coming out Monday to look at things again. I think he wants to plant some more things.''

"Does he," Phoebe said. More tears were coming out of the girl's eyes. Vicki felt very nervous. The 20 Vol wasn't supposed to burn so badly it made you cry. Was Phoebe crying about something other than her hair?

Vicki went to the kitchen for a few minutes and washed her hands. Schnoodle woke up and came in, looked up at Vicki curiously. "I'm sorry," Vicki said. "I'm sorry, my little sweetheart. But I haven't got any more hair for you!''

The dog whined softly.

Vicki came back into the conservatory and got some cotton. She wiped off the bleach in one place and checked the color. Things seemed like they were going along okay. There were still tears coming out of Phoebe's eyes.

"I'm sorry it hurts, sweetheart," Vicki said, and took Phoebe's hand.

Phoebe just nodded.

After fifteen minutes, Vicki checked the bleach again. The hair was now light, like the color of straw. Gently she walked Phoebe back over to the sink and had her bend over it so that her head was facing upward. The frothing bleach on top of Phoebe's head had the consistency of light blue cake frosting. Vicki rinsed out the bleach and started to shampoo it.

As she did so, Vicki noticed several disturbing things. Apparently she had been on the phone with Dwayne longer than she thought. Half of Phoebe's head was very, very bleached. The scalp underneath was red and raw. This was very strange. She put some shampoo into it and lathered it. As she rinsed out the shampoo, Vicki noticed that there was a lot of hair in the sink.

She swallowed. There was a lot more hair in the sink than there should have been. She ran some more warm water over Phoebe's head. There was a whole area in the back of Phoebe's head, just below the ear, that looked like it had been scalded clean. There were two other patches near the back where Phoebe was almost bald.

"Oh my god," Vicki said.

"What?" Phoebe said. "What's oh my god?"

"Oh nothing," Vicki said. "I was thinking about something else entirely. You look great. Sorry if I scared you."

"Well, gee. Don't say stuff like 'oh my god,' okay? You're freaking me out."

But Vicki was the one who was freaking out. More and more hair was falling out. She put a little conditioner in Phoebe's hair, still wondering what the hell was going on. She looked over at her collection of bottles. There was the container of 40 Vol.

Vicki swallowed again. It wasn't supposed to be 40 Vol, it was supposed to be 20. Forty was what you used on wigs and stuff, hair that was not attached to a real human head. No wonder Phoebe had started crying. Jesus. It was a miracle all her hair hadn't burned off entirely.

"You know," Vicki said. "I don't like the way your hair is falling." It was the truth, although what she meant was she didn't like the way her hair was falling *out*.

"Yeah?" Phoebe said. She still sounded nervous.

"I just want to cut one little place in the back again," she said.

"Okay," Phoebe said. Vicki led her back to the chair, combed Phoebe's rapidly thinning hair, and started cutting the entire perimeter except for the bangs.

She's going to strangle me, Vicki thought. Her heart was pounding in her throat. Depending on how badly this turns out, there's no knowing what Phoebe might do. Maybe she'll tell Wedley about Dwayne. Oh god no, Vicki thought. She could not bear the thought of causing poor Wedley more harm.

Suddenly, the thought occurred to her: maybe I *did* do it on purpose. Is that possible? Is there something in me that wants to do something so terrible to Phoebe that she'll tell Wedley on me? If the truth were out then it would be possible to leave him. Maybe burning off Phoebe's hair with the 40 Vol was part of some secret psychological scheme to help her run off with Dwayne again. It wasn't out of the question. She would do almost anything if it meant that she could be Dwayne's lover, feel his enormous presence throbbing inside her again. Vicki was going to figure things out soon, and when she did, actions were going to be taken. She wasn't about to let her stepdaughter ruin her plans.

Vicki went to work with the scissors. By the time she finished the second cut on Phoebe's hair, Vicki felt that she had concealed her error pretty well. She'll figure out pretty soon that her hair's a lot thinner, Vicki thought. But she won't recognize these burned out patches until they start growing back all prickly. Maybe by that time everything about Dwayne will be out anyway. And anyway, once I dye it, this won't look so bad. All these preppy girls have pretty thin hair anyway. Maybe having her hair burned off is exactly the thing Phoebe wants.

Again Vicki took Phoebe over to the dryer and sat her down for a while. While Phoebe sat there under the enormous shower cap and its accompanying esophagus, Wedley came home.

"Hi, girls," he said, peeking into the conservatory. Phoebe couldn't hear a word he said, could only see his mouth opening and closing. He gave Vicki a big kiss on the cheek, then headed down into the basement. He was holding a new exhaust hose for the clothes dryer.

It was going on six o'clock when Vicki finally started applying Frivolous Fawn to Phoebe's head. She smooshed it around for a while, then left it there for twenty minutes. Phoebe waited in silence, as the honey-colored guck slowly grew dark. Phoebe's stomach was growling, and some of the Springsteen tunes she had been listening to earlier in the day came back to her mind. *You and me we were the pretenders/We let it all slip away/In the end what you don't surrender/Well the world just strips away.*

At last Vicki raised Phoebe out of the chair again, put in a conditioning rinse, rinsed that out, then slapped in some sculpting lotion. Vicki combed and blow-dried the whole thing with a boar's bristle brush, looking at the results of her labors.

It really didn't look too bad. If the wind blew suddenly Phoebe might find out there were a couple of bald spots, but someone else would have to see them and tell her about them. Over the next few days, though, if more hair fell out there might be real trouble. It was hard right now to predict how bad things were going to get.

"Okay," Vicki said at last. "Why don't you go look at it?"

Phoebe stood up, a little afraid. "You're sure you're done?" she said. Vicki nodded, and looked at the clock. They had been there over four hours.

Phoebe went into the bathroom to check out the mirror. The phone rang again, and Vicki picked it up.

"Vicki," the voice said. "It's me again. Dwayne."

Wedley walked across the kitchen, humming. He went over to the counter and got out a Waterford crystal tumbler, then poured some Jameson's Irish whiskey into it.

From the bathroom came a sudden wail, a bloodcurdling, crystal-shattering shriek.

"I'm sorry," Vicki said. "You'll have to call back."

"Oh my god," Phoebe screamed from the bathroom. "I don't know who the hell I am!"

"Vicki," Dwayne said. "I have to tell you. The way I feel."

"I know about that," Vicki said. "You told me before. Remember? You just did."

"Hey, Vic," Wedley said, holding up an empty glass. "Highball?"

"I feel different now," Dwayne continued, in Vicki's ear.

"You do?" She nodded at Wedley, who started to mix her a gin and tonic. "What? What is it?"

"More," Dwayne said. It sounded like he was about to swoon over onto the floor.

"More?" Vicki said. "More what?"

"Here, darling," Wedley said, handing his wife the highball. He patted her on the ass. "Let's sit down and have some peanuts." He smiled. "When you're off the phone, of course," he added considerately.

Phoebe screamed again. There was the sound of her feet running in panic up the stairs.

"Yeah," Dwayne said. It sounded like he was sobbing. "I feel even more."

"I'm glad," Vicki said, madly in love with him. She wanted to reach into the phone and grab hold of Dwayne's great chest. "I'm so glad!"

"That's all," Dwayne said.

"I'm glad you called," Vicki whispered. "I have to go."

She hung up the phone. Wedley was smiling at her.

"Who was that?" he said.

"Landscapers," she said.

"They're terrific!" Wedley said. "Calling on Saturday night! Boy, that's commitment!"

"They're coming out again Monday," Vicki said. "They have more things to plant."

"Excellent," Wedley said. "I'm so glad!" He raised his drink, and Mr. and Mrs. Harrison clinked glasses. There was a clear, high-pitched *ting*.

Phoebe Harrison, aged fifteen, came into the room. She had put on her Dillinger Academy green tunic for the full effect. Wedley couldn't believe it. His own daughter had miraculously become a perfect, honey blond girl. Phoebe looked like she might, at a moment's notice, drop everything and start playing field hockey.

Vicki looked at Phoebe with more alarm. She had done a very good job of hiding her mistake, she thought. In a couple more days the full effects of her transgression would be clearer, but for now her errors were still invisible.

Phoebe, however, was consumed with sobs. She stood there in front of Wedley and Vicki, her face red, tears dripping off her chin. She was doing her best to get herself under control, but she was still weeping uncontrollably.

"There there," Wedley said. "There's my girl! I've never seen you look prettier! I haven't! You look absolutely perfect! Yes, sir, you're Wedley's little Frivolous Fawn!"

Vicki prepared herself for the worst. It was all going to come out now. The affair with Dwayne. Her sabotaging of her stepdaughter's hair. In a single moment all these terrible things would be revealed.

"So," Vicki said to Phoebe. "What do you think?"

Phoebe snuffed back the tears and wiped her eyes on the back of her hand. Schnoodle wagged his tail.

"Oh god," Phoebe said, still sobbing. "It's perfect."

WINTER STARS

THE PLEIADES

*This group of faint stars looks, at first,
like a tiny silver cloud.*

By February, Phoebe's sister, Demmie, was more than willing to admit that stealing the dog had been a mistake. It was never pleasurable to stuff someone's pet in a sack, but kidnapping Buddy had been downright atrocious, an insult to the brain. He sat around Demmie's apartment with this sad look, gnawing on his legs, and whenever she tried to play the guitar he put his head down and smacked on his lips with a bitter expression, as if he did not like his own taste. Demmie didn't blame him. She wouldn't have wanted to have eaten the dog, even when it was younger.

She had had a number of jobs in the eight years since she stole Dwayne's appliances and went out in the world to become a famous musician. The first thing she had done was to hock the appliances, which had given her enough cash to make a deposit on this horrible apartment on Lombard Street, near what was supposed to be Philadelphia's bohemian district. The idea was to live as cheaply as possible until she could form a band and live off the millions from her recording contracts. It took forever to get the Poison Squirrels together, though, and even once they had attained something of a following, Demmie couldn't quit her day job. The Poison Squirrels had had their day, and still the world seemed unchanged and unimpressed.

For a while she worked in a bookstore. Her friend Billings, whom she had met on her way out of town, on the day that she left home, had worked there, too. They got to eat their lunches together. The best job in a bookstore was standing in the stockroom ripping the covers off paperbacks that were to be returned to their publishers unsold. This process was called stripping. There was something indescribably satisfying about stripping the covers off books, especially since, as almost everyone knew, the majority of them were contemptible cheese. It was less enjoyable to be out on the sales floor, where Demmie had had to face the book-buying public. Demmie's job was to sit at a little information counter and answer any questions people asked her. She wore a button that said ASK ME ANYTHING. Usually people would ask her about the names of books or authors, but once in a while they'd come up with unsettling, weird questions. A woman with a huge strawberry birthmark on her cheek had once come up to Demmie and asked, "Hey, you. Why do you work here?"

Demmie just shrugged sadly and told her she did not know.

Compared with literature, stealing dogs and cats was a pretty good deal. It was remarkable what people would pay just to get their stupid pets back. They once got five hundred dollars for a snake with legs. The only time they made a serious mistake, other than when they got Buddy, was the time they took someone's chimpanzee. It turned out to be a lot more difficult than you'd think to hold one hostage. For one thing, you had to keep washing its clothes all the time. Maybe it was just upset about being away from its owners, but this chimpanzee, whose name was Ted, kept smashing its bananas in its pants.

Other than Ted, though, Buddy had turned out to be the biggest headache. She hadn't known she was breaking into her Uncle Pat's house until they got inside and saw the pictures of Phoebe and herself and her mother and father on the piano. Billings had picked up a photograph of Phoebe and said, "Hey, is this you? You used to be cute!"

She wanted to smash the picture over Billings's head, but even through the panty hose which she was wearing over her face she could see that Billings was right. Phoebe, whom she had not seen in eight years, now looked very much the way Demmie had looked at her age. In the photograph, Phoebe had big black blow-dried hair and lots of makeup. Demmie recognized this look. When you were fifteen, it was your way of telling the world that you weren't happy with the way things were working out, that you wished that there was some alternative to this world where things hadn't been screwed up so much by the adults.

Goddammit, Phoebe, she wanted to say. There is no other world.

God what a loser, she thought. I mean, it's one thing to go around stealing people's pets and holding them for ransom, but to break into your uncle's house without knowing it, and steal your own family's dog, that's just despicable. She had felt so low about it that she hadn't been able to call up Uncle Pat and ask him for the money. One time she even went as far as the family's old house in Centralia, with the hope that she could break in and leave Buddy there, sort of as a surprise for Wedley and Phoebe.

When she got to Centralia, though, she learned what she had half-feared to be true all along. Her father and her sister didn't live there anymore.

"Come on, Demmie," Billings said. "We're late."

Demmie looked up at him. He was wearing leather pants and a vest; Demmie was wearing a jumpsuit. The two of them would have been very fashionable except that it was February and they didn't have any coats.

Demmie grabbed her guitar case and walked down the stairs to the street. Billings carried Buddy in his arms. The dog was too old now to descend stairs on his own.

Outside it was snowing softly. They looked down the street for the other members of their band.

"Where are they?" Demmie said. "I'm cold."

"Buddy's freezing, too," Billings said, looking at the old dog.

"Yeah, but he's got hair," Demmie said.

"I know what he's got," Billings said. "Don't act like I don't know what he's got."

"What's he got, Billings?" Demmie said.

Billings shrugged. "Hair," he said.

Demmie folded her arms and rubbed her biceps with her palms. Her leopard-skin jumpsuit didn't even have any pockets. Last fall, Billings and Demmie had agreed that as soon as the Poison Squirrels got paid for their next gig, they would buy her a winter jacket, but it had turned out to be almost four months before anyone wanted to pay to hear them play again, and in the meantime there had been a lot of expenses, not the least of which was Snausages. He sure liked those things, especially the ones flavored with liver and cheese.

"Don't try to understand 'em," Billings said quietly, singing the theme from *Rawhide. "Just rope 'em up at random."*

"Hah?" Demmie said, blowing onto her fists. A cloud of steam rose in front of her face in the cold winter air. "What did you say?"

"I said, 'rope 'em up at random,' " Billings said. "Want some gum?"

"It's 'rope 'em up and *brand 'em,*' " Demmie snapped. "It's 'brand 'em,' not 'random.' Why the fuck would they rope 'em up at *random,* asshole?"

Billings heaved a sad sigh and jumped up and down to keep warm. He hated it when Demmie got all bossy like this. All he wanted to do was offer her a stick of gum and she acted like he was a psycho.

But Billings did not respond. He just looked down the frozen street, as if he had not heard a thing. There were no cars coming.

He turned toward Demmie. "They rope them up at random," Billings explained, softly. "Because they don't know which ones are the ones they have to rope up. This way they just rope the ones up that they get because it doesn't matter. Once they rope them up they can do whatever they want with them. Maybe even let them go, sometimes. That way they have a choice."

"Billings," Demmie said. "Get a grip."

He sniffed. "Gee, Demmie," he said. "Sometimes I think you don't love me at all hardly."

Buddy moaned softly.

"It's not about love," Demmie said. "How many times do I have to tell you? It's not like we're fucking married."

"I wish we were," Billings said. "I do! I wish we could have a whole fambly!"

"Don't start," Demmie said. "You're pissin' me off."

"You're the one who's starting," Billings said. He pulled some of his beard hair into his mouth and sucked on it. "You'd think I was the fuckin' Elephant Man the way you act sometimes."

"Can we please please please not have this discussion now?" Demmie said. "I got stuff to consider."

Buddy moaned. A green Ford Falcon station wagon pulled over. Something was wrong with the exhaust manifold, causing the car to be enveloped in a grayish cloud of toxic fumes. Limmburjay, the bass player, got out. He was wearing leopard-skin pants and no shirt.

"Eee-yo!" he said, and raised a palm high in the air. Demmie slapped it. He held the same palm up for Billings to slap, but Billings just scuffed some snow with his foot.

"I don't wanna go slap," Billings said.

"Hey, man," Limmburjay said. "What's wrong? You okay?"

"She don't love me," Billings said. "Never has, never will."

"Well, duh," Limmburjay said. "I mean, jeez, Billings, everybody knows that!"

Demmie picked up her guitar.

"I mean, like, this is supposed to be news?" Limmburjay said. He shook his head and laughed. "Boy oh boy! I mean, way I figure, she wouldn't give two hoots if you got shot in the head! Really!"

"Let's go!" Angelique said from the backseat. She was a good-looking black woman with a crooked Mohawk. "Come on! It's cold!"

"She would so," Billings muttered. "Give two hoots. She doesn't know how many hoots she'd give."

Demmie put her guitar case in the back of the station wagon and climbed in. Billings lifted Buddy out of the snow and put him on the floor. Oxx hit the gas. The seven of them—Billings, Demmie, Oxx, Limmburjay, Chim-chim, Angelique, and Buddy—lumbered down Lombard in their little gray cloud.

"This gig is going to be great," Limmburjay said. "We are going to wipe the floor with this place!"

"Oh boy," Demmie said sarcastically. She reached into her handbag, removed a piece of lunch meat that was tied to a piece of string, and placed the baloney necklace around her neck. "I can't wait. I'd describe myself as trembling with excitement. Yes, trembling, that's the word." She turned to Angelique. "How do I look?"

"Bitchin', Scabbaxx," Angelique said. Scabbaxx was Demmie's stage name.

They were performing that night at a seedy club on Market Street called The Fire Station, which at one time had been a firehouse but was now filled with chairs, drunks, and female dancers who didn't wear much more than firemen's hats. It wasn't exactly a prestige booking.

"I have news," Oxx said serenely. He was one-half Apache, and the other half was something with a very deep voice. Oxx served as their manager, at least when he wasn't preoccupied with his other job, which was feeding acorns to the prairie dog at the Philadelphia Zoo.

"News," Demmie said. "Why I'm so excited!"

"I got us another gig," Oxx said. "Next week. Some high school prom, for the Dillinger Academy. It's at the Franklin Institute. They're paying eight hundred."

"Wow," Demmie said. This was a pretty impressive booking, as these things went. The Franklin Institute was the city's science museum. This gig would be a lot more upscale than The Fire Station, anyway, and they could be reasonably certain that they would not have to witness anyone sliding down the poles when the sirens went off.

"It's on Valentine's Day. They call it the Valentine's Day Massacre. All the kids are supposed to wear gangster clothes. We could wear gangster clothes, if we had them."

"Whyn't we just wear our normal stuff!" Billings said, excited. "That would work!"

Chim-chim sighed loudly. "Doesn't matter," he said. "Existence is meaningless."

"Hey, Chim-chim," Angelique said. "Are you okay?"

"Aw, don't disturb Mister Philosopher," Demmie said. "The deep thinker! Mister College Professor!"

They were turning right on the parkway now, headed toward Logan Circle. On the left was a fountain, and a famous sculpture of the letters L-O-V-E stacked up in a block. The *O* was tilted at a forty-five-degree angle.

"Hey look, everybody," Billings said. "The City of Brotherly Love!" He wanted all the members of his band to notice the statue. It was important.

The members of the Poison Squirrels watched LOVE pass them by.

"I'm pulling over," Oxx said. "I gotta take a whiz."

"You know, we could rearrange those letters if we wanted," Chim-chim said with a kind of morbid hopefulness. "We could change the letters in LOVE so they spell VEAL. That would make the bastards sorry. That would teach them all a lesson they wouldn't be sorry to forget, if they all came out one day to find their precious LOVE transformed to VEAL!"

Buddy whimpered softly.

There was silence for a moment as the Falcon slowed to a halt. Then Billings said, "But, Chim-chim." He cleared his throat. "Like, there's an *A* in VEAL, man."

Chim-chim was silent for a moment; then his lower jaw started to quiver. Suddenly he began to cry.

"Buh, buh, buh," Chim-chim said.

"Nice going, Billings," Limmburjay said.

"Yeah, way to go!" Angelique snapped.

"Don't you care about his feelings?"

Chim-chim covered his face with his hands.

"Hey," Billings said. "I'm being realistic!"

"Shut up," Angelique said. She went over to Chim-chim and held the sobbing man's head against her shoulder. "Just shut up!"

Chim-chim reached up and stroked Angelique's Mohawk with his fingers.

Oxx jumped out the door onto the Benjamin Franklin Parkway in order to urinate on a statue. Billings followed him.

Demmie sat in the station wagon with the sobbing guitarist and Limmburjay and Angelique and her family's very old dog. Chim-chim looked at Demmie, tears pouring from his eyes.

"There there," Demmie said. "It's all right. Really." She stroked Chim-chim's hair.

"You really believe that?" Angelique said.

"What?" Demmie said.

"That everything's going to be all right." She looked at Demmie as if Demmie had some pipeline to the future that Angelique did not possess.

"Yes," Demmie said softly, still stroking Chim-chim's hair. "I do." She looked out the window at the sculpture of LOVE. Billings was peeing on it.

Chim-chim sniffed. "Stupid Billings," he said, trying to gain control of his tears.

"Stupid jerk!" Chim-chim said. "Stupid goon. All I wanted to do was spell VEAL and he wrecks *everything*!"

"I know," Demmie said, trying to imagine the future. Buddy moaned softly from the floor. His tail twitched. "I know."

THE SERPENT HOLDER

He's got a lot on his mind.

Duard was sitting at his desk in his bedroom in Centralia, attempting to study for the SATs. He was having a hard time. For one thing, he didn't quite understand the questions. *Crispy* is to *bacon* as *sticky* is to what? There were five choices: boulder, cola, pinecone, aspirin, panda. None of them made sense. If you wanted to go to college you were supposed to put them in a sentence. All right, so you might say, "I'd like some crispy bacon." Following that logic, then, you might say, "I'd like some sticky aspirin." If you had a headache and kept dropping the tablets on the floor, some sticky aspirin would solve your problems. That way you could hold on to them. Or maybe you'd say, "I'd like some sticky pinecones, please," if you were out eating at some restaurant. But you wouldn't want to eat a pinecone; it would be unrelentlessly crunchy. Duard checked in the answer box at the back of his preparation booklet. The correct answer was panda.

Maybe they got sticky when they got left out in the rain at the zoo. That could happen.

The other reason why Duard was distracted was because a copy of the Elizabeth's Enigma catalog had showed up in the mail today, addressed to his brother's late girlfriend, Edith. Elizabeth's Enigma was a mail-order store that specialized in lingerie. He had seen it lying there in the kitchen, had placed his schoolbooks casually down upon it, and then when he went upstairs following his after-school snack of Hostess cupcakes and Mountain Dew, he had carried it with him. Now the catalog was lying next to his desk while he was attempting to study. He knew that it was wrong to read it, because it wasn't stuff boys were supposed to find out about until after you were married. Still, Duard found it extremely educational. Some of it was almost astonishing, like the French Wench Body Cincher Trimmed with Orange Buds. *The puckered knit accents the more ample bustline.*

Duard blinked. He knew what would happen if he kept thinking about it. The next thing he knew his pants would be down around his ankles and then he'd be in trouble. It was wrong to do it, he knew that. He was certain that he was the only boy in tenth grade who ever touched himself in this manner. What was wrong with him, that he couldn't concentrate? These SATs were important, and on the basis of Duard's trial scores thus far he wasn't going to do very well. On the last sample test he took he had gotten a 375, which wasn't very good. How many points did you get for writing down your own name? 200. Duard was not looking forward to Harvard, not unless he could stop thinking about the Elizabeth's Enigma catalog and get down to business.

Duard decided to give up on the analogies and attempt some of the math problems. He hated word problems worst of all because they posed complexities that did not seem interesting to him. If the situations they described were important, then that might be a different story. But these problems seemed designed for no other purpose than to give him a headache. A train is heading toward Victoria Station at a hundred kilometers an hour. Its speed decreases by half its square root the first hour, then increases by five integers each succeeding moment. If the circuit of the train's approach is a closed polygon, at what moment does the train reach this Victorian treasure? Its romantic Victorian-style corselette comes with a French-cut panty.

Duard put down the SAT preparation book. Maybe the problem was that he was consciously avoiding the catalog. Maybe if he just looked at it for a minute then he could forget about it. The important thing was to agree right off the bat that he wasn't going to touch himself, that that was simply out of the question. All he was going to do was just glance over things so he'd know what was what, and then he could get back to work with an open mind.

Duard opened the catalog at random. There was a whole page of women standing there in their brassieres. But these weren't like any brassieres Duard had ever seen. Oh my goodness gracious, Duard thought. This isn't anything like I ever expected.

Nipples are left exposed in this all-lace cowgirl bra, made exclusively for women who spend a lot of time on horses. Select the matching silken chaps or the body-hugging nylon lace breeches. Both have an open crotch.

Duard looked up suddenly. No, he said. I'm not gonna do it. I'm not. They can't make me. The women in the catalog just looked back at him. Come on, they said. What the heck? Who's gonna know?

The lace bodysuit is bursting with surprises. Fingerless gloves complement this slickery ensemble. The matching thigh-high boots accompany the matching teddy trimmed with nuts and bolts.

Please don't make me, Duard thought, pulling off his pants. I want to go to Harvard. There's no way I can go to Harvard if you keep pulling my pants off. Can't you see I'm trying to work? I'm trying to improve myself?

Be a frisky feline in this Day-Glo ensemble. This cupless underwired cat suit entices with a butt-baring thong back. The gartered legs are held tightly in place with sheer rubber grippers.

Duard pulled his underpants down to his knees. Yes, that felt better, sort of. He tried to picture Dominique as a frisky feline. Little ears. Black whiskers. Her cupless tattooed breasts bursting with their vinyl surprises. Long tail twitching around her back. Digging in the litter box. *Goddammit Duard,* she said. *Where's my scratching post?*

He was just about to proceed with the next step when he saw the brain lying across the room on top of his dresser. The brain. He remembered the night that Dominique had given it back to him. *I'm sorry, Duard. I don't want your brain anymore.*

"Is it because you don't love me anymore, Dominique? Like, what did I ever do to make you change? Nothing."

"No, that's not it," Dominique said. "It's just because I think it's gross. Whenever I see it I get kind of sick to my stomach."

Duard tried to be understanding. I mean, if she thought it was gross, then that was plain enough. He didn't want her to keep it if she thought it was disgusting. On the other hand, didn't she see that it was important to him, that it was the first thing he had ever given a girl that he would rather have kept himself? Maybe the trouble started when he bit her in the tattoo studio. He couldn't really blame her for being sore. It really wasn't very courteous, if you thought about it, biting people.

Duard thought about the way Dominique's finger tasted, like something in a can. The next thing he knew, Phoebe drove off with his car. He hadn't told her he was using Crisco instead of motor oil, though. It was no wonder the Swinger died near Hershey. That Crisco made your engine think you wanted to fry something, or maybe make a cake. You couldn't expect a car to go very far when it was confused.

Recently, he had heard through Dwayne that Phoebe had moved back with her father in Valley Forge now, that she had become a little preppy. Still, Duard couldn't imagine that happening to Phoebe, at least not on the inside. He liked Phoebe a lot more than he wanted to admit, if only because they were both orphans after a fashion. Phoebe knew what it was like to grow up in a family like his, with a brother as whacked out as Dwayne, and a sister as lost as Dwenda. He wished that Phoebe hadn't moved away. Now he would never know her. He wondered what Phoebe would look like in some of this stuff. Cute, maybe.

Thinking about Phoebe, and the brain, and Dominique, had cooled things off a little. Feeling ashamed, he pulled his pants back on. This was not the way to behave at all, not if he wanted to work for the government when he grew up.

He opened his SAT book again and tried some of the logic problems. *Mr. Whiskers is standing in the inner circle. Mrs. Poodle is in the circle next to Mrs. Wilson. Mr. Fun-Hog won't stand next to Mrs. Garrigle. Mrs. Poodle smokes Camels. Mrs. Wilson won't stand next to a smoker. There are two groups of three circles. Where is Mrs. Garrigle standing?*

Duard knew that in order to do these problems, you had to draw a little diagram. He drew two big circles, adjacent to each other, and then drew two small circles right in the middle of them. In the middle of the tiny circles he drew two even tinier circles. He looked at them carefully.

Duard's lower lip began to tremble. He looked back at the paragraph to make sure he had followed the instructions properly.

He had drawn two breasts, complete with nipples and areolas. It's not my fault, he thought. They *made* me draw them. It's for school.

He got out a red pencil and shaded in the areolas and nipples. Mr. Whiskers was standing on a nipple. Mrs. Poodle and Mrs. Garrigle were on the opposite breast. He wondered if this could possibly be right. He flipped to the back of the book to find the answer, but while he was at it, he checked the Elizabeth's Enigma catalog again because that had lots of pictures of breasts in it and that would be helpful to make sure he had gotten it right. *The padded push-up bra creates buttery-soft lift. The vinyl slit cups look wet.* Goddammit, Duard thought again, standing up. This is really annoying. He pulled off his pants again, then yanked off his underpants and jumped onto his bed. For a moment he reconsidered, put his feet on the floor, and then put his underpants back on. Nah, what the hell, he thought, then pulled his underpants off again. Still, he thought, maybe I shouldn't. But what could it hurt, just this once? Well maybe a lot. Maybe it's the kind of hurt that doesn't bother you now but then when you're thirty or something and you want to have a baby you'll find out you can't because you used up all your sperm when you were fifteen. That could easily happen, at least he thought it could.

When the phone rang, Duard was naked. He was hoping that Dwenda or Dwayne would pick it up, but for some reason they just let it ring and ring. Maybe they knew he was naked up in his bedroom and they wanted to punish him for it. You see? Maybe in the future you'll think twice.

Duard picked up the telephone, hoping that the person on the other end wouldn't be able to tell he was nude from the sound of his voice. Boy, Duard thought. Am I glad they don't have picturephone yet.

"Hello, is this Duard?" Duard said. "Sure it is."

"Hi, Duard," Phoebe said. "It's Phoebe."

"Phoebe," he said, immediately regretting the fact that he was naked. He wondered if he could get his underpants back on without her hearing it. If she heard the elastic in his waistband snap, though, she might get suspicious.

"How are you?" she said. Something in her voice sounded funny, almost as if she were nervous. Yeah, that'll be the day, Duard thought. When someone like Phoebe gets nervous talking to a guy like me, sitting around buck naked reading the Elizabeth's Enigma catalog.

"Am I good?" Duard said. "I think so. I feel good I guess."

"I feel good, too," Phoebe said. "I hope you don't mind me calling like this. It's just been so long since I talked to anybody from home. I feel like I'm a million miles away."

"I heard you moved," Duard said.

"Yeah," Phoebe said. "I'm staying with my father now, and his wife. Well, you know. Vicki. I guess you know all about her."

"Yeah," Duard said. "Do I know all about her? I do. How do I feel, when I think about what Dwayne's doing? Not good, I can tell you that. Your father still doesn't know? That they're doing it all behind his back?"

"Yeah," Phoebe said. "I think so. I'm not sure, sometimes, though. Wedley might just be putting on a big show, pretending he doesn't know. Maybe he thinks it would hurt me, if I knew. He's trying hard to give me a stable home life now. It's sad to watch him sometimes."

"Does Dwayne ever think about what he's doing," Duard said. He was reaching down to pull on his underpants now. Slowly he slid them up his legs.

"Anyway," Phoebe said. "How's school? How's everybody? What's Dominique up to? Is she still mad at me for taking off that night?"

"I don't know," Duard said. "How are me and her getting along now? Not so hot. She's still sore I bit her."

"Oh really?" Phoebe said. There was something unmistakably unremorseful about her voice. "I mean, I'm sorry. That must be tough for you."

"I don't know," Duard said. "The worst part was the taste. Sort of like tuna fish oil." Duard thought about the night Dominique got Phoebe tattooed. Something about it struck him as odd.

"I'm sorry about that night," Duard said. "When we went to Rusty's."

"Sorry?" Phoebe said. "Why should you be sorry?"

"Because I should have stopped it. I knew you didn't want it. I thought maybe you'd get out of it on your own. But I just let her do that to you. Why don't I have any courage and junk?"

"You have courage, Duard," Phoebe said. "It took a lot of brav-

ery to bite Dominique. If you hadn't of bit her I might never have
gotten out of there.''

"Yeah, well," Duard said. He had gotten his underpants back on
now and felt a little more confident.

"Listen, Duard," Phoebe said, her voice quavering. "They have
this dance at my school. It's called the Valentine's Day Massacre. If
you aren't doing anything on Friday night, the fourteenth, would you
go to it with me? Please?''

Duard felt incredibly guilty at lying there only in his underwear.
Phoebe was asking him out, and what was he doing? Reading about
open cups and rubber grippers. Serves me right, Duard thought. I'll
never think about this stuff again, *ever.*

"Is that the best invitation I've ever gotten?" Duard said. "Might
be. You're the best, Phoebe. I'll be there. Do I miss you?''

"I miss you too, Duard," Phoebe said. "I'm so glad you can make
it. I'm warning you, though, it's formal. You're supposed to wear like
gangster clothes if you can get them. This is what they do at Dillinger
instead of a prom.''

"Can I get gangster clothes?" Duard said. "I might. There's a
Mister Formal shop in town, or at least there used to be until it
washed away. Where did it go, when it washed downstream? Somewhere else, that's all I know.''

Even as he agreed to Phoebe's invitation, Duard realized that he
had already promised his brother to baby-sit Dwenda that night. Still,
he would not turn down Phoebe's offer. He would have to make
other plans for Dwenda.

"So what's your new school like?" Duard said. "I heard it's all
hoity-toity.''

"It's hoity-toity all right," Phoebe said. "I mean, you wouldn't
believe some of these girls. Still, the teachers are really good. You
wouldn't believe how much I'm learning.''

"Learning, in school!" Duard said, stunned. He shook his head.
"I can't imagine what that's like. I mean, wow!''

"You won't recognize me anymore, Duard," Phoebe said. "I'm blond now. I cut off all my hair and dyed it."

"Is that different?" Duard said. "Has to be."

"Yes," Phoebe said in a small voice. "It's different."

"Do I bet you're still pretty, Phoebe?" Duard said. "Did I ever know anyone I thought was as pretty as you? Not that I can think of."

Phoebe didn't know what to say. She sat at her end of the connection, blushing.

"I'm too tall," she said, finally.

"Hey, do I like you tall?" Duard said.

"Oh, you're so nice, Duard. But I don't know. Sometimes when I look in the mirror I don't recognize the person I'm looking at. Sometimes I think I'm going crazy. Jeez, all I want to do is fit in!"

"Oh, well, that doesn't make you crazy," Duard said. "When I look in the mirror, who do I see? Beats the hell out of me. Some guy, I guess."

Phoebe laughed. "I'm glad you're coming, Duard," she said. "I can't wait to see you."

"I can't wait to see me either," Duard said. "We are finally going to get mental together. Just like I predicted!"

"Well," Phoebe said. "I'll see you Friday. Can you pick me up?"

"I'll get you," Duard said. "I'll get you then."

They said good-bye and hung up the phones. Duard looked at the catalog, still sitting on the bed, and decided to put it away. He was too old for things like this now. Who knew what would happen, once he went to this dance with Phoebe? He looked at the brain, still sitting on top of his dresser. It was a good thing he had gotten it back. Things were about to change.

He was on the verge of sitting down at his desk, to do some more of his SAT problems, when he reconsidered his decision about the catalog. If things were really going to be so different for him from now on, then perhaps it would be appropriate to take one last look inside, to bid this all adieu. *Miracle escalator pads lift buttocks up and out.*

Duard went back to his bed and pulled off his underpants again. It was important in life to say good-bye. *The bikini top inflates through a hide-a-way nozzle concealed in the cleavage. Check it out!*

Phoebe, back in her bedroom, stood there holding the telephone in one hand. Duard had actually said yes! She could not believe it. On a small piece of paper before her she had a list of all the things she had wanted to say to him. Tell him I'm blond. Ask about Dominique. Find out about school. Invite him to dance. This last item was underlined seven times.

And he had answered, and he had sounded just like he always did. The impossible had come to pass, and he had broken up with Dominique. She could not believe her good fortune. Now, in about a week, she would be picked up and taken to the Massacre. She would show the other girls at Dillinger what the boys from Columbia County were really like. She hoped Duard would make a good impression.

In her joy and disbelief, Phoebe spun around her room. She watched all her posters and books and her bed and the window rotating past her vision. Her eyes rested on a small picture on the bureau, a photo of her going over a jump in a horse show when she was nine. She remembered that horse, and the feeling of weightless dizziness she felt when Misty cleared the jump. She felt something like that now. Phoebe put her hand on her head, wondering for a moment what had happened to her hard hat. Then she remembered: it was still in the attic in the house in Centralia.

She ran downstairs to tell her father the news. There was sound coming from Wedley's bedroom. She knocked on the door, then burst in, overjoyed.

"Hey, Pa, the greatest thing just happened!" she cried. "I'm going to the Massacre after all! And you'll never guess with who! It's the most amazing thing!" She was so happy she was practically singing.

Unfortunately, Wedley was not in the room at the time. Wedley was miles and miles away, in Rosemont, at the offices of Mister Chimney.

Vicki lay naked on her back, her arms extended over her head, clutching the bars of the brass headboard. Sweat was dripping off her breasts. Her legs were spread wide. Dwayne was sprawled on top of her. He was naked, too, except for a green hat that said: JOHN DEERE. Dwayne looked up at Phoebe with a curious expression.

"Uh-oh," he said. "Vicki."

"Dwayne," Vicki moaned. Her eyes were tightly shut. "Dwayne, Dwayne, Dwayne."

Phoebe ran out of the room, frightened, disgusted, and ashamed. She ran down the stairs, through the kitchen, past the range, where a pot of Stove Top baked potatoes was burning, through the back door, and out into the street. Dwayne's van was parked in the driveway, complete with its stepladder and the sign that said DWAYNE'S SERVICES. As she ran she muttered, *oh my god oh my god oh my god.* Tears gathered in her eyes and ran down her cheeks as she ran through the cold winter air.

I should just keep running forever, Phoebe thought. I should just run until I reach a place where no one knows my name. Still, even as she thought this, she knew it was impossible. Even if she ran for two days, she'd only wind up at Phartley Park again, with its smells of fried dough and the screams of children trapped on the Sky Master.

A car pulled up slowly behind her. Oh Jesus, Phoebe thought. The creep in the Miata. Now, of all times, to have to be humiliated by this weasel.

She turned angrily toward the car and yelled.

"Leave me alone! Whoever you are, just leave me alone! Can't you see that things are hard for me?"

The person behind the wheel rolled down the window. "I'm sorry, Phoebe," the woman said. "I didn't mean to bug you."

"Ma?" Phoebe said, looking at her. "Ma?"

Emily Harrison was terribly thin. Phoebe could see the bones around her eye sockets. For all that, though, it was strange how familiar she seemed, as if it had not been nine years since Phoebe had seen her mother last, but a few hours. Her eyes were a remarkable pale blue. Her hair was tied into a long braid down her back. When she smiled, Phoebe was full of a mysterious recognition.

"Jesus, Phoebe," Emily said. "What'd you do to your hair?"

Phoebe looked at her, and at the car. This moment seemed like a wavering dream to her, like the surface of a lake seen from its depths, shafts of sunlight twisting through the reeds and past the fish. Was it only a moment ago that she was talking to Duard, and he was telling her she was pretty? What had happened to the world, that everything had suddenly taken on this odd shine?

"I mean, it's very nice," Emily said. "It's just not what I was expecting."

"What were you expecting?" Phoebe said. She was suddenly self-conscious about her appearance. She was still wearing her Dillinger Academy tunic and knee socks. What if Emily took one look at her and decided that Phoebe was no longer worth knowing?

"What do you think, Phoebe?" Emily said. "Do you want to take a ride with me?"

Phoebe, standing there in the cold in front of her father's house, thought about the awful scene she had just witnessed. Vicki lying on her back, her sweaty breasts pouring in every direction. Dwayne with his John Deere cap. The objects in her bedroom spinning around her.

"Yes," Phoebe said. "I think I'd like that."

Phoebe walked around to the far edge of the car and got in. Emily reached over and hugged her daughter. For a long time the two of them sat like that, embracing, as the car's engine idled. Then Emily kissed Phoebe on the forehead, and put the car into gear.

"Let's ride," she said.

NORTHERN CROWN

Small but graceful.

In the eight months since his wife had left him, Patrick Flinch had almost become accustomed to living alone. He had finally begun to live on something other than microwaved pizza, and no longer slept on what had been "his" side of the bed. The silence of the house was still difficult to adjust to, though. Phoebe had returned to live with her father. Even Buddy was gone. Pat was alone in the big house with the paintings of his ancestors, most of whom looked like people you wouldn't have wanted to have known, even before they were dead.

It was the overbearing quietness of the place that made having the mice so annoying. He'd be reading in bed, tired after a long day at his restaurant equipment company, and then he'd hear the rustling of the tiny paws in his walls. He thought he could hear their little tongues lapping their own fur, cleaning themselves. Their teeth were constantly being sharpened upon the studs and the electric cables in the wall. He wondered if mice ever got an electric shock when the teeth got past the insulation. There would be a quick puff of smoke and a single moment when you could see the mouse skeleton illuminated. After that, nothing. Rodent radon.

When he came downstairs Wednesday, on the morning of the day that Phoebe called Duard, he found nothing reassuring about the soft squeaking he heard from under the sink. This could only mean that the Havahart trap that he had purchased had been successful in capturing its prey. These new traps were supposed to be more humane—they trapped the mouse alive, so that you could dispose of it in some dignified manner. It was a lot better than having the traditional traps, which slammed down on the mouses' tails, enabling them to run around the house dragging the trap behind them, like some newlywed's car hauling around tin cans and tires and a sign that said, JUST MARRIED. SHE GOT HERS TODAY; HE'LL GET HIS TONIGHT! It was likewise an improvement over poisons, which even if successful resulted in the mouse curling up somewhere and decaying, filling the house with a distinct and mournful aroma.

The problem with the Havahart trap, though, was that you had to release the mouse somewhere. Unless you got in the car with it and drove miles and miles away, Pat figured that the mouse would sooner or later wind up back in your house again, chewing into the bread box and leaving little turds in the sink. The alternative wasn't all that great, though—what would happen if the cops pulled him over and they figured out that he was driving a mouse around in his car? They would realize pretty quickly that he was a man who lived alone.

So, instead of opening the cabinet underneath the kitchen sink, Pat went upstairs to the library and checked the other trap, the one under the bookcase. He figured he might as well know whether he was going to have to drive around with one mouse or two. This one was empty, though, just like the rest of the house. He looked at the picture of his great-uncle over the fireplace. Over here was the place where he had stood in the morning sunshine, inhaling the smell of skunks. Isabelle had come down the hallway in her pink T-shirt and asked him what he was doing. He was still trying to figure out an answer to that one.

Pat sighed and went downstairs. He knew that he was particularly susceptible to jags of melancholy these days, and decided to do what he could to avoid another one. It was hard not to fall victim to these moods, though, with his wife off on her around-the-world-cruise and his niece off in Valley Forge. He was amazed how much he missed Phoebe; he missed her even more than Clara. All the time he had loved his niece without realizing the depth of his affection. The way she used to spend hours in the bathroom doing her hair, the way she used to sprawl all over chairs while she talked on the phone, the seriousness with which she tackled her homework—all of these were now missing from his life. He felt like he had been washed up naked and stupid on a tiny island, so small there wasn't much more to it than a single palm tree with one coconut.

Even Buddy's absence hit him to the core. He didn't understand what had happened to the dog. One day he was in the basement sleeping next to the water heater, the next day he was gone. Was it possible that the dog's intricate plan had at last been realized, that after twenty-three years Buddy had finally succeeded in devouring himself whole?

Pat went downstairs, wearing his gray suit and scuffed up wing tips, then walked outside in the cold. He picked *The Philadelphia Inquirer* off his driveway, then climbed the stairs back up to the house.

He made some coffee, then sat down with the paper. He always read the magazine section first, because the news in it was gentle, usually having to do with the misbehavior of celebrities and features on oddities like the woman in Camden who made hats out of ice cream. There were recipes for dishes he did not intend to make, and reviews of books that he did not anticipate reading.

Today, on the front page of the magazine, however, was a large article entitled *Local Artist's Work Really Takes Guts*. Underneath the headline was a photograph of Isabelle Smuggs standing next to her work.

He thought he could almost see the nervousness in her eyes as he looked at her picture. Still, there was something both comic and apologetic about her stance. Perhaps it was because she was standing next to a guillotined plaster of Paris head of Jimmy Stewart. According to the article, this is what she was doing now—a whole series of guillotined heads. I don't know, Isabelle, he thought. If it makes you happy, I guess.

Underneath the sink he heard the squeaking of the captured mouse. He was going to have to think of something to do with it. Pat got up and poured himself another cup of coffee.

Isabelle's work was being premiered at a show that opened this Friday night, Valentine's Day, at the Art Alliance. The opening was not open to the public, the article said. It was by invitation only.

Well, Pat thought. So much for that. For a moment he had considered showing up at the opening, hoping to catch her eye. Maybe they could talk about things. He wondered if she would be wearing the same dress she was wearing in the photograph. He kind of hoped so. It made her look beautiful.

Maybe that's the one good thing I can do in life, she had said to him, as they lay there by the Catawissa River in the aftermath of their passion. Maybe if I teach you the stars I won't be such a jerk. She had told him the story of being in Miss Bolgin's class, about not knowing what planet she lived on. The teacher asked her if she was living on Mars and she had said, yeah, maybe. The class laughed.

He thought about his old school, James Buchanan High. They had finally closed it in 1979, and there it stood with its windows boarded up for ten years. Finally they blew it up. Even well into his forties, Pat could not think of the dynamiting of his high school with anything less than pleasure. How long do we stay in the shadow of our adolescence?, Pat wondered. The rest of our lives?

The doorbell rang, and Pat jumped. It was especially eerie to have the silence of the dark house broken these days. He felt his heart pounding in his throat. Pat looked at himself in the mirror, to make sure he didn't look insane, then went to the front door and opened it. A woman of indeterminate age was standing on his threshold, holding a vacuum cleaner.

"Good morning, how are we today, sir!" she said, exhibiting a cheerfulness completely out of proportion to the situation.

"I'm all right," Pat said, thinking about the magnitude of this statement's falseness. He was not all right. He was in a lot of trouble.

"I'm glad!" she said. "I'm very glad! Listen, are you interested in keeping drug addicts off the streets and ending crime in this neighborhood?"

No, Pat wanted to say. As a matter of fact, drug addiction and crime are things I'm emphatically for.

Instead, he shrugged and said, "Sure."

"I'm glad!" She beamed again. The woman had a very intelligent face, Pat noticed, but there was something strange about her eyes, which were surrounded by tired purple circles. It didn't look as if she got out much.

"My name is Wendy Walisko," she said. "And I have the opportunity to go to Acapulco, Rio de Janeiro, or Morocco! Isn't that great?"

"Yeah," Pat said.

"Well, aren't you nice to say so! We're going to get along great, Mister—"

"Flinch," Pat said. "Patrick Flinch."

"Pat," Wendy said. "I'm showing people the Vacu-Master Ten Thousand today. I get ten points just for demonstrating it to you. I'm only four points short of a trip to Acapulco this morning! If you let me show you how it works, I'll go over the top. You won't have to buy a thing! Won't you help me go to Acapulco?"

She looked away for a moment.

"My whole life, I've wanted to go there."

Pat sighed. "All right," he said.

"Oh, but you're too nice. I'll get ten points and I'll get the vacation! I'm too happy to believe!"

She came into the front hallway, looked around at the decaying parlor with the piano and the long oak staircase. "Wow," she said. "What a place this is."

"Yeah," Pat said. "It's a place all right."

"Well, the Vacu-Master Ten Thousand could come in handy around here, that's for sure! You'd find it a real boom!"

"A what?"

"A boom. Here." She dug into her purse and got out a plastic Baggie and poured the contents on the floor.

"Jesus!" Pat said. The bag contained an awful-smelling pinkish semi-liquid glop that seemed to have little worms and nuts floating in it. There was a large stain of the stuff on the hall carpet now, spreading outward.

"Now I know what you're thinking," Wendy said. "You're thinking how is an ordinary vacuum cleaner going to clean up this mess, am I right?"

"That's right," Pat said. "That's what I'm wondering."

"Well, watch this," Wendy said, and unrolled the vacuum's long electric cord. She walked over to a wall socket and plugged it in.

Wendy moved back to the vacuum, grasped the long nozzle, and said, "Prepare yourself for a miracle."

She flicked the switch. Nothing happened.

Wendy looked up at Pat, flicked the switch another couple of times. Still, nothing happened.

"Hey, is that outlet on? You're sure there isn't like a wall switch or something for it?"

"I don't think so," Pat said.

"Let me try another outlet," Wendy said, but before she could get to the wall, the vacuum suddenly sprang to life. A light near its mouth illuminated the pink glop on the carpet.

"There we go!" Wendy said, and sprang back to the vacuum. She grasped the handle, but even as she did the thing died again.

"Darn it," she said. The pink glop on the rug looked like it was soaking pretty deep into the pile now. Pat wasn't sure, but it seemed as if the color of the rug was changing at the stain, as if the glop itself was burning off the dye.

The vacuum again sprang unexpectedly to life, and the hose jolted and jumped like a striking snake. Wendy moved the head of the vacuum over the stain, and there was a liquid, slurping sound, like someone sucking the bottom of a drink with a straw. This was followed by a sudden metallic clank. The vacuum went dead again.

"Damn this thing," Wendy said, her forehead crossed with irritated wrinkles.

The vacuum sprang to life again, but it was making a strange sound, as if its nozzle had somehow inhaled a small animal. Wendy kicked the engine. Some smoke began to spew out of the back, and Wendy tried to flick off the power switch. This, however, appeared to have no effect. She kneeled next to the machine, flicking on and off the switch, as black smoke filled the front hallway.

"You want me to unplug it?" Pat said, yelling over the high-pitched whine.

"What?"

"The vacuum?" he said. "You want me to unplug it?"

"I don't know!" Wendy said. Her face was filled with a kind of morbid hopelessness now, as if she had resigned herself to sitting in Pat's hallway for the rest of the day, watching smoke fill the house. "It's not supposed to do this!"

Pat walked over to the wall and unplugged the vacuum.

Disconnecting the plug, however, had no immediate effect. The machine still belched black smoke, its engine roaring and clanking, and the few ounces of the pink glop that had been sucked into the vacuum earlier now started oozing from the rear vent. Wendy stood up and kicked the machine. "Shut up, you!" she said. "Damn it, you're not even plugged in! Shut up!"

But the vacuum continued to whine and smoke and glurt pink liquid onto the carpet. Wendy was very upset, and picked the machine up by its canister.

"I said shut up!" she yelled. "Why don't you just shut up!"

Wendy threw the machine angrily across the hallway, and it landed on the staircase. Still whining and puking, the vacuum rolled down the steps. Wendy ran over to it, kicked it a second time, then threw it up the stairs again. The sound of the engine seemed to change, as if the gears were seizing up inside. The vacuum tumbled down the steps, and the hose broke off. Some dusty pink liquid oozed out of the place where the hose had been. Wendy picked up the vacuum and threw it up the stairs a third time. The engine choked as it hit the steps, sputtered, and died. The motor rolled down the stairs, extinguished, and fell onto the hose, which was still lying, broken, on the bottom step.

"Stupid piece of junk!" Wendy said. Tears were running down her face. "Goddamn piece of shit!"

She sat down on the bottom step, among the ruins of the Vacu-Master, and sobbed into her hands.

"It's all right," Pat said. "Don't you worry."

He rubbed his chin with his hand. "Listen. How much is one of these vacuums anyway?"

"Two hundred dollars," Wendy said, shaking her head. "Can you believe that? Two hundred dollars for this piece of garbage."

"Well," Pat said. "I do need a vacuum."

She looked at him, wiped her tears away with the backs of her hands. "You mean you'd buy one? You'd actually buy one?"

Pat thought to himself. He had hundreds of thousands of dollars in the bank, and no mortgage. What would it cost him to help this woman? Was a vacuum cleaner that did not work such a high price to pay?

"Sure," he said.

She looked at him suspiciously. "Why?" she said.

"I told you," he said. "I need a vacuum."

"Oh," Wendy said. "That's just too good to be true." She stood up, and brightened. "I'm so happy! I don't know what to say! I feel like singing something!"

"And now you get to go to Acapulco," he said.

"Oh that," Wendy said, waving her hand through the air. "That's just a bunch of garbage. If I get the points I'm only eligible to enter the lottery for the trip. Usually what I wind up with is another vacuum cleaner. Then I got to sell that one, and they give me two more. Then I sell *those*, and I have to sell *four*. The more vacuums I sell, the more I wind up with. That's how the lottery works."

"Well, you write up the paperwork," Pat said, "and I'll buy one. I'm glad you showed up this morning. I was just about going bonkers in here."

He had not meant to say anything quite this personal. Pat feared that he had betrayed the fact that he was buying her vacuum out of pity. Still, this Wendy did not seem to resent it.

"I'm glad I showed up too," she said. "You're kind."

"Well, I don't know about that," he said.

"Oh but you are," Wendy said. Her eyes widened as if she were looking at him for the first time. "Have you lived here long?"

"My whole life," he said. "Except for a few years in my twenties. I lived in New York then."

"This is a hard place to leave," Wendy said. "I can't imagine living anywhere but this part of Pennsylvania."

"You live in Buchanan?"

"Centralia."

"Oh."

"Hey," she said nervously. "Patrick. Do you like making stuff up? I do."

Pat looked at her curiously for a moment. "What do you mean?" he said.

"Never mind," Wendy said. She looked around the house. "This is a pretty place," she said. "It's so huge."

"It's too huge," Pat said. "I get a little nuts in here, all by myself."

"You can get nuts in little places, too," Wendy said softly.

"Yeah," Pat said. "I bet that's true."

"It is," Wendy said.

"Well, listen," Pat said. "I'm on my way to work. If I give you my card, can you have that delivered here?"

"Oh yes," Wendy said. "I'll bring it by personally, once your order's in." She smiled crookedly. "I can't wait to see you again."

"Yes," Pat said. He reached into his pants and got out his wallet, then removed one of his cards and handed it to her. "I'd like to see you again, too."

"Well," Wendy said. "I guess I'll see you later."

"Yes."

She picked up the pieces of her broken vacuum and left. Pat stood in his front hallway for a moment or two, looking at the stain on the Oriental rug. Then he went back into the kitchen, where the mouse under the sink was still squeaking. He drank a little more coffee, then he looked at the picture of Isabelle in the paper.

Pat felt as if someone were holding his heart in a fist, slowly squeezing down on it with enormous fat fingers. It's inconceivable, he thought. Women really can't imagine the magnitude of the love that men have for them. Our whole lives are spent like this, floating on the merciless clouds of our desire.

He went upstairs to put on his tie. Before he got to his bedroom, however, he paused before the guest room, what had once been the room where Phoebe spent her days. He walked to the window; outside Wendy Walisko was still trying to pack the pieces of her vacuum back in her car.

Pat picked up the necklace from the bureau, the silver chain with the blue crystal that Emily had given her daughter long ago. He closed his eyes and made a wish. For a long moment, Pat stood there, his eyelids squeezed together, the crystal held to his forehead.

Nothing happened.

Patrick Flinch lowered the necklace, put it back down on the bureau. Well, I don't blame Phoebe for leaving this here, he thought. This thing is busted.

CEPHEUS

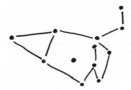

*Cepheus is rather dim. His brightest stars are
all moving away from him.*

Wedley Harrison drove toward home in the Lincoln Town Car, listening to WFLN-FM, Philadelphia's classical music station. A very distinguished announcer was introducing his program, which was entitled "Strike Up the Band." He pronounced "Band" in a way that made it sound like "Bond." The man cleared his throat ostentatiously, then began to play a piece by John Philip Sousa.

Damn I love the Philadelphia suburbs, Wedley thought. I love Swarthmore. I love Merion Station. I love Bryn Mawr. I love Nether Providence. I love Newton Square. I love Hatboro. Well, maybe this was stretching things too far. Actually he wasn't that crazy about Hatboro.

He leaned on his horn. He had entered the long stretch of Lancaster Pike in Wayne near the Farmer's Market and the McDonald's. Even in the year and a half since he had moved here he had already seen it get more congested, and the residue of snow and slush in the

road wasn't making things any easier. An enormous new superhigh-
way, I-476, had opened recently, cutting a merciless swath through
the suburbs. Now Philadelphia was just like any other East Coast city,
with its beltway surrounding it like a force field. I sure feel sorry for
the people who live next to it, Wedley thought. For centuries the
wealthy had surrounded themselves with farms and fields and mansions. Suddenly they wake up one morning and they've got a highway
out the window. Wedley was glad he lived in Valley Forge, some distance away from the new highway, which everyone, for unknown reasons, called the Blue Route. It would be a few years still before Valley
Forge got like Wayne, which was ironic, since Wayne had been named
in the first place after General "Mad" Anthony Wayne, the Revolu-
tionary War soldier who rode into battle holding a cake in one hand.

He got past the traffic light at Sugartown and Lancaster and
changed the radio station to WRTI, the jazz station out of Temple
University. In the old days it was run by Black Muslims, who had
the best taste in music that he had ever heard. They called it "The
Freedom Sounds." Then some idiot decided to get rid of all the Muslims and they called it "The Point." A few years went by and they
changed it again, simply called it "Jazz Ninety." The music was still
good, but it wasn't quite the same when the DJ's name was Bob instead of Sameer. It had been hard to get WRTI then, on his hi-fi in
Centralia, but it came in on clear nights. He remembered sitting
around his house on hot summer evenings, listening to the crickets
and cicadas, drinking a beer with his shirt off, and listening to Sameer
and "The Freedom Sounds" coming in from Philly. Those were the
days.

On his right was something called the Rib-It, which was the Main
Lion a few years ago, and before that was the Covered Wagon. The
Covered Wagon had been there for years, had originally been a tav-
ern on the Conestoga trail west to Pittsburgh and beyond. He had
taken Emily to the Covered Wagon to see Count Basie in the seventies. The Count was a tiny gleaming man who sat like a frog on his

piano bench and played the piano with one finger. Wedley had wanted to dance all night, but Emily didn't like big-band music. She kept going up to the Count and asking him if he couldn't play something a little more up-to-date. Count Basie just shook his head and smiled, and kept playing his piano with one finger.

He turned down Waterloo, and passed the Devon station. Graffiti on the overpass read: ARLO FOR PRESIDENT. On the left was a house with a big chimney, one of the last ones he had swept himself before promoting himself to the front office. He remembered that it had been a particularly nasty job, and he'd had to use almost a whole bottle of Ko-Mate deglazer before he got the soot off of it.

The car phone rang. Wedley punched in the speakerphone.

"Hello?" he said.

"Hello?" said a woman's voice. "Is this Mr. Harrison?"

"Yes," he said.

"I wanted to talk to you. About business."

"Well," Wedley said. "I thank you for your call. Unfortunately, we're closed up for today. Could you give me a ring tomorrow? We open at eight-thirty."

There was silence on the line for a few moments. Wedley wondered if she had hung up.

"Where *are* you?" the woman said, irritated. "It sounds like you're in a fucking toilet."

"I'm on a speakerphone," Wedley said, suddenly embarrassed. "I'm in my car."

"You have a phone?" she said. She sounded outraged. "In your goddamn car? What kind of car are you driving?"

"A Lincoln, actually," Wedley said.

"A Lincoln!" the woman swore. "Jesusgod, Wedley!"

"As I said," he continued, politely. "We're closed now. Call me back tomorrow, won't you?"

"This isn't about chimneys," the woman said. "It's about Buddy. You know. Your dog."

Wedley froze for a moment. He picked up the phone and held it to his ear, then turned off the speakerphone.

"Who is this?" he said.

"A friend," she said. "We've got your dog. Buddy. We'd like to talk terms."

"Why don't you speak to my brother-in-law," Wedley said, slowly. "Patrick Flinch. He's responsible for that dog now."

"Oh, come on, he's not responsible for diddly," the woman said. "The guy's a mess."

"Who are you?" Wedley said. "What do you want?"

"I told you," she continued. "This is a friend. You give us the money, we'll give you the dog back. If I were you I'd hurry. He doesn't look too good."

"Well of course he doesn't look good," Wedley snapped. "He's like twenty-five years old or something."

"Oh, I see," the woman snapped. There was something familiar about her voice. "That means he's just supposed to die? Is that it? Sorry, Buddy, you're twenty-five years old now, we won't pay your ransom? Jesus, it's not like we're asking for a million dollars. Not now anyway."

Wedley sighed. "How much are you asking?"

"I don't know," she said. "Maybe fifty bucks. What do ya got?"

Wedley's heart raced. The woman on the line was his daughter Demmie.

"Listen, miss," Wedley said. "Why don't we meet? Sit down, talk together. You sound reasonable."

"Of course I'm fucking reasonable," she said. Wedley shook his head. It was definitely his daughter. "How could anybody who'd kidnap a disgusting dog like this be unreasonable?"

"Where can I meet you?" he said.

"Next Friday," she said. "Where are you going to be next Friday?"

Wedley thought. On Friday he was chaperoning the St. Valentine's Day Massacre. He would be surrounded by kids in tuxedos with zits and bubble gum and machine guns.

"I'm going to be at the Franklin Institute," he said. "I'm chaperoning a dance."

"That's what I heard," Demmie said. "We'll be there, too."

"Where?"

"Franklin Institute. How about the giant heart? We'll meet you in the left ventricle. Nine o'clock. You got that?"

"Nine o'clock. Left ventricle. Hey, listen. Uh—"

"What? What is it?"

"How do I know you've got Buddy? This could be anybody calling."

"Oh, Wedley," she said. "Of course I've got him. What do you want me to do, put him on the line?"

Someone in the background said something. It sounded like *yeah put him on the line he likes to talk on the phone sometimes what's so wrong with that.* Wedley strained to hear. Demmie put her hand over the receiver for a moment; it sounded like she was arguing with someone who was not very bright.

"Hello?" Wedley said. "Hello? Sweetheart? Are you still there?"

"I'm here," Demmie said, into the phone.

"Are you all right?"

"Of course I'm all right," she said. She sounded a little upset. "Don't call me sweetheart."

"I'm sorry, miss," Wedley said. He was approaching home now. "You reminded me of someone. Someone I used to love very, very much. Someone I still love."

"Yeah," the woman said. There was a long pause. It sounded like Demmie was trying to get hold of herself. "I'm glad for yuz."

"Maybe if you see this person I was thinking of, you could tell her I'll always love her. That anytime she wants to come home, she has a family waiting for her."

"A family, right!" Demmie said bitterly. She laughed. "Oh, you are breaking me up, Wedley! I think I'm gonna split a gut laughing!''

"You tell her things change. People can make mistakes. That's not the end of the world.''

"The end of the world,'' Demmie said softly. "What do you know about the end of the world, Mister Chimney?''

The man in the background said something again. "Shut up,'' Demmie whispered again. He heard a low moaning sound that Wedley recognized. Buddy.

"You tell her all that, all right?'' Wedley said. He was pulling into his driveway now. A van marked DWAYNE'S SERVICES was parked by the back door.

"Listen,'' Demmie said. "I got your dog, see?''

"I understand that,'' Wedley said. "You've made that clear.''

"So don't start sniveling about some stranger you don't even know, okay? You listen to me for a change.''

Wedley pressed the button that opened the electric garage door opener, then pulled the Lincoln into the carriage house.

"I'm listening,'' Wedley said.

"You don't know me,'' Demmie said. "You've never known me.''

"He knows Buddy!'' the man in the background said.

"Shut up,'' Demmie whispered to him. "Can't you shut up?''

"You tell her what I said,'' Wedley repeated. He turned off the engine. "You just tell her.''

"I gotta go,'' Demmie said. "You be there.''

She hung up.

Wedley sat in the car for a full minute afterward, holding the receiver in his hand. Then he got up and went into the house.

"Hello?'' The place seemed deserted. "Phoebe? Are you there, darling?''

Her book bag was lying on its side in the kitchen. A pair of school textbooks had fallen out: *Introductory Astronomy* and *Human Psychology*.

He walked up the stairs to the second floor, calling his daughter's name.

There were voices coming from the bedroom. This gave him some sense of encouragement. Perhaps Vicki and Phoebe were having a conversation, getting to know each other. Relations between the two had been somewhat strained since Vicki burned some of Phoebe's hair off last September.

He swung open the door.

Vicki was lying buck naked on the bed. Her cheeks were flushed red. Some perspiration glowed at her hairline.

"Oh my god, it's Wedley," Vicki said. She didn't sound happy about it.

"Vicki," he said. "What are you doing?"

"I was . . . ," she said. Her gaze shifted around the room. "I was, uhh, waiting for you, darling."

"Me?" Wedley said. "You were waiting for me?"

"Oh yes oh yes oh yes. Come to me, Wedley!"

Wedley was not quite sure what was going on here, but he had a theory.

"Have you seen Phoebe?" he said.

"Phoebe?" Vicki said. Again she looked at a number of unexpected corners of the room. "I'm not thinking about Phoebe!" she said. "I'm thinking about you!"

"She isn't home," Wedley said. "Did she go out somewhere?"

"Oh," Vicki said. She raised her index finger in the air. "Yes. She did say she was going out. Just a little while ago."

"Out?" Wedley said.

"Yeah. Jogging. That's right. She went for a little run."

"It's a little late for her to still be out jogging," Wedley said. "She's usually back by now."

"Yeah well," Vicki said. "Go figure." She looked deep into his eyes. "Oh, Wedley," she said. "I'm not thinking about Phoebe." She reached down and held her breasts. "I'm thinking about you." Her nipples slowly grew erect. "I'm thinking about you, Wedley," she said.

"Oh, Vicki," Wedley said, sitting down on the bed next to her. "I'm thinking about you, too."

"Then don't you want to make love?" Vicki said. "Please? Can't you see how I'm waiting for you?"

Wedley smiled. What the hell. He took off his coat and his shoes, then yanked off his tie. As he unbuttoned the collar and the cuffs of his starched white shirt, Vicki sat up for a moment.

"I have to just take care of one little thing," she said. She got up and walked toward the bathroom in the corner.

I'll bet, Wedley thought, and took off the rest of his clothes.

Vicki went into the bathroom and made some sounds so that Wedley would think she was putting in her diaphragm, which had, of course, already been in place for several hours. She looked over at the large hamper in the corner. The top was not all the way down. Dwayne's eyes peeked out at her from the crack beneath the lid. He was wearing a cap that said: JOHN DEERE.

"It's too small," Dwayne whispered. "Vicki. There's clothes in here."

"Sshhh," Vicki said. "We're in trouble."

"Maybe if I threw some of these pants on the floor I could fit better. But then maybe he'd get curious about all the clothes on the floor. If he tries to put them in the hamper he'll find me. He'll know I'm not just some clothes, Vicki!"

"Quiet," Vicki said. "Listen. I'll get him all riled up. When things get going, you get out of the hamper and climb out the window. You can follow the roof over to the awning over the back door, then jump down and get back in your truck. You got that?"

"Uh," Dwayne said. "Yeah. You'll get him riled up. Then—uh—then—"

"Then you get out of the hamper."

"I'll get out," he said. "Should I try to put some of these underpants on the floor first? I'd have more room if I got rid of some of
these underpants."

"What did you say, dear?" Wedley called from the bedroom.

"Nothing!" Vicki said. "I'm just getting ready! I'm so excited!"

"I'm excited too!" Wedley said.

"Forget the goddamn underpants," Vicki said. "Wait ten minutes then climb out the window. You got that?"

"Wait ten minutes," Dwayne said. "Then—uh—"

"Climb out the goddamn window."

"Climb out the—"

"The window, Dwayne. Say it."

"I'm going to wait until you get things going. I'm going to wait
ten minutes."

"Then you're going to climb out the window."

"Then I'm going to climb out."

"The window."

"Yeah."

"Good."

"I got it," Dwayne said. He popped his head out of the hamper.
"This is exciting!" he said. "It's like some show!"

"Quiet," Vicki said.

"Vicki," Dwayne said, pulling some of the underpants at the bottom of the hamper out, and throwing them on the floor.

"What?" Vicki said.

"I feel special," he said. There was a sock on his head.

"Good, Dwayne," Vicki said. She put the underpants back in the
hamper and closed the lid.

"Hey," Dwayne said. "It smells like old clothes in here. Some of
this stuff needs washing."

"It's a hamper, Dwayne," Vicki said.

"I know what it is," Dwayne said, sounding hurt. "Don't act like I
don't know what it is."

"What is it then?"

There was a long pause.

"Listen," Vicki said. "I gotta go."

"Okay," Dwayne said. "I'm waiting here. You're getting things going. I'm waiting ten seconds then jumping out the window."

"Ten minutes," Vicki said.

"Right."

Vicki left the bathroom, walked back to her husband.

"Hello, sweetheart," she said again. "I'm sorry I took so long!"

"Me too," Wedley said. He kissed her. "Me too."

Vicki climbed on top of Wedley. He gently licked her neck.

Jesus, Vicki thought. She was surprised and embarrassed to find herself moved by her own husband. I must be out of my mind. Screwing Dwayne and then Wedley within the same hour. It's not adultery I hate so much, but the lying, the duplicity. If only there were a way of coming clean with Wedley about the whole thing. If she explained to him the confusion her heart had felt, wouldn't he have sympathy for her? Would the fact that she had lied to him make his understanding her impossible?

She shuddered and collapsed on top of him. Wedley and Vicki kissed softly, then more vigorously. He rolled over on top of her. Even at forty-nine, Wedley was still a good-looking man, full of life. Since they had come to the Main Line he seemed to have been injected with adrenaline. Is it me, Vicki thought, that's brought him all this confidence, power, and joy? If she told him about Dwayne, would it all just as quickly dissolve?

But for a few minutes Vicki forgot about the idea of Dwayne. Wedley was holding her in his arms, adoring her, making her body jolt with electricity. He entered her quietly and gently, and she moaned. Wedley had always been good in bed, at least once he got used to having sex again. It had taken a few weeks in the beginning to get him used to being with a woman once more. He hadn't slept with anyone since Emily left him, eight years before that. She wondered whether Wedley ever thought about Emily now, if he ever closed his eyes and imagined he was making love with her instead.

Vicki reached over her head with her outstretched arms and grasped the bars of the great brass bed. "Oh, Wedley," she said. "Oh my god, it's my husband!" She gnashed her teeth in pleasure.

"Vicki," he said.

There was a soft thump across the room, then another. Vicki opened one eye and tried to look around Wedley's shoulder.

The hamper appeared to be moving. Dwayne was shifting his weight around inside it, in sudden heaving thuds, so that first one end of the hamper, then the other, slowly walked across the room.

"No," Vicki said. "No!"

The hamper thumped forward again. Now it was practically right next to the bed. The lid opened partway. Dwayne's head peeked out, watching Vicki and Wedley in jealousy and dismay.

"No?" Wedley said, slowing down. "What's wrong? Am I doing something wrong?" he said.

"No," Vicki said. "You're wonderful. You're driving me crazy."

Dwayne looked very angry at this point. He popped the lid of the hamper open completely. Vicki thought she understood. He was going to go out the bedroom window, instead of the one in the bathroom. This was going to be more difficult than she thought.

"Go," Vicki cried softly. "Hurry."

"Hurry?" Wedley said. "You want me to hurry?"

"Just go," Vicki said. "Go!"

Dwayne got out of the hamper and stood behind them for a moment. Wedley and Vicki were speeding things up. He understood. She wanted him to hurry. She wanted him to go. He looked over at the window, then back at the couple.

"I'm coming," Wedley said.

"You're going," Vicki said, looking at Dwayne.

"I'm coming."

"You're going."

Wedley collapsed on his wife and exhaled heavily. Vicki held her husband against her breasts. She loved this part of sex better than the sex itself. The best thing in the world was to lie there with your lover, hovering on the outskirts of sleep, being still once more. Unfortunately, it was a little hard to enjoy this moment with Dwayne standing less than three feet away.

Dwayne cocked his head to one side, sort of like a bloodhound. He looked at the lock on the window. It seemed to make him sad somehow.

Still, this sudden melancholy seemed to have an illuminating effect. Dwayne gave up on this window, and turned slowly and walked back into the bathroom. Vicki did not hear the bathroom window open, but she was aware of a new gust of cold air blowing into the house. She hoped that Dwayne would manage to get down to the ground safely.

"Wedley," Vicki said. "I love you." She hated herself for saying this, but in spite of everything it was still true. How was it possible to be in love with two men at once?

Wedley looked surprised. He wondered whether she thought she was fooling him. Did she really think he was ignorant of his own betrayal? He had known ever since the first day. It was hard for a woman to get the smell of cement mixer off her clothes.

"I love you too, Vicki," Wedley said sadly.

"Oh, Wedley," Vicki said, looking out the window. "I feel so sorry for you sometimes."

From outside came the sound of Dwayne's van starting up and driving quickly away.

CASSIOPEIA

According to legend she was once a queen.

L ight snow was falling as Emily drove her daughter through Valley Forge. Jazz played softly from the radio.

Phoebe couldn't stop looking at her mother. Emily didn't look anything like she had expected, and yet there was something about her appearance that was inevitable. Above all she was shocked by her mother's height; she had not recalled Emily being so tall and thin. Well, Phoebe thought, now I know where I got it from. She wondered if anyone ever called her mother Icky.

"How's your father?" Emily asked.

"Fine," Phoebe said.

"Is he really?" Emily said. "Or are you just saying that? You don't have to spare my feelings, believe me."

"I don't know," Phoebe said. "I don't really know how he is. I'm not sure if *he* knows."

"What's his wife like? He did remarry, didn't he?"

Phoebe gritted her teeth, remembering that her most recent view of Vicki had also featured an image of Dwayne lying on top of her, wearing his John Deere hat.

"You don't like her?" Emily said. She squinted at her daughter. "Don't mind me. I shouldn't ask."

"I *hate* her," Phoebe said. She heard her voice crack. "She's screwing someone else, behind Wedley's back. She's awful."

"Poor Wedley," Emily said.

They drove down Devon State Road and stopped at the light just before the intersection with 202.

"It's been hard for you, hasn't it," Emily said. The light changed.

"Well of course it's been hard for me," Phoebe said. "What did you expect?"

"I don't know what I expect," Emily said. "I guess I sort of hoped it would be easier for you and Demmie without me. I knew Wedley would have trouble, but I figured all of you would land on your feet. Even as little girls you and Demmie were resilient."

"Resilient?" Phoebe said, annoyed. "Yeah, I guess so. We're resilient all right."

A sign on the left said: VALLEY FORGE NATIONAL HISTORICAL PARK.

"You're angry, aren't you," Emily said.

"What?"

"You're angry." Emily looked at Phoebe sadly. "I was hoping you wouldn't be angry, not anymore."

"Well of course I'm angry. What do you think? You think it's been easy without you?"

"I didn't think it would be easy," Emily said. "But it wouldn't have been easy if I stayed either."

"Where have you been all these years? What have you been doing?"

"Oh, you don't want to hear the whole schmear, do you? It's boring."

They drove down the Baptist Road, through hundreds of acres of cleared open pasture. The snow had covered the ground and the trees.

"You want a little tequila?" Emily said. She reached into the back and got out a bottle of Cuervo Gold. Holding the steering wheel with one hand, Emily held the bottle to her face with the other and took a good slug. "Here," Emily said. "That'll put hair on your chest!"

"No thank you," Phoebe said, looking out the window. "I don't want hair on my chest."

Emily turned left onto Valley Creek Road. "It's just an expression," she said softly.

"I know what it is," Phoebe said.

They drove in silence through the park. After a few minutes they got past the large open field and traveled onward between the two small mountains at the park's western end, Mt. Joy and Mt. Misery. A large, white covered bridge loomed up out of the snow at them. It was dark inside. Phoebe couldn't see the road at the far end of the bridge. A large sign on the bridge said: 1865.

Emily turned right, avoiding the covered bridge. They drove parallel to Valley Creek, now frozen and covered with ice. A man on cross-country skis was gliding over the top of the creek. His steaming breath puffed from his face.

"Did you ever read that story about the Headless Horseman?" Phoebe asked her mother.

" 'The Legend of Sleepy Hollow,' " Emily said. "That's Washington Irving. Disney made a cartoon of it. It used to scare the hell out of you when you were little."

"It did?" Phoebe said. "I don't remember that."

"Oh yeah," Emily said. "We used to watch the *Wonderful World of Color* on Sunday nights. Make some Jiffy Pop and sit around watching that. When you saw that Ichabod Crane get killed by the Headless Horseman, you screamed. We shouldn't have let you watch it. We shouldn't have let you watch any television, actually. The light goes right through you."

Phoebe thought about this, then shook her head. "I don't remember any light going through me."

"Well, I don't know," Emily said. "Maybe it was your sister."

They passed a small footbridge that crossed the stream. A small sign read: SITE OF VALLEY FORGE IRON WORKS. DESTROYED, 1777.

"This is some car," Phoebe said, also thinking that the Miata was probably not the best vehicle to be driving during a snowstorm.

"It's Russell's," Emily said. "You think I could afford a car like this, you're crazy."

"Who's Russell," Phoebe said. "Is that like your boyfriend or something?"

"Something like that," Emily said.

"And you're in love with him, right?" Phoebe said.

"What?" Emily seemed to have been taken by surprise. She laughed a long, liquid laugh. "Me, in love with Russell? Don't be ridiculous." She snorted. "He's disgusting."

"How can he be your boyfriend if you think he's disgusting?" Phoebe said.

"I don't know," she said, shaking her head. "It's a mystery."

They turned right at the light on North Gulph Road, then followed the park tour road past Washington's headquarters.

A police car parked in the lot next to Washington's headquarters suddenly flashed its lights on and pulled out into the road behind them.

"Shit," said Emily. She downshifted and began to drive more quickly. Phoebe felt the power of the car's engine push her back in her seat.

"What are you doing?" Phoebe said. Emily didn't answer. She floored the accelerator and pulled onto the Inner Line Drive. In a moment they were traveling at high speed through dark snowy woods. A log cabin with three old cannons in front of it rushed past them.

Phoebe looked behind them. The cop car did not appear to be following them. "Ma, it's all right," she said. "There's no one there."

But Emily just kept driving through the woods. She had a strange expression on her face that frightened Phoebe. Emily stuck her lower jaw forward so that she had an underbite. Every few moments she glanced in the rearview mirror with a look of unspeakable dread, as if she feared that something terrible were following her. Looking at her mother, Phoebe thought for a moment of Ichabod Crane, watching the far end of the covered bridge growing further and further away.

They screeched and slid in the snow, wheeling around hairpin turns, climbing higher up the ridge. More cannons and soldiers' huts appeared out of the night, standing there abandoned by the roadside. The sun had gone down entirely now, and it was getting hard to see. The snow was beginning to fall heavily.

"Ma," Phoebe cried, looking back. "There's nobody there."

"Yeah," Emily said. "That's the worst part of it, the way things aren't there."

"Ma," Phoebe said. "What are you talking about."

"Listen," Emily said urgently. "Just because we can't see them doesn't mean they aren't after us."

They drove down out of the inner line defenses and passed the huts of the Conway Brigade on their right. A huge statue of General Steuben loomed out of the night at them. Snow was gathering on the general's hat.

On the right now was another immense field, full of cannons and the huts of soldiers. On the other side of the street was the Washington Memorial Chapel, a large church with a carillon tower.

Phoebe's mother drove on, her lower jaw stuck out like a bulldog's. Phoebe could see the muscles in her mother's jaw clenching and unclenching. She kept looking in the rearview mirror.

They reached a small intersection. Straight ahead, at the top of a small hill, was the Kennedy-Supplee Mansion, which was a fancy restaurant that served stuff like crabmeat on pear slices. Emily turned left, then turned down a small drive. An old train station stood there. Its windows were boarded up with plywood.

"Come on," Emily said, stopping the car. She turned off the engine, and opened her door. "Bring the tequila."

"Ma," Phoebe said. "Where are we going?"

"Hurry," Emily said, grabbing the bottle herself. "We don't have much time left."

Emily slammed her door and walked quickly toward the train tracks. Phoebe stumbled after her. There was a distant rumbling down the rails. The bright headlight of a freight train's engine shone on them, illuminating the closed-down station with a harsh yellow glow.

The station appeared to have been built in the late 1800s, with the moderate flourishes of Quaker Victorians. A blue sign on the side of it said: VALLEY FORGE PARK STATION. Graffiti had been written on the yellow bricks of the station's walls with brown spray paint.

The engine bore down upon them, occupying the middle of the three tracks. The engineer looked out the window at them. He did not smile. He's probably wondering what the hell is wrong with us, Phoebe thought. Two women standing here at this abandoned station, in the snow. Does he think we're waiting for a train?

The engine groaned past, and the station grew dark again as its headlight moved onward. The noise from the boxcars and tankers, though, was still huge and absolute. Phoebe felt her heart beating in her breast, and thought for a moment about the tattoo she had, the one that said FEEBY. What would her mother think if she knew she had gotten it? Phoebe's cheeks burned with shame.

Down the tracks, Phoebe could barely see the outline of a destroyed stone mansion, fallen into ruins. The roof was missing entirely, and small saplings were growing through what had once been the rooms on the first floor. Empty windows punched through the stone walls. A chimney was collapsing inward upon itself. Phoebe swallowed. *Centralia.*

The freight train thundered past the abandoned house. There were yellow boxcars that bore red, white, and blue shields from the Union Pacific. After these came black tankers, marked DuPont Ti-Pipe Titanium Oxide, and ACF Center Flow. A small sign on the tankers read: CAUTION: DO NOT STEAM WITH BOILING WATER. Then came another long line of boxcars: Canadian Northern, New Orleans, Pacific Belt Railroad. Railbox: The National Boxcar Pool. Chessie System. Southern Serves the South. The empty cars boomed and rang as they passed through a switch.

Phoebe had stood still for a moment, frightened by the massiveness and the volume of the passing freight, transfixed by the old abandoned house; in doing so, she had allowed her mother to run onward, almost out of sight. It was easy enough, though, to follow her footprints in the snow. She had gone past the station and was climbing through the woods, up a small hill. Phoebe remembered some legend about the men at Valley Forge being so cold that they had no shoes, that their footprints in the snow had been red with their own blood.

The abandoned station, Phoebe now saw, sat right on the banks of the Schuylkill River. A large bridge loomed out of the sky over her head, traversing the river on three stone supports. Something about the bridge filled Phoebe with dread. It looked spooky, hanging there in the winter sky. A few hundred feet beyond it was an even larger bridge, filled with screaming cars heading down 422 toward the Pennsylvania Turnpike. That was what was so unnerving about this one, Phoebe thought. There weren't any cars on it.

Phoebe walked through the woods, marching uphill through the snow. When she got to the top she found herself on a small road. At the end of the road was the entrance to the bridge, which was closed off with hurricane fencing. Emily was climbing it. She already had one foot over the top, and in another moment would descend onto the other side.

A sign read: DANGER. BETZWOOD BRIDGE CLOSED.

"Ma," Phoebe called. "It's closed."

Emily dropped down onto the other side of the bridge and began to follow it out across the train tracks and the river.

Phoebe ran to the bridge and watched her mother through the hurricane fencing. It was no wonder the Betzwood Bridge was closed. It had to be at least a hundred years old; the roadbed consisted of rusting iron grates. The Schuylkill River moved frigidly many hundreds of yards below. The bridge couldn't have been more than two lanes wide, and must have been originally built for horses and carriages. Phoebe could see large holes in the iron grate from where she was standing. All around her was a tremendous racket, from the speeding cars on the other bridge, and from the ringing, roaring freight train underneath her. As if to reemphasize the unpleasantness of the situation, large orange and white cans blocked off the entrance to the bridge, and more signs saying DANGER: KEEP OUT were attached to the hurricane fencing.

Goddammit, Mother, Phoebe thought, and climbed the fence.

It was harder than it looked to get over it, partly because it was snowing and the fence itself was very cold, which made it difficult for Phoebe, who was not wearing gloves or, for that matter, a coat. She was still wearing her tunic from school. Her legs were bare above her knee socks.

Phoebe dropped down onto the grilled surface of the Betzwood Bridge. She thought she could feel the bridge bouncing from the impact of her weight upon it. A hole in the gridwork to her right opened into nothing.

"Ma?" she said, following her mother out into space. "Ma?"

The snow was falling quite hard now, and it was not possible to see the opposite bank of the Schuylkill in this darkness. Headlights from the cars on 422 sent a dome of glowing light into the winter sky from the other bridge. Phoebe walked slowly out, feeling acutely the distance from land that each step along the old Betzwood Bridge brought her.

She found Emily sitting in the snow at the center of the bridge, her feet dangling off the edge.

"Hey," she said to her daughter.

"Hey," Phoebe said.

Emily handed Phoebe the bottle of tequila.

"Thirsty?" she said.

Phoebe took the bottle from her and raised it to her lips. She liked the tequila. It tasted kind of like acid.

Emily looked out at the river below. The snow was disappearing as it hit the water.

"Why do you think that doesn't freeze?" Emily said. "You think the water moves too fast or something?"

"Maybe," Phoebe said. She took another drink of tequila and remembered being at a party at Muffy Pennypacker's house where one boy had shown everyone how to drink it. He put a little salt on the top of his hand and held a lime slice in his fingers. "Or maybe it's too polluted."

"Yeah, that could be it," Emily said. "Government puts fluoride in things now. That could melt snow, I guess."

Phoebe sat down in the snow next to her mother. She felt it melting into the back of her skirt.

"I'm cold," she said.

"Yeah, well," Emily said. "You go outside without a coat, you get cold."

"Aren't you cold?" Phoebe said. Emily wasn't wearing a coat either.

"Yeah," she said. "But it doesn't bother me so much. You get used to it."

On the bank below them, the freight train was slowing down. Now a long line of coal cars was traveling past. Phoebe could see that the cars were empty.

"You know where they're headed?" Emily said, taking another swig of the tequila. "Those coal cars? Centralia."

Phoebe nodded. It was entirely possible.

"I see them all the time now," Emily said. "Ever since I moved back."

"You moved back?" Phoebe said. "Where? To Centralia?"

"Yeah," Emily said. "I'm in the old house. You know, you and Wedley and Demmie left a ton of stuff up there, just lying around."

"Wait," Phoebe said. "You mean you're back in our old house?"

"Uh-huh," Emily said. "Me and Russell."

"Who's Russell?" Phoebe said.

"I already told you. We been seeing each other. Anyway, you know him. That's how I found you. He's got that tattoo parlor."

Phoebe took the bottle of tequila from her mother and drank another mouthful of it. She thought for a moment.

"Rusty?" she said. "That's who you left Pa for? That guy who looks like Mr. Clean?"

"I did not leave your father for Rusty," Emily said. "For heaven's sakes, Phoebe. I already told you. He's disgusting!"

"Then who did you leave us for?" Phoebe shouted. She heard her voice crack, and hated herself for it. "Somebody else?"

"Somebody else," Emily said.

"Who?" Phoebe said.

"Me. I left your father for me, all right?" She paused, and took a long slug of the tequila. "Listen, Phoebe," she said. "I don't expect you to forgive me. I did it, all right?"

"But don't you know what you did to us?" Phoebe said. "Do you know what it's been like?"

"Ah, honey," Emily said. "All I can say is, if I'd stayed it would have been worse. I would have gone nuts, I mean just totally stark raving nuts. Ripped our house apart with a chain saw. Strangled your father with a lariat.''

"But why?" Phoebe said. "How come?"

"I don't know, Phoebe," Emily said. "I guess I'm just not cut out to be a housewife."

"A housewife? That's what you think you would have been, if you'd stayed with us?"

"Of course that's what I would have been. What else would I have been?"

Phoebe shook her head. "Jesus, Ma," she said. "A housewife!"

"Phoebe," Emily said, taking her daughter's hand.

Phoebe wrenched her hand back away from her. "Fuck you," she said. She felt hot tears on her cheeks.

"Phoebe, I'm sorry," Emily said.

"Did you hear me," Phoebe said. "I said fuck you!"

"I heard what you said."

"Well good, because I meant it!"

For a while they just sat there on the edge of the bridge. Emily stared at her daughter, watching her cry. Phoebe didn't look at her.

"So where did you go," Phoebe said. "After you decided we weren't worth the trouble?"

"Atlantic City," Emily said.

"Atlantic City?" Phoebe said. She looked at her mother with an even deeper disgust. It was one thing for her mother to have thrown her family over, but for her to have thrown her family over for Atlantic City was unforgivable. At the time she'd left, they didn't even have gambling.

"Yeah," Emily said. "I went there because it was as far as I could get on the money I swiped from Wedley. I got a little room there in a hotel they were tearing down."

"How could you have stayed there," Phoebe said, "if they were tearing it down?"

"I stayed there before they tore it down," Emily said. "After they tore it down, I lived somewhere else."

"Somewhere else in Atlantic City?"

"Yeah. At first."

"I suppose you were with a whole bunch of different guys all this time? Living it up?"

"I wasn't living it up," Emily said. She took Phoebe's hand. "I used to walk on the beach, every day, thinking about you and Demmie and Centralia. I used to look for shells and stuff the sea washed up. I collected things. Pieces of glass. The candles from someone's birthday cake. One time when I was out there this horse swam right out of the water, walked up on the beach, and looked at me. I was thinking I could rope it or something and bring it to you. You know, how you always liked that story, *Misty of Chincoteague*? It was kind of like that."

Phoebe looked at her mother like she was from another planet. "Ma!" she said. "I don't want some horse you found! Jesus!"

"Well that's good," Emily said. " 'Cause a couple minutes later the guy who owned it swam up and yelled at it."

"Why did he yell at it?"

" 'Cause it wasn't supposed to be swimming, honey. I think it must have jumped off of some ship." Emily smiled for a moment. "You should have seen this sailor guy trudging up on the beach after his horse, dripping wet. Boy, was he mad."

"Well, that's just what I've felt like, as a matter of fact," Phoebe said. "Like some guy who had his horse jump off a boat."

"I don't know, Phoebe," Emily said. "I guess my sympathies were with the horse."

"Why?" Phoebe said. "How can you side with the stupid horse, when some guy is worried about it, wondering whether or not it's drowned?"

"You don't know what it must have been like for that horse on that guy's ship, Phoebe. Maybe they kept it there against its will. You think that's a sensible place for a horse? On a goddamned *boat?*''

Phoebe smiled, and regretted it. ''All right,'' she said. ''Maybe it is a stupid place for a horse.''

''Of course it's stupid,'' Emily said. ''What you want is to find someplace with *hay.* A *barn* or something. That's where you want to keep a horse.''

Phoebe looked at her mother. ''So that's what you've been doing for the last nine years? Walking on a beach in Atlantic City, rescuing horses?''

''I walked on a beach in Atlantic City for a few years. Then I walked on a beach on Treasure Island. You know where that is, Treasure Island?''

''Ma,'' Phoebe said, annoyed. ''That's in *Pinocchio.*''

''It is not in *Pinocchio,*'' Emily said. ''It's underneath the Oakland Bay Bridge. There's a naval base there. I had a job in the mess hall for a while. That's where I met Rusty.''

''I still can't believe you're living with him. I mean, boy. What a loser!''

''Yeah well, maybe he's about what I deserve, Phoebe, you ever think a that? Maybe going out with someone like Rusty just about serves me right.''

''Serves you right?'' Phoebe said. ''For what?''

''For giving up on you and your sister. And Wedley. Ah Jesus, Phoebe, I can't explain it. I'm a screwup, basically, is what this is all about. I'm a total screwup. You want any more of an explanation than that I don't have one.''

Emily looked over at Phoebe. She reached out with one hand, and ran her fingers through her daughter's hair.

''God, you're so pretty, Phoebe,'' she said. ''I wish I'd been pretty like you.''

Phoebe shrugged. ''I wish I wasn't so tall.''

"Oh, you'll be glad you're tall, one day. Once the boys catch up to you. It's kind of nice to be able to tower over them, anyway. It's always worked for me."

She looked at Phoebe as if remembering her daughter from another life.

"Hey," Emily said. "Hey, Phoebe. Do you like your name?"

"My name?"

"Yeah. Did Wedley ever tell you why we named you girls Phoebe and Demmie? It's for the two moons of Mars, Phobos and Deimos. I thought it was pretty. I bet he never told you that."

Phoebe sat there, amazed. She had never known that there was a story behind her name. "No," she said. "He didn't."

"Well, maybe he forgot. But I didn't." Emily swung her braid down over one shoulder. "There's something important you shouldn't forget about outer space."

"What's that, Ma?"

There was a pause. "It's fun."

Emily took one more slug of the tequila, then stood up. "Let's get out of here," she said. "Aren't you cold?"

"Of course I'm cold," Phoebe said. "I'm freezing."

"Well, you should have said something. Let's get off this bridge. It gives me the creeps."

"I did say something," Phoebe said. "You said it didn't bother you."

"Well of course it bothers me," Emily said. "Everything bothers me."

They walked toward the riverbank, being careful to avoid the large holes in the bridge's grate. Again Phoebe was sure she could feel the Betzwood Bridge swinging back and forth as they moved.

"You know somebody killed themselves off this bridge," Emily said. "A couple of months ago. Jumped right off the edge and killed themselves. It was in the papers. The article I read said they didn't even hit the water. Some woman. They said she was despondent."

Phoebe looked through the grate below her feet and saw the rocky shore of the river. It didn't surprise her at all.

It was harder to climb the hurricane fencing this time, perhaps because they were cold, or perhaps because they had consumed all that tequila. When Phoebe was halfway down the far side, Emily reached up and took her daughter under her arms and lowered her to the earth. She moved forward and encircled the girl with her arms. Emily and Phoebe stood there for a while in a big embrace. Emily kissed Phoebe on the forehead.

"You know I love you, kiddo," she said. "I'll always love you."

Yeah, Phoebe thought. *You sure have a weird way of showing it.*

They walked down the hill again toward the old train station. A blue Conrail caboose trailed at the end of the enormous freight. As it receded down the tracks, the night finally became quiet again. It was a relief to be freed from the incessant, lumbering noise.

"So how long have you been with Rusty?" Phoebe said, as they walked along the tracks toward the car. "A long time?"

"No, no, heavens, no," Emily said. "I only met him last summer, just before I came back east. I'd never stay with him for that long, are you kidding? All his mumbo jumbo about his men's group and kidnapping people and all the rest of it. He's messed up. I'm not kidding. It's the navy. It does that to people."

"Well, I don't know," Phoebe said. "How should I know about the navy?"

"He's crazy about me, though," Emily said. "Every time I think I'm going to head back west, he threatens to come with me. He says he's going to kidnap you so all three of us can go out west together, to Nevada. You must have seen him trailing you, in the Miata. He says he's been out to get you a bunch of times, only every time he's about to kidnap you you turn and look at him and give him the finger."

"I do give him the finger," Phoebe said. "I don't want to go to Nevada. I want to get out of high school and go to college and get the fuck *out* of here."

"I don't blame you," Emily said. "Not one bit."

They got in the car and drank more tequila as they waited for the engine to warm up. Phoebe felt as if her skin were frozen solid.

"I sure would like to be with you more often, Phoebe," Emily said. "This was fun, wasn't it?"

"Kind of."

"Hey, kiddo, can I ask you a question?" She put the car in gear and drove out of the closed-down train station.

"Sure," Phoebe said.

"You think Wedley would ever take me back?" Emily turned right onto Outer Line Drive. They passed the visitors' center and another long line of soldiers' huts.

Phoebe looked out the window at the log cabins and the snow-covered cannons. "I don't know," she said. "Would you ever come back to him?"

"Oh, Phoebe," Emily said. "Of course I would. I'd come back to him in a second, if I thought he'd forgive me. You think I like living like this?"

"I don't know, Ma," Phoebe said. "Maybe you do. I mean, you wouldn't have left him if you didn't mean to."

"Yeah," Emily said. "But I wouldn't leave him *now*. Not if he took me back. God, I'd love to have a regular house, and just make you lunches and shit. There's really a lot worse than that. Oh, Phoebe, the things that I could teach you!"

They passed the National Memorial Arch on their left, an enormous Arc de Triomphe standing in the midst of a snow-covered field. On the top of the monument, bathed in spotlights, were the words NAKED AND STARVING AS THEY ARE, WE CANNOT ENOUGH ADMIRE THE INCOMPARABLE PATIENCE & FIDELITY OF THE SOLDIER.

Emily punched in the cigarette lighter and dug around in her shirt pocket for a pack of cigarettes. "You smoke?" she asked her daughter.

"No, Ma," Phoebe said.

"That's good," Emily said. "You don't want to start. See, there's another thing I can teach you."

Emily put the cigarette on her lip, then raised the lighter to her mouth. She sucked on the cigarette with her thin, hollow cheeks. Phoebe could see from where she was sitting that her mother had the wrong end in her mouth, and had lit the filter.

They passed through the Pennsylvania Columns, a pair of soaring monuments with eagles at their crests.

"Ma," Phoebe said. "You're smoking the filter. Look at what you're doing!"

"What? Oh for heaven's sakes." Emily rolled down her window and threw her cigarette out into the snow. She punched in the lighter again.

On the right was a large statue of General Anthony Wayne. Emily held the lighter to her face; it illuminated her mouth and nose with its orange glow. "Hey," she said, looking out the window. "There's Anthony Wayne. They say he was nuts. You believe that, that he was nuts?"

"I don't know," Phoebe said.

"Well," Emily said. "You should."

A cop car suddenly turned on its headlights and pulled out behind them. "Shit," Emily said.

"Just relax, Ma," Phoebe said. "It's probably nothing. Last time it wasn't anything either."

"That's 'cause we escaped."

The cop turned on his siren and flashed his spotlight in Emily's rearview mirror.

"Shit, shit, shit," Emily said, pulling over and pounding her hands on the steering wheel. "Give me that bottle."

"Ma," Phoebe said.

"Give it, goddammit," she said, and grabbed the bottle neck. She looked at Phoebe, whose mouth was hanging open. "Remember what I told you?" she said.

"No, what?"

"I'm a screwup," she said, then opened the door and began to run.

"Hold it right there," the cop said over the loudspeaker on top of his squad car. "Stop running, now."

But Emily was already disappearing across the battlefield, her long braid trailing behind her like the tail of a kite. She was headed up a small rise toward the position of Scott's Brigade, at the far western end of the Outer Line Defenses.

"Stop or I'll shoot," the cop said. There was the sound of gunfire as the cop fired a warning shot into the air. Jesus, this isn't possible, Phoebe thought. They aren't actually going to kill her, are they?

Emily stopped running, halfway up the hill, and put her hands up.

"Come back down here nice and slowly," the cop said. All of this was being shouted through his megaphone. The cop hadn't even gotten out of the car yet.

"All right, ma'am," he said, finally, standing up. "Put your arms up against the car and spread your legs." As the one cop frisked her, another one got out of the car and shone a flashlight around in the Miata. Phoebe squinted as the light shone in her eyes.

"Looks clean," the second cop said. They were putting handcuffs on Emily and putting her in the back of their squad car. A long time passed by as the cops sat there with Emily in the backseat, talking into their radios. The blue and red strobes on top of the car whirled around and around, turning the face of General Anthony Wayne different colors.

"All right," the second cop said at last, coming forward to talk to Phoebe. "We're going to have to take your mother in. She's intoxicated, and driving without a license. Can you get yourself home, miss?"

Phoebe said that she could. "I live near here," she said. "I'll walk."

"All right," the cop said, and turned.

The policeman got back in the car, and then they drove off. The last that Phoebe saw of her mother, she was sitting in the backseat, looking out the window.

It was funny, Phoebe thought, as she walked home through the swirling snow. Being abandoned, left to fend for herself like this, ought to have made her angry at her mother, ought to have filled her with rage and disgust. But she didn't feel anything like that. As her mother vanished, Phoebe just put her hands in the pockets of her tunic and started walking more quickly. The way Phoebe figured it, Emily had been gone for so long that losing her again just felt like things were getting back to normal.

ORION THE HUNTER

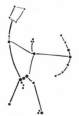

*Orion is heavily armed, with a raised club, a shield,
and a sword dangling from his sparkling belt.*

Isabelle Smuggs stood alone in the second-floor hallway of the Philadelphia Art Alliance, looking at herself in a large ornate mirror. As she considered the low-cut black dress she had chosen for the evening, she concluded that the only thing wrong with it was that she was the person wearing it. It was impossible for her to observe her reflection without seeing into her own interior. You impostor, she thought. Spilling out of your clothes like some cheesy Italian fountain. For a moment she felt dizzy, and put one hand on her temple. She was perspiring. I only hope, Isabelle thought, turning away, that others see me more kindly than I see myself. It would be just my luck if some lovers came along and tried to throw some coins in me.

From downstairs came the sounds of many people, meandering through the gallery, observing her work. There was the far-off, echoey sound of cocktail glasses clinking, some laughter. The throbbing noise of the crowd rose up the staircase and reverberated in the empty upper stories of the museum. What are they thinking down there? What is the verdict on the things that I have made? Are people laughing in contempt at the futility of my labors? Choking back the stunned saliva of their derision? Have I made them hog-boiling mad?

Of course it wouldn't have been surprising to Isabelle if her work made people want to boil hogs in scorn. These pieces were supposed to be disconcerting, to make the viewer consider the possible nature of his or her own atrociousness. Although she was proud of what she had done as an artist, as a human being it was a little embarrassing. It was hard to respond to people when they asked you what you had had in mind when you created a work of art that made them sick to their stomachs.

Throughout the first floor of the museum, on elegant marble pedestals, was a series of celebrity heads, guillotined at the neck. Their tongues, which were purple, were sticking out. Each of the heads wore a kind of surprised, disappointed expression, as if his or her feelings had been hurt by the idea that someone would want to behead someone so fabulously mythological. The Nancy Reagan looked especially disillusioned. Next to her was a chagrined Jimmy Stewart and a flabbergasted Leonid Brezhnev. Lyndon Johnson was bending over to show everyone the gallbladder scar on his belly. But his belly wasn't there anymore.

The centerpiece of the show was Isabelle's ex-lover, Mr. Barton Sumac, whose severed head was the largest, and most disgusting, in the entire series. She had put a lot of time into that one. She had sent an invitation to the opening to Sumac, not expecting him to show, and of course he hadn't. Still, it was pleasant to think about the huge, offensive smarty-pants lumbering around the hall, sniffing at her work, squinting at it and passing judgment, until he came at last to his own, contemptibly severed head. She didn't think he'd like it.

Isabelle had mixed feelings about her show. She liked the statement that these floating heads seemed to send. Still, there was something tediously gruesome about them that got on her nerves. In her heart she wished that she could have painted huge canvases full of flowers, or tried to capture the light reflecting off the water in Tahiti. Unfortunately, those things had been done. It wasn't her fault that beheading people was the only thing left. Nevertheless, she wished that she had had the heart to be a little less original in her art and a little more generous.

For a moment the gravity in the room seemed to fail, and Isabelle had the unpleasant sensation of floating through space. It's like that time I chased my hubcap off the edge of that cliff, Isabelle thought. Last time this happened I wound up in Wendy Walisko's basement, in the company of her invisible boyfriends. She still recalled with some disgust the feeling of their imaginary fingertips on her cheek. A few moments later she had screamed and ran for the door in panic.

Isabelle put one hand on the banister. In a moment she would descend back onto the gallery floor. She would begin again the process of accepting compliments, inquiring after her guests' pursuits. There would be Victoria Ballinger, whose watercolors hung in the Philadelphia Museum of Art. There would be Antonio Bellarosa, the ex-curator of the Rodin Museum. There would be Thomasina Feltzer, who wrote the society column for *The Philadelphia Inquirer.* There they were, and there she would be, chatting with them, maintaining just the right balance between humility and arrogance. Waiters and waitresses circled through the crowd, offering people platters of sushi and little plastic packets of imported soy sauce. Was it really possible that she was the focus of all this attention, a woman who, if a knife were held to her throat, couldn't sensibly explain who she felt she really was?

"Isabelle!" cried a voice from the bottom of the stairs. "Isabelle!"

She looked down the steps, and there she was: Marybeth Backup, her father's second ex-wife. The woman was wearing what looked like an oversized rubber inner tube. It was a skin-clenching, strapless, vinyl dress that only some waiver of gravity kept attached to her upper body. Her arms were covered from fingertip to elbow in black velvet gloves. The woman waved a small pink napkin at Isabelle, like she was trying to flag a train.

Jesus, Isabelle thought, smiling her so-glad-to-see-you smile, descending the stairs. I guess Marybeth gave up on analyzing people's colors. It wasn't so terrible that she was here, though, especially since Isabelle was paralyzed at that moment in a fog of self-loathing. Marybeth was a good reminder of the fact that there were less appealing alternatives to being yourself.

"Izzy!" Marybeth shouted, and kissed the air on either side of Isabelle's head, making a soft kissy-smacky sound as she did so. "Muh!" she said. As she bent forward to kiss Isabelle, a purse swung forward off her left shoulder. The purse was so small she couldn't have kept much more than a pack of matches in it.

"But this is all too divine!" Marybeth said, practically shrieking. "I had no idea you were so talented!"

"Thank you, Marybeth," Isabelle said, looking toward the floor. "You're nice to come." Isabelle thought: it would have been even nicer if you had been invited.

"But I wouldn't have missed it for the world," Marybeth shrieked. "I would prefer to have died, I honestly would!" Other people were looking over at Marybeth Backup, and noticing that Isabelle had reappeared among them. The level of murmuring in the gallery seemed to rise.

Marybeth clasped Isabelle's arm and tenderly ushered her toward her statues. "But you must tell me all about them!" They paused in front of the decapitated Jimmy Stewart, his head bathed in soft blue spotlights. "I think they're stupendous!"

She looked at Isabelle, waiting for her to explain all about the deep hidden meaning of the sculpture. Isabelle just stood there, blushing. It became clear after a few moments that this would not do. People were waiting for her to say something.

"Well, this one here is Jimmy Stewart," she said finally. People kept staring at her. She recognized one onlooker, Richard St. James, the sculpture critic for *The New York Times*. Jesus, she thought. The *Times* is here.

People were waiting for her to say something else, to shed further light on her intentions and the possible interpretation of her work. "You know, Jimmy Stewart," Isabelle said, softly. "The actor."

"Oh sure," Marybeth said. "Everybody loves him!"

Suddenly Richard St. James cleared his throat. "So, Miss Smuggs," he said. "What is your intention then? What are you trying to tell us by cutting off this man's head, a man so beloved by all?"

"Yeah," muttered a young man with a ponytail. "What's the matter with you?"

"Nothing's the matter with me," Isabelle said, feeling her cheeks burning. "I'm totally normal."

There was an unpleasant murmuring in the crowd. The critic from the *Times* rubbed his chin.

Isabelle felt her heart pounding in her chest. She looked down at her dress, hoping that the thumping was not visible through the material. That would be really awkward.

Then the critic spoke. "It's ironic," he said softly.

"What?" said Marybeth. "What did he say?"

"He said it's ironic," said the man to her left.

"Hmmm," muttered a woman with vertical hair.

"You know," said the man with the ponytail. "I think he's right!"

Everyone started speaking very quickly. Marybeth clasped on to Isabelle's upper arm. She whispered in Isabelle's ear.

"I'm so proud of you, dear."

The man from the *Times* cleared his throat. "And yet," he said. "I think this work goes beyond irony. By removing the heads of those who are most beloved to us, there is in a sense a way in which the sculptress has left us with that which is most essential. There is a kind of insipid quality to these floating heads which makes us wonder about their position in space. If, for instance, these are heads without bodies, then what are we? Bodies without heads? The heads which speak for all of us are the heads which we do not have. In our culture, one has to lose one's head to have one at all. I think this is what Miss Smuggs has so adeptly—and so honestly—shown us here tonight!''

There was a short pause, and then the man with the ponytail said, "That's what I think, too!''

"Couldn't have put it better,'' said a woman in yellow.

"It's exactly how I feel.''

They all turned to Isabelle and applauded.

"Aw,'' she said. "It's just plaster.''

Marybeth pulled on Isabelle's arm. "Let's get ourselves a drinky-poo,'' she said. "I don't know about you, doll. But I kinda feel like getting *smashed*.''

Marybeth had her gloved fingers dug so deeply into Isabelle's arm that it was impossible to escape her. They moved toward a bar operated by two crisp young men in red bow ties and white linen aprons, and Marybeth ordered a martini. Isabelle got some more seltzer.

"Congratulations,'' Marybeth said to Isabelle, clinking glasses with her. "Now let me tell you all about me!''

As Isabelle stood there, surrounded by the crowd of people admiring her labors, Marybeth proceeded to tell her the story of her recent life. She seemed determined to go into some detail, too. After she had divorced Isabelle's father, she had married a man whose occupation could only be described as millionaire playboy. His name was Lockwood Winthrop, and he owned two professional baseball teams and a small town on Nantucket. He was not present at Isabelle's opening, Marybeth said, because he was white-water rafting in Libya.

"I'm glad to see you're getting along,'' Isabelle said at last, wondering when and how she could detach herself from Marybeth Backup. For an instant she remembered standing at the top of the stairs alone, listening to the crowd noise, watching herself in the mirror. Some part of me, Isabelle thought, is still up there. Trapped in that mirror.

Marybeth was now jamming piece after piece of sushi down her throat. A waiter walked by with a platter stacked high with little packets of soy sauce. There seemed to be thousands of them.

"Now you must tell me," Marybeth said, and paused. She looked around the floor to make sure no one was watching her, then grabbed the top of her strapless inner tube and pulled it back up, which, all things considered, was a good thing, seeing as how Marybeth's top was about to collapse around her navel with a sound like *boing*. "I know you'll forgive me for asking, Isabelle. But how is your father? Dear, dear Quentin?"

Dear Quentin? Isabelle thought. The man who dumped you for one of his own students, the guy who got caught by the dean of faculty wearing a baby bib? That's Dear Quentin?

"He's fine," Isabelle said. "I think he's getting married again."

"That's what I heard. The nurse, what is her name? Clara?"

"That's her," Isabelle said. "They're off on a cruise together."

"And do you suppose he's really in love this time? Do you think it's possible?"

"I don't know," Isabelle said. "You know how he is. He's mercurial."

For a moment Isabelle thought about her dad, wondered what he was doing right now. It was like him to miss the most important night of her life. She had been disappointed by him so many times that she no longer felt much hurt when she found herself the victim of his inconsideration. She suddenly wanted to talk to Marybeth Backup, have a real conversation with her. What had it been like being in love with him? How had she survived his infidelity and rejection? What prescription for self-healing did Marybeth possess that eluded and frustrated Isabelle? Was it possible to ask in words that this Marybeth would understand? Was being superficial really the best means of survival? She wondered if it could be achieved, if she might find some mending inner superficiality if only she were able to dig down deep enough.

But at that moment, Marybeth saw someone she knew across the room, an incredibly short woman on extremely high pumps. "Oh, there's Nanette," she said. "I've got to go. It's been terribly wonderful talking to you! You're a smash!" She kissed either side of Isabelle's face again without actually touching it, and said, "Muh!" Then Marybeth Backup flittered into the crowd, leaving Isabelle alone.

For the moment, no one descended upon Isabelle to take Marybeth's place. She felt like an outsider, like some kind of intruder on an event that she had no connection to. Looking around the gallery, she saw that the place was beginning to thin out. The show was a success. When it officially opened, tomorrow, she could be reasonably sure of good reviews, and good attendance, perhaps even some sales. It was almost too good to believe. After all these years, she had hit the jackpot.

And as if a voice were speaking to her from the beyond, something in her soul suddenly screamed at her: *Well big deal. You're still a fake.*

The extremity of this emotion caught her completely off guard. Even in the midst of this huge public success, even as I'm surrounded by strangers begging for the opportunity to tell me how much they admire me, I still feel like a failure, a fake. Why is that? Well, maybe it's because I know something about myself that these other people do not, which is, namely: I'm a *quack.* Again she felt perspiration creeping down her temple. She felt suddenly gawky and ridiculous in this ostentatious dress. It's me, she thought. That's the problem.

And at that moment, through the crowd, she suddenly saw the face of Patrick Flinch.

Shit. What the hell was he doing here? She had done her best to put him out of her mind since that disastrous day last summer. They had had that lovely morning, a moment stolen together by the stream, full of love and sex and warmth. Then, as if in response to this, had come a series of repercussions so ridiculous and punishing as to be almost contemptible. His wife had left him; his niece had returned to live with her father. And that wasn't all of it. He had wound up inside a mayonnaise box and got chased by cows.

He was coming toward her, through the crowd. She felt dizzy. Oh god, why does he have to be here, and why now, at the very moment when I feel like I'm about to escape from my own body like a vaporous gas?

Pat stumbled forward. He was wearing a huge brown suit that made him look even larger than he was, which was pretty big. Pat's trousers were held up by a shining belt. He didn't look good.

"Hi, Izzy," he said.

"Hi," said Isabelle.

"You look great."

"So do you."

They stood there for a moment, swaying. Pat licked his lips.

Then they both started to speak at the same moment, each of them saying the other's name.

"Isab—"

"Pat—"

"Go ahead."

"No, you."

"No, you."

"No, you."

"I'm glad to see you," Isabelle said.

"Me too," Pat said. "To see you, I mean. I miss you."

"Well," Isabelle said. "You shouldn't."

"I know," Pat said. He looked around. "Your work is beautiful."

"Beautiful?" she said. "You think so?"

He looked over at the head of Amelia Earhart. "Yeah," he said. "In a scary kind of way."

She followed his gaze. "Yeah," she said. "It is a little scary, I guess." She shook her head. "Sometimes I can't believe that I'm the person who makes all this stuff."

"You can't?" he said. Pat looked at her. She was as beautiful as he remembered her, perhaps even more so. It pained him to see her so nervous in front of him.

"No," she said. "I mean, it all looks pretty strange to me. I mean, like, decapitated heads? Sometimes even I don't know what I'm up to."

"Well," said Pat. "It's eye-catching stuff. I got to give you that."

"Yeah," Isabelle said. "It is that."

"Listen," Pat said. "I just wanted to say—"

"You don't have to say it—" Isabelle said.

"You don't know what I was going to say," Pat said.

"Oh, Pat," Isabelle said. "I think I do. I'm sorry. But I don't think it's a good thing for us to be together."

"I know that," Pat said. "I know. The last time we saw each other, things—you know. They weren't good."

"You mean like your wife left you. You mean like you got caught inside that mayonnaise box. All that?"

"Yeah," Pat said, and nodded. "I'm sorry."

"I'm sorry too," Isabelle said. "I kind of flipped out. I don't know. Maybe I shouldn't go out with men. Maybe there's something about me."

"What do you mean?" Pat stammered. "You you you think you should go out with wuh wuh wuh women?"

"No," Isabelle said. "I don't want to go out with women. I just don't want the men I'm attracted to to have to get chased by cows."

"I wouldn't get chased by cows a second time," Pat said softly. "I mean. If there was a second time."

"Patrick," Isabelle said, feeling the blood coming to her face. "I don't think there should be a second time. I'm bad luck. You saw. I think we're better off apart."

Pat just stood there. It looked like someone had let all the air out of his suit.

"Please," Isabelle said. "That's the way I want it. I'll go crazy if I'm responsible for one single more thing. I'll explode."

Pat sighed.

"Okay," he said. "I just wanted to say I'm proud of you. Of your work, I mean. I am."

"Thank you," Isabelle said, trying not to mumble. "I'm glad you came."

"Me too," Pat said.

"Patrick," Isabelle said. She stepped toward him, held one hand up to his cheek. Softly she moved forward, and they kissed. They stood there for a long time.

"Okay," Isabelle whispered.

"Okay," Pat said.

She turned her back on him, and moved quickly away. She did not want to see him standing there, alone among the innards. Isabelle walked through the diminishing crowd, looked at the steps leading upstairs. There on the landing was the large oval mirror where she had been trapped earlier.

Jesus, Isabelle remembered suddenly. *It's Valentine's Day.*

She felt very weary all of a sudden. I think I better lie down. Isabelle went to the foot of the long staircase. Most of the crowd was leaving now anyway. No one would miss her if she just went up to the second floor of the gallery and lay down on one of the long benches. All of this adoration was draining. It was a lot more interesting to create these things than to let people see them.

Isabelle Smuggs stumbled up the stairs in her gown and entered a quiet room filled with Cézannes. There was a large, wall-size painting of some lilies floating in a river. She took off her earrings and lay down on a leather couch, looking at the water, sweeping slowly downstream toward some village in France. Gee, Isabelle thought. I wish I could have painted that. The river drifted gently past the reeds.

★

She woke up hours later to hear a sudden crashing sound, like something shattering on the floor. She sat up. It took a few moments for her to remember where she was. The gallery was dark now. Isabelle glanced at her watch. It was almost nine-thirty. From downstairs she heard the sound of someone groaning.

What the hell? she thought. She stood up, feeling the strange disorientation one feels from napping late in the day. Isabelle Smuggs moved out into the hall, paused before the oval mirror again.

This time she did not recognize herself.

Well, she thought. You see that? That's you. She opened her purse and got out some lipstick. That was the least she could do before facing the closing-up crowd, the caterers, and the gallery's director. She hoped that things had continued to go well during her absence.

Wurf, said a voice from downstairs.

She turned and looked down the long staircase at the gallery. The show appeared to have been over longer than she thought. All the lights were out, and were it not for the streetlights shining in through the windows in the front hall, the gallery would be pitch dark. The place looked like it had been cleaned up already. The bar was gone, and the floor had been swept clean.

And the sculptures were missing.

She inhaled sharply for a moment, wondering if this could possibly be true. Perhaps it was just the dim light that made the place look so vacant.

Isabelle moved down the stairs as quickly as she could in the ridiculous cocktail dress. She paused briefly to take off her pumps, and then, holding her shoes in one hand, bounded down into the gallery.

It was true. The main hall had been completely cleaned out. Jimmy Stewart, gone, Nancy Reagan, gone. Her heart pounded in her throat. It couldn't be. Not after all she had been through, not again.

Perhaps the curator had put everything in the vault for the night. For safety.

But then she heard the muffled scream again, and she turned her face to the side gallery.

There, at the far end, was a large man holding a linen sack. He was unscrewing Madonna's head from its stand with a huge monkey wrench.

Against one wall, tied to the radiator, lay Patrick Flinch, his mouth gagged. *Wurf,* he said again.

"Hey, you," Isabelle said, running toward the thief. The man was wearing an ascot. "What do you think you're doing?"

The man looked at her suddenly with a curious expression. Isabelle recognized that look. Often, as he had painted her, Barton Sumac's face had assumed that attitude of guilt and arrogance. Even now, as he looked back at her, Sumac seemed to be reducing her, miniaturizing her in his imagination.

For an instant they all stood there—Isabelle watching Sumac, holding the linen sack that contained her work; Barton Sumac, frozen and caught in the act of thievery; and Patrick Flinch, gagged and groaning against the radiator. Isabelle heard the pipes clanking in the old building, and realized at that moment that the radiator was probably on, and hot.

Wurf, said Pat, through his sock. The radiator he was tied to began to hiss violently.

"Hello, Isabelle," Sumac said. "My little protégée!"

"What do you think you're doing?" she said. "What the hell is this all about?"

"What do you think, my dear," he said. "I'm stealing your work. Just as I have always managed to have your work stolen, pilfered, and pulverized. It's fun!"

"Fun?"

"Of course," Sumac said, placing Madonna's head in his sack. "I only think it's fair. After the way you behaved. Running out on me.

Causing me such abominable stress. Did you really think I'd allow your star to rise?''

"My star?" Isabelle said.

"What would have been your star, I mean," Sumac said, and sighed. "To think how much of my greatness I gave to you. To think of the months I stood there, painting you. Only to receive your scorn, your dismissal! When I see your breasts on canvas, do you know how it makes me feel now?''

"No," Isabelle said, looking at him in amazement.

"Not good," he said. "I can tell you that."

He nodded, then sprang suddenly, still holding his sack. Sumac ran to an open window and jumped out into the street. Isabelle ran after him and reached the window. Sumac threw his bag into the back of a car. She saw several other sacks already sitting there in the passenger seat. He jumped behind the wheel and started rummaging through his pocket for his keys.

At that moment there was probably enough time for Isabelle to jump out the window, run over to the curb, and jump into Sumac's car before he drove off. It was even possible that with the right combination of luck and strength she would be able to stop him before he hit or shot her. It was necessary for her to act quickly, to spring up and out the window, while time remained. It was her last chance of saving her creations.

And yet Isabelle stood there, unable to move. There was something else, something she had forgotten. Simply running outside and conking this guy on the head was the wrong solution to the current situation. There would still be something incomplete.

Wurf, said Patrick Flinch. *Herf merf.*

Aw, Christ, no, Isabelle thought, even as she turned to him. That's what I'm waiting for? To rescue Pat?

The car's engine started with a roar.

"Goddamn you to hell," she said, moving toward Pat. "Asshole! Idiot!" Behind her she heard the sound of Sumac's car tearing off into the street. "You aren't even supposed to be here! You weren't even invited!"

She pulled the gag off of his face.

"Stop that guy," Pat said. "He's stealing all your stuff!"

"Well *duh!*" Isabelle yelled at him. "You think I don't know that!"

"Well hurry," Pat said. "You can probably still catch him! Go on!"

"Shut up," Isabelle said, looking around for something with which to cut through Pat's ropes. "Just shut the fuck up."

"Don't be mad at me!" Pat said. "I didn't steal your stupid guts!"

"Oh, so now my work is stupid, is it?" she said. "Now it's all coming out! Now we're getting someplace!"

"I didn't say that," Pat said.

"Yes you did! What's the matter with you? You think I'm deaf? Of course you said that!"

"Well, that's not what I meant!"

Isabelle threw one of her shoes at him. The pump bounced against Pat's belly, then rolled onto the floor. "Well," she said. "Could have fooled me, pal!"

Pat looked at her, heartbroken. "I was trying to help you," he said, miserably. "I was trying to stop him."

She looked at him with even more fury. She threw the other shoe.

"Ooff," he said.

"Well, great job, Pat!" she said. "I mean, outstanding!"

"You don't have to yell at me," he said. "I was just minding my own business. Standing outside. Then I saw this guy drive up. He busted in the window and started creeping around. I followed him and almost got him."

"You almost got him," Isabelle said. "Gee, I'm so impressed."

"I had him," Pat said. "I had him right in my hands!"

"So?" Isabelle said. She picked up a small plastic knife off the floor.

"He hit me," Pat said. "One of the statues. I think it was that Jimmy Stewart. Smashed it right on my head."

"You're kidding! You busted the Jimmy Stewart? That was the best one!"

"I didn't bust it!" Pat said. "He conked me with it!"

Isabelle started sawing through the ropes. It was going to take a long time with this plastic knife.

"It was your head it smashed on," she said, bitterly.

"That's not the point," Pat said.

"Oh yeah? What's the point?"

Pat shrugged. "I don't know," he said.

"Well," Isabelle said. "You should."

"Who is that guy?" Pat said. "What was all that about your breasts?"

"He painted me," Isabelle said, flushing red with anger. "I used to date him."

"Why would you date him?" Pat said. "He's awful."

"I don't know why!" Isabelle yelled. "Let's just say my judgment isn't very good sometimes, okay? Let's just say I have a habit of falling in love with the wrong people, with cretins and morons. Does that make me inhuman? Does that mean I'm so different from everybody else?"

Pat's face fell. "I'm sorry," he said. "I didn't know you thought I was a moron."

"Oh shut up, Patrick," she said. "I didn't mean you. I mean, I didn't even get to go out with you. You and me never even had a goddamn chance."

Pat shook his head. "That's really low," he said. "Stealing somebody's guts."

"You don't know the half of it. I'm ruined now, ruined. Tomorrow all the reviews are going to run, people are going to show up here, and what will they find? Nothing! A big empty space with some fat guy tied to a radiator!"

Pat shrugged. "You'll have me freed by then," he said. "Won't you?"

"Not at this rate. Goddamn this stupid knife!"

"Anyway," Pat said. "We can still catch him. I know we can."

"Aw, what do you know? How can we catch him?"

" 'Cause," Pat said. "I put some soy sauce in his gas tank."

"You what?"

"Soy sauce," he said. "That'll slow him down. I think so, anyway!"

"Soy sauce?" she said again.

"From the sushi appetizers. There were all those packets left over. I figured I'd take some home with me. When I saw him break into the gallery I figured something was up. I poured them in his tank just to slow him down."

"You know how much soy sauce it would take to affect his engine, Pat? Do you know? A lot!"

"Well." Pat nodded. "There were a lot of those packets."

Isabelle stared at him and kept sawing at the ropes with the tiny plastic knife. She wondered how long it was going to take to provide Patrick Flinch with his freedom. The tool that she was using had not really been designed for this purpose.

The pipes connecting to the radiator began to clank and hiss more furiously. Pat wiggled against the baffles.

"Hurry," he said.

PERSEUS

*Perseus is close to Cassiopeia, his future mother-in-law,
and to Andromeda, his fiancée. With one hand
he makes a beckoning gesture.*

" "Of all the loves," Billings sang into the microphone. "I have won or have lost. There is one love I should never have crossed. Test, test, test."

"Hey, Billings," said Limmburjay, heaving an amplifier onto the makeshift stage in the Great Hall of the Franklin Institute. "I could use a little help here."

"She was a girl in a million, my friends," Billings crooned. "I should have known she would win in the end. Testing! Testing!"

"Ah, don't bother him," said Angelique. "He's practicing."

"Since when do we practice?" said Chim-chim.

"Since when do we work?" said Demmie.

"I'm a loser," Billings continued.

Oxx was screwing the cymbals onto the stand, testing the fit of his bass drum pedal.

"Ahem, are you the Poison Squirrels?" said a woman in a white dress, walking toward them. She had such magnificent posture that it was impossible not to be impressed by it. All the members of the Poison Squirrels looked up at the regal, elegant woman, thinking: Wow. This woman has really good posture.

"*I* am Mrs. Hobson," she explained. "The *head*mistress."

"I'm a loser," Billings said.

"Dear chap," Mrs. Hobson continued. "I'm so sorry."

"He's not really a loser," Chim-chim said, softly. "He's lying."

"He's not lying," said Angelique. "That's just a song."

"Maybe it's just a song," Oxx said. "But he's not lying."

"Ah. Lovely." She flashed a quick smile that did not seem to be an indication of pleasure. "Now I am sure you want to know the rules," Mrs. Hobson said. She cleared her throat. "Yes. The rules. The boys and girls at the dance tonight will respect you for enforcing them."

Oxx looked up as if he did not understand. "Rules?"

"Of decorum," Mrs. Hobson continued. "Why yes indeed."

"Huh, rules," Oxx said. He picked his nose.

"First of all," Mrs. Hobson said. "No boy or girl shall be allowed on the statue of Mister Franklin." She looked over at the massive marble statue behind them, and gestured with a pencil. "That is he."

"Duh, like we know who Benjamin Franklin is," Billings said.

"Of course you do, my good man," Mrs. Hobson said. "And yet in the past we have had the experience of young people climbing onto the statue, sitting in Mr. Franklin's lap, putting gum on his head, things like that. I am sure you see. It is tedious."

"Gum?" said Billings.

"On his head," Mrs. Hobson confirmed, sadly. "We cannot tolerate that. If you at any time see anyone climbing onto Mr. Franklin we would appreciate it if you would stop playing immediately and then say clearly into a microphone, 'Attention, young persons, off of Mister Franklin, this instant!' Something along those lines? Well, you are professionals, I am sure you can improve on this."

"We can improve on anything!" Billings said, cheery.

"Secondly, we hope that you will observe general standards of decency and good taste in your choice of repertoire this evening. I know you understand. As I said before, I know that you are professionals."

"Us?" Chim-chim said.

"Of course we're professionals," Limmburjay said. "We just don't work much."

"I see," Mrs. Hobson said. "Still, I know you will use good judgment. No songs about Satan worship, then, for instance?"

The Poison Squirrels looked at each other and shrugged.

"Nothing about, oh, you know. Murdering people and laughing about it. No songs about nuclear waste. Carnal knowledge of animals is another topic you might wish to avoid. There's really a rather long list, isn't there? Do be dears, won't you? Just play songs that are nice, and that demonstrate what I am certain is your well-defined sense of intuition and good taste."

"Nice?" Oxx said. He was starting to turn crimson. "Nice?"

"Oxx," Demmie said. She turned to Mrs. Hobson. "Of course," she said. "We're professionals."

"Thank you too much," Mrs. Hobson said. She stepped down from the stage. "I just know you'll be a hit." She looked back at Demmie and Angelique for just a moment, regarding their aluminum kitchen funnel brassieres. "Oh, and dears? Will you be wearing, uh, those?"

Angelique and Demmie looked at each other.

"Yeah," Angelique said. "It's part of our look."

"Must you?" Mrs. Hobson said. "That is, I don't wish to interfere. But if it's all the same to you. Would you mind? I'm sure you could find something else to wear, couldn't you? Those are good girls."

"But it's our look!" Angelique said.

"It *can't* be comfortable," Mrs. Hobson said. "No indeedy."

Demmie and Angelique looked at the ground, somewhat ashamed.

"It's not," Angelique said, quietly, flushing.

"I just want you to be comfortable!" Mrs. Hobson sang. "That's all. I want you to feel right at home! You wouldn't wear those—ah—things in your house now, would you? Heavens no."

Angelique muttered something.

"What was that, darling?" Mrs. Hobson said. "I couldn't quite hear that."

"I said I have a shirt in my car," she said, downcast. "Okay? In my *car*."

"Me too," Demmie said.

"Oh," Mrs. Hobson said. "How charming." She cleared her throat. "I do hope as well that you have the accompanying and appropriate foundation garments to complete your presentation? Of course you do."

Angelique and Demmie looked at each other for a moment, then nodded.

Mrs. Hobson turned to leave them, walked halfway across the dance floor, then stopped once more. "And he," she said, pointing toward Limmburjay with her pencil.

"Me?" Limmburjay said.

"I'm sure you'll put on a shirt."

"A shirt!" Limmburjay shouted. "A shirt!" He threw his guitar on the ground. "That's it!"

"Hey, man," Billings said. "Easy."

But Limmburjay was very angry. He poured lighter fluid on his guitar and got out a pack of matches.

"What is he doing?" Mrs. Hobson said. "You tell him there's no smoking."

"No smoking!" Limmburjay said. "I'll tell you if there's smoking or not, you ol' douche bag!"

"Ladies," Mrs. Hobson said, turning toward Angelique and Demmie. "Do speak with him."

Limmburjay, however, was having some trouble getting a match lit. After a few moments of failure, he threw the matches on the ground and yelled in Mrs. Hobson's direction. "You know, lady, you've got some fuckin' nerve, don't ya! A *shirt*! I mean, *fuck you!*"

"I know, dear fellow," Mrs. Hobson said. "It must seem so old-fashioned to you! I am sorry that my mores have agitated you so!"

"It's not fashion," Limmburjay yelled. "It's the whole fascist *system*! I mean, a shirt, that's like a symbol, a symbol of the whole goddamn *situation*! Well, our music's about *fightin'* stuff like shirts! We're here to change things, lady! If you don't like it you can lump it! You understand? Lump it, that's what I say!"

"Limmburjay," Demmie whispered hoarsely.

"My boy," Mrs. Hobson said. "If and when I lump it, I shall instantly notify you by telegram. Until then, do be quiet."

"Don't worry," Angelique said. "We'll find him a shirt."

"I'd rather *die!*" Limmburjay said.

"You lamb," Mrs. Hobson said and turned. She walked briskly away from them.

"I'm not wearing no goddamn stupid shirt, you hear!" Limmburjay said. "I'm not knuckling under to *her,* or to anyone!"

"He can wear mine," Billings said. "I don't need one."

"I'm changing, right now," Angelique said.

"I'm coming," Demmie said. "I can't wait to get out of this goddamn thing, if you want to know the truth."

"Me either," said Angelique. "I've always *hated* these things, actually."

"Go ahead," Limmburjay said. "*Sell out!* See where that gets you!"

"I always wear a shirt," Chim-chim said, tuning his guitar. "It's pants I could do without."

"This gig here," Billings said. "I think we gotta wear shirts and pants. Both."

"This *sucks*," Limmburjay said.

"Shut up," said Oxx.

"You shut up," said Limmburjay.

"I didn't say anything," Chim-chim said.

"That's what I mean," said Limmburjay. "That's it exactly. The whole goddamn *situation*."

Angelique and Demmie walked across the huge ballroom. The caterers were putting the final touches on the place. A long table at one end held an assortment of hors d'oeuvres and punch bowls. Beyond this were several dozen tables with white tablecloths and candles. Over their heads, the high, curving ceiling was held up by great marble columns. The place really did look nice, Demmie thought. It's a shame the Poison Squirrels are playing.

They passed out into the main entryway. Through some bars to her left she saw the outline of the Human Heart exhibit, across from the planetarium. She remembered being a Brownie, almost twenty years ago, and being driven down to the Franklin Institute of Science with her whole troop on a yellow school bus. She recalled how gruesome, grotesque, and wonderful the enormous heart had been, how she and the other girls in the troop had run from chamber to chamber, up the blue stairs into the giant lungs, then back into the heart again. They had gone through the exhibit over and over again, the whole time hearing the ear-splitting *thuh-thunk, thuh-thunk, thuh-thunk* of the great valves pumping.

Demmie and Angelique went outside and walked down the long marble stairs toward Logan Circle. There was the Poison Squirrels' Falcon parked illegally on the curb.

"What do you think, Demmie?" Angelique said, as they climbed inside the car to get a pair of shirts. "Is this the end of the line, or what?"

They squatted down in the backseat so as to keep from attracting too much attention. Angelique sighed with relief as she got rid of the funnels.

"I don't know," Demmie said. "I can't see how much longer we're going to keep going like this. It's no fun anymore, is it?"

"It's not," Angelique said, sitting up. "I remember when we first started. What was that, 'eighty-four, 'eighty-five? Almost eight years ago. Right when you and Billings first came to the city. I thought we were gonna be on the cover of *Newsweek* by the time I was twenty-five. I'm not kidding! I really, really believed it! We weren't so bad back then, were we? Remember when we first started playing, and everybody paid attention? Remember when we were right there, in the middle of the whole *scene*?"

"Yeah," Demmie said. "I remember."

"So where did we screw up?" Angelique said. "Like, what did we do that was so wrong that we wound up like this?"

A white linen sack on the floor of the car moved slightly. There was a thick, unpleasant smell of sulfur.

"Good dog, Buddy," Demmie said.

Buddy lifted his head, which then appeared at the open end of the sack. He looked mournfully at Demmie, then Angelique.

"Poor old thing," Angelique said. "Is your father really going to give you the money for him tonight?"

"Said he would," Demmie said. "Nine o'clock."

"And you don't think he knows it's you?"

"I don't know," Demmie said. "You know, if he did know it was me, that wouldn't be the end of the world. Sometimes I miss him."

"Uh-huh," said Angelique. "You're lucky your father's alive. I wish mine was."

Buddy moaned softly. Demmie patted him on the head.

"Ah shit," Angelique said. "Shit."

Demmie looked over at her. Angelique was crying.

"Hey," Demmie said. "Hey. What's the matter, girl?"

"Aw shit," Angelique said again, tears dripping onto her lap. "I didn't want this."

"It's okay," Demmie said. "We didn't know."

"I just wanted to get famous," Angelique said. "Is that asking for so much?"

"I don't know," Demmie said, stroking Angelique's back. "Beats me."

"We'll never be famous now. This is the end of the line. This sucks."

"You don't know," Demmie said. "Anything is possible."

"No, Dem," Angelique said. "That's not what I mean." She turned to her friend. "I'm fucking pregnant."

Demmie's mouth opened wide, then closed. "For real?" she said. "Pregnant? Is that a good thing?"

"A good thing?" Angelique said, in anguish. Tears flooded her eyes. "How could that be a good thing?"

"I don't know," Demmie said. "I think about having a kid sometimes. I don't think that would be so bad."

"We aren't talking about you," Angelique said. "We're talking about me!"

"Oh, Angel, I know," Demmie said, putting her arm around her. "I know. I'm sorry."

"I don't even know who the father is! Jesus, what if it's Chimchim! I mean—give me a break!"

Angelique sobbed on Demmie's neck for a few moments, while Demmie looked up at the steps of the Franklin Institute. What would happen if she stopped resisting Billings, if she actually took him seriously and tried to settle down? Would it be possible to maintain a relationship with a man whose only known passion, other than that which he had for Demmie himself, was for chewing gum?

At last she turned to Angelique again and asked her, "So what are you going to do?"

"Oh, for god's sakes, I'm not going to have the baby! I mean, get real!" Angelique shook her head. "I'm just waiting until we get paid for tonight, and then I'm going down to the clinic. Tomorrow probably." Angelique looked up at Demmie. "Hey, Dem? Like, you wouldn't want to go down with me, would you, tomorrow, when I go, I mean?"

Demmie put her hand on Angelique's back. "Of course I'll go," she said. "You want me, I'll go with you."

"Oh forget it," Angelique said. "I don't even have enough money for it. Even after they pay us tonight there's still no way."

They sat there in silence for a moment. Demmie thought about the winter coat she had hoped to buy.

"I can loan you the money," she said. "I mean, I'm getting paid tonight, too. If we put it all together we'll have enough."

"Oh, Dem," Angelique said, hugging her friend, dissolving once more into tears. "You're a real friend." She wiped her eyes. "I guess I made a mess of things, didn't I?"

"It's not your fault," Demmie said. "It's nobody's fault."

Angelique wiped her eyes on the back of her hand. She looked back toward the institute. "I guess we better get back inside."

"You go ahead," Demmie said. "I got to make sure Buddy's okay first."

"All right," Angelique said, and got out of the car. "You know that Billings is a lucky guy. You should give him a chance sometime."

"You think so?" Demmie said.

Angelique shrugged. "I don't know. Way I figure, you got to love somebody. May as well be a person that likes you."

Buddy groaned softly, as Demmie watched Angelique ascend the stairs to the museum. He grunted for a moment, as if in pain, then exhaled. There was brown stuff on his muzzle.

Buddy groaned again.

"Good boy," she said, and patted him on the head. He looked at her with some concern.

"Yeah, you." She patted him. "What do you think? Should I give Billings a chance?"

Buddy fell over, and started eating his paws.

"Atta boy," Demmie said. "Good dog."

The doorbell rang downstairs, and Phoebe heard her father going to answer it. "Hello, Duard," Wedley said.

"Hello, Mister Harrison," Duard said. "Am I here?"

Gee whiz, Phoebe thought. He's early.

She looked at herself one last time before descending the stairs. She was wearing a pinstriped jacket from one of Wedley's suits and a miniskirt that she had made out of the pants. Wedley had said she could borrow the suit for the prom; he hadn't exactly given Phoebe permission, though, to hack his pants apart with pinking shears. Still, the results were impressive. Look at me, she thought. I'm a gangster's moll.

"Phoebe," Wedley cried from the bottom of the stairs. "Your date is here."

One hand trailing along the banister, Phoebe descended the stairs.

There, in the front hallway, stood Duard, wearing a pinstriped suit, holding a violin case. Her father stood to Duard's right; the two men smiled proudly at her.

Phoebe reached the bottom of the stairs, leaned forward, and kissed Duard on the cheek.

"Hi, Duard," she said.

"Huh huh huh hi," he said. He shoved a small, square box into her hand. "Like I got you this. Is it a carnation? Probably."

"Why, Duard," Phoebe said. "How cool."

"I better get ready," Wedley said. He was one of the chaperones for the dance. "You look great, darling," he said. "Magnificent." For a second Phoebe thought she saw tears in his eyes.

"Thanks, Daddy," Phoebe said.

"Excuse me, you two," Wedley said. His voice was cracking. "Excuse me." He ducked into the kitchen.

Phoebe stared after her father for a minute.

She turned to Duard. "Pin it on me, will you?"

"Wuh, wuh, wuh," Duard said.

"Here," Phoebe said. She removed the corsage from the box. It was not a carnation; Duard seemed to have invested in a small, beautiful orchid. It was tied up with a pink ribbon.

She held up the orchid and gave Duard the pin.

Duard took it from her, then stood there looking at her bust. The Y in FEEBY was just creeping out of her jacket. It looked like Duard wanted to attach the orchid to her, but he was afraid to proceed, unsure of what would happen if he put the pin in the wrong place.

"You want me to help you?" Phoebe said.

"Wuh," Duard said. "No. I'm thinking."

She took his hand and guided it to a safe spot. He was shaking.

"Am I a little nervous?" Duard said. "No. What makes you think that?"

"You look great, Duard," Phoebe said.

"What would Dominique think if she saw us here like this now, huh?" Duard said. "Sore, I bet."

Phoebe thought about Dominique for an instant, remembered the feeling of that needle cutting into her skin.

"Why, Phoebe," said Vicki, sweeping into the room. "However gorgeous do you look!"

Vicki was wearing a ridiculous jumpsuit, a shimmering, gold lamé thing that looked like she should be standing next to the grand prizes on a television game show. Vicki was Wedley's date.

"Thank you," Phoebe said.

From outside came a sudden blasting of an air horn. Phoebe jumped.

"Jesus," she said. "What's that?"

"Something I have to tell you," Duard said. "Could I get some-one to watch Dwenda for the night? No. Could I borrow a decent car, either? No. The Swinger is busted again."

"What are you saying, Duard?" Phoebe said. "What are you talk-ing about?"

There was another blast from the air horn.

Oh no, Phoebe thought. Tell me it isn't so.

"We better get going," Duard said. "Unless we want to be late."

"You kids run along," Wedley called from the kitchen. "We're right behind you."

Phoebe looked out the front door. There in the driveway was a cement mixer. Dwayne was behind the wheel. Little Dwenda looked out the window on the passenger side, one tiny outspread palm held up against the cold glass. On the door of the cement mixer were the words DWAYNE'S SERVICES.

"Dwayne's giving us a ride," Duard said sadly.

Russell Hawkins thundered down Kelly Drive in the Miata, imagining the air of Nevada in his lungs.

"Just one more thing, though," Rusty said, out loud, as he ap-proached Logan Circle. He quickly opened the glove compartment and removed the bottle of chloroform and a small rag. It was going to be easy.

This was going to be a wonderful evening. He had tried to obey the laws of society since his release from Skagville, but when you came right down to it, tattooing people just wasn't as satisfying as kidnap-ping them. Anyway, Phoebe was practically family.

He trembled with excitement at the idea of putting her in a linen sack. That was the best part about kidnapping someone, was that first moment, when you pulled the bag down over their heads. Clipping out letters from the newspaper to make a ransom note was satisfying, too, but still could not compete with that first initial plunging of the victim into darkness. You pulled the bag down over their heads and they said something like, *hey, what's the big idea,* or maybe *hey, cut it out,* and that was the moment when you hit them with something heavy. Tonight he had his gun with him for this very purpose. He wouldn't shoot the girl, just bonk her with the handle. It was more satisfying that way, at least it was for the person doing the bonking. Rusty felt connected to the very first man when he did this, felt the tie of kinship back to the days when cavemen dragged women around by their hair and ate big pieces of chicken. He had talked a lot about his feelings with his men's group, and it was surprising how much support he got, at least until they threw him out. Most modern men suffered from a kind of psychic wounding on account of women telling them that doing stuff like clubbing people and locking them in closets was bad, that it was somehow something you should be ashamed of. Rusty was glad that he had finally broken through that wounding and had at last learned how to speak for himself using his own mouth instead of someone else's.

Still, it was lonely being the only person with his mouth. What he needed most was the company of other men, companions who would share and understand the awful burden of his pleasures. It was a terrible thing, being a man alone in this world.

In the middle of the road ahead of him stood an agitated stranger. The man held his hands up in the air, urging Rusty to stop. He didn't seem like the kind of person you could refuse. Rusty pulled over.

"I say," the man said, coming over to the car. "Sorry to bother you, my good fellow. My car seems to have malfunctioned. Could you give me a lift?"

He nodded toward the side of the road, where even now gray smoke was billowing from the tailpipe of his car. There was an unpleasant smell, sort of like burned-up soy sauce, in the air.

"I'm Barton Sumac," the man said. "The artist. Perhaps you've heard of me."

"I'm Rusty," he said. "Ha ha ha."

"What's so funny?" Sumac said. "You've heard of me?"

"Naw," Rusty said.

Rusty and Sumac looked at each other. "Heavens," Sumac said, staring at the tattoos which covered Rusty's arms. "You're very intricate, aren't you."

"Aw," Rusty said, and blinked. For a moment Barton Sumac stared into the other set of eyes, tattooed on Rusty's eyelids.

"So can you give me a ride? As I say, my car is in a state of malfunction."

"I can see that," Rusty said. He ran his fingers over the top of his smoothly shaven head, then nodded. Rusty unlocked the door.

Sumac climbed in and rested the sacks containing Isabelle's sculptures on the floor and in his lap. He picked up the bottle of chloroform and the rag.

"On your way to a job of some kind?" Sumac said.

"Yeah, you could say that, yeah," said Rusty. "I don't think of it just as a job though. More like an ancient hairy ritual."

Sumac pulled out his gun and pointed it at him.

"I think you might postpone that ritual," he said. "I think it's best if you go where I say."

But Rusty just threw back his head and laughed. His large gold earring swung from his earlobe. Reaching into his jacket, he pulled out his own gun, and pointed it at the artist's head. "Come on, brother," Rusty said. "You and me are all the same."

Sumac looked menacingly at Rusty for a moment, then hiccuped suddenly. The bag fell out of his lap, and the decapitated plaster head of Erma Bombeck rolled onto the floor. The two men, guns still drawn, looked at her, then at each other, then at Erma Bombeck again. Then they burst into a mutual laughter.

"You know," Sumac said. "I feel good!"

"Ha," Rusty said, shifting into high gear. "Funny."

"Who?" Sumac said. "That Erma Bombeck? You think she's funny?"

Rusty just shook his head. "Nah," he said. "Not really."

★

Sitting in the cement mixer, Dwayne held his little sister in his arms. "Baby has ten little fingers," he sang to her. "Baby has ten toes."

"Toes," Dwenda said.

"Drinks and swears, busts up chairs. Baby has ten toes."

"Toes."

"Huh huh huh," Dwayne said. He wasn't really enjoying himself, but he did not want his baby sister to think badly of him. He felt a little guilty about bringing a six-year-old out here to Philadelphia just so she could sit in a cement mixer all night. Phoebe and Duard had gone inside to the dance almost an hour ago now. The Massacre was in full swing.

He looked up at the Franklin Institute. A man with a large linen sack was walking up the stairs. To the man's left was a couple, heavily locked in an embrace. The woman, who couldn't have been more than seventeen, raised one hand and placed it on her lover's cheek.

Dwayne sighed. "Edith," he said softly. "My coconut."

"Coconut," Dwenda said. She reached forward and pulled one of the knobs off the radio, then put it in her mouth.

Dwayne had a strange moment, sitting in his cement mixer, re-membering the ghost of his old lover, Edith. She had jumped out of a plane eight years ago. Yeah, Dwayne thought. But she never hit the ground, not in my heart. She was still falling.

Dwenda looked up at her brother and spat the radio knob at him. It bounced off his cheek.

"Ha," she said, smiling. The little girl's eyes glowed. She really did look cute, Dwayne thought. He was glad he had dolled her up for the prom tonight. Dwenda was wearing a little pink dress, white tights, and black sandals. She had a pink ribbon in her hair. It was good, Dwayne thought, for a little girl to have the experience of dressing up and going to a big dance. Even if instead of actually going to the dance you had to sit outside with your brother inside some cement mixer. It was something, anyway.

"Hey," Dwayne said. He had an idea which he hoped would clear the air. Vaporize his thoughts of Edith and get back to the important thing, which was the extramarital affair he was conducting with Vicki behind Wedley's back. Maybe if he ran the cement mixer, that would shake things up. Get the drum spinning, maybe let Dwenda work the controls. What little girl, given the chance, wouldn't like working a cement mixer? None that Dwayne knew. Anyway, Vicki would like it, if she came outside for him, once she escaped from Wedley. She would come for him and there he would be, all ready to pour concrete, anywhere she wanted.

"Hey, Dwenda," he said to his sister. "See this?" He pointed to the emergency brake. "You ever want to roll down a hill and flatten something, you just pull back on this lever. You got that?"

"Flatten something," Dwenda said.

He picked the girl up in one arm and jumped down onto the pavement of Logan Circle. "Come on," he said. "You're old enough to know how a cement mixer works."

"Cement mixer," Dwenda said.

He flipped open the control box at the rear of the truck. "Now this lever here," he explained, "that's your diluter. Controls how much water you got in the mix." He showed her another switch. "This one here's the power. Starts the drum, uh, spinning."

He flipped it on. There was a low humming sound.

"And this lever on the bottom," Dwayne said, excited, "increases or decreases the speed of the the the the drum."

He paused. There were many more controls to explain, but Dwenda wasn't paying attention. She had wandered off to the far side of the truck again to look at the Franklin Institute. There was the sound of a woman's heels on the pavement.

"Mommy," she said, pointing.

"Dwayne, darling," Vicki said. She stood there in her gold lamé jumpsuit. "I got away as soon as I could."

"Uh—" Dwayne said, looking at her. He was about to call her Edith, but that was the wrong name. Edith was the dead one. What was her name, this woman who stood in front of him, this woman he had sacrificed everything for?

"What are you doing?" she said, looking at the truck.

"I got it started," Dwayne said, apologetically. "Vicki." That was it. Vicki. "I started it spinning."

"But, darling," Vicki said, walking up to Dwayne and putting her arms around him. "Whatever for?"

Dwayne shrugged. He looked over her shoulder at the slowly spinning drum of the cement mixer.

"I did it for you," he said, softly. "It's a present."

"Why, Dwayne," Vicki said. "How thoughtful."

They kissed. After a few moments, Dwayne looked at her again. "If you want," he said quietly, "I can pour some cement for you."

"Oh, Dwayne," Vicki said.

"I can set up the chutes. If you want I can pour some cement right on the street. If you want it."

"Oh, Dwayne, yes," Vicki said. "I want to pour some cement with you." She leaned forward and kissed him. Her tongue disappeared into Dwayne's head.

After a moment Dwayne detached himself from her and looked over her shoulder at the mixer. "You want it wet?" he said. "I should add more water if you want it wet."

"Oh, Dwayne," Vicki said. Her face was almost scarlet now.

"You know what else we could do," Dwayne said. "If you really want to feel special."

"What, Dwayne?" Vicki said. She licked his neck. "Tell me."

"I mean if you want. We could like—get *in* the mixer."

Vicki looked over at the drum. "Oh my god," she said. "Oh my god." She clutched at her own breasts.

"I think I'd have to slow it down, though," he said, thoughtfully. "A cement mixer's one thing you don't want to be inside of if it's going too fast. You know. Safety first."

"Oh, Dwayne," Vicki said. "You're so right."

Dwenda scuffed the curb with her Buster Brown sandals. From a great distance came the sound of a rock and roll band playing.

"Safety first," Dwenda said.

★

George Billings sang into the microphone. The Poison Squirrels were rocking behind him. Demmie's arm was windmilling in the air. Limmburjay, playing the bass, was wearing a Franklin Institute T-shirt with the inscription I LIKE SCIENCE. Oxx played the drums. Angelique played the keyboards. Chim-chim was staring into space.

The song Billings was singing was one he had written himself:

> *Down in Pennsylvania there's an awful slob.*
> *Making chocolate muffins is his daytime job.*
> *By night he makes Saran Wrap in a business suit.*
> *Throws his little children down the laundry chute.*
> *On weekends he's the lizard king in shopping malls.*
> *Drops his chocolate chips and don't care where they falls.*
>
> *Bye, bye, bye, bye.*
> *Bye, bye, bye, bye.*
> *You're stupid.*
> *You're going to die.*

Mrs. Hobson, standing erect by the punch bowl, felt reasonably sure that the St. Valentine's Day Massacre of the Dillinger Academy for Girls was progressing in an orderly fashion. No one had climbed into the lap of the Franklin statue yet, which was an accomplishment. And none of the girls had thrown up, at least not out in public, which was where it mattered.

She noticed Wedley Harrison, Phoebe's father, leaning against one of the marble columns. The man did not look well; to be quite honest about it, he looked a little bit drunk. This would not do. It did not matter how inebriated one was. The important thing was, no matter what the circumstances, to continue to exhibit good posture.

"Mr. Harrison," she said, walking up to him.

"Aw, Mrs. Hobson." Wedley groaned. He did not sound glad to see her.

"And how are we this evening?" she said.

"Aw," Wedley said. "You don't want to know."

"But of course I do," she said. "That is why I asked the question. To learn."

"Well, let me see. I think I can tell you. I think I can. But you have to know the facts."

"The facts," Mrs. Hobson said.

"Yeah." Wedley blinked, as if he had been underwater for a moment. "Are you sure you can take 'em?" he said. "They aren't pretty."

"I am prepared to face the worst, Mr. Harrison," Mrs. Hobson said. "Fire away!"

"You're sure?"

"Positive!"

"Even if it turns your stomach, you want to know. Even if it makes you want to choke."

"I will stand with you, Mr. Harrison, in the face of all the things you are even yet to say!"

"All right, then. Here it comes."

"Bombs away, Mr. Harrison!"

"All right, then," Wedley said. "It's about my wife, Vicki?"

"Yes. Of course. The beautician. Charming girl."

"She's out screwing some guy in the parking lot inside of a cement mixer."

Mrs. Hobson gave her quick, pained smile. "But, Mister Harrison," she said. "Everyone knows that. You're referring to Dwayne. Duard's brother."

Wedley looked around the dance hall. Some of the other chaperones were standing in pairs, talking. An elderly woman looked at him and shook her head. "They know?" he said. "Everyone knows?"

"Dear chap," Mrs. Hobson said. "A cement mixer is not something a fellow can keep to himself. Am I correct? Of course I am."

"Well, you want to know how I am?" Wedley said. "There it is. You know already. Everybody knows. Apparently."

"I'm afraid so," Mrs. Hobson said. "But listen. Mister Harrison. Wedley. There's something else I must tell you. It is a matter of some urgency."

"What?" Wedley said. "I'm listening. You got something to tell me, Mrs. Hobson? I'm all ears."

"I do," she said.

Wedley waited for her to speak. He wished at this moment that he had another black Russian.

"I'm telling you," Mrs. Hobson said, her teeth clamped together, "that you'd better stand up straight. Or there will be actions taken. Do you understand me? Actions."

Wedley's eyes raised.

"What did you say?" Wedley said. "You want me to stand up straight."

"I do," Mrs. Hobson said. "It's a disgrace the way you're slouching. Disgusting."

"I'm sorry," Wedley said.

"You should be," Mrs. Hobson said. "It's nauseating."

"What's nauseating?" Wedley said. "That I'm sorry?"

"No," Mrs. Hobson hissed. "That you're slouching."

She stormed off.

Wedley watched her recede into the crowd and tried to stand up a little straighter. So much for Mrs. Hobson.

He downed the rest of his drink and started walking toward the heart. The appointed time had arrived. It only took a minute to walk across the crowded dance floor, toward the exhibition hall. There was a velvet rope and a small sign that read: MUSEUM CLOSED. NO ONE BEYOND THIS POINT.

Wedley ducked under the rope. The heart was easy to find; all he had to do was follow the loud, throbbing pulse. The thing was huge, almost two stories high. Great veins wriggled on its surface. The venae cavae and aorta stretched high into the ceiling, connecting into a pair of blue lungs. The entrance into the heart was a door which opened into the inferior vena cava.

Slowly, shyly, Wedley Harrison stepped forward into the right auricle.

Back on the dance floor, the Poison Squirrels finished playing "Johnny B. Dead," and Billings said, "We're going to play one more tune and then we'll take a short break. This one's for all the lovers in the audience."

The teenagers began to flee the dance floor.

The band began to play a slow song, a piece written and sung by Chim-chim. It was a real gut wrencher, performed in three-four time. Chim-chim stepped up to Billings's mike and sang:

> *There is a reason we carry our lunches*
> *In boxes and bags that we tie up with string*
> *Someone is talking but no one is listening*
> *The words that they tell you here don't mean a thing.*

You picked a fine time to leave me, loose wheel.
Picking the daisies and dreams of the crazies
Are just pretty phrases for me.
You picked a fine time to leave me, loose wheel.
Being funny is no fun at sea.

The remaining couples on the dance floor wrapped themselves around each other. Some were already sobbing openly. It was hard to tell in some cases if they were weeping because of the intensity of emotion evident in Chim-chim's song or if it was due to the fact that the young man sang a little bit like Jim Nabors. Phoebe and Duard danced as close as they could without actually having dated much, which wasn't very. After a few bars, Duard looked over at Phoebe and said, "Maybe we should sit down for this one."

"But I don't want to just sit down, Duard," Phoebe said. "Let's walk around, do something."

"Okay," Duard said. "Does that sound like fun? I don't know. Am I still nervous? A little!"

They went over to the punch bowl and drank a couple of cups of sweet red liquid. Across the ballroom floor Phoebe saw Stacy Merriwhether and Donna Moherr throwing up on one of the marble columns. Their dates were standing by, holding their pocketbooks for them. The boys seemed embarrassed, but it wasn't clear if this was because their dates were throwing up or because some of the other guys might look over and see them standing there holding pocketbooks. Across the Great Hall, Muffy Aurora Pennypacker and Reid Smyth were climbing into the lap of the enormous Benjamin Franklin.

"Stop it, you two," Mrs. Hobson said. Phoebe thought that she meant Muffy and Reid, but she didn't. She was referring to Stacy and Donna.

"Boy," Duard said. "What a crowd."

"It sure is different from Centralia," Phoebe said.

"Yeah," Duard said. "No kidding." He finished his punch. "Do you ever wish you went to school with us again, back at New Buchanan High?"

"Sometimes," Phoebe said. "But most of all what I want now is to just get out of here and go to college. I can't wait to be on my own."

"I wish I could go to college," Duard said. "But how likely is that? Not much."

"You could get a scholarship," Phoebe said. "You can apply for financial aid."

"Yeah, right," Duard said. "That's only for smart kids. Not for the dummies."

"You're not a dummy, Duard," Phoebe said.

Duard smiled at her. He thought about the evening when he had attempted to study for the SATs and wound up deep inside Elizabeth's Enigma instead. If he had any guts he would have ordered one of those cat suits for Phoebe, given her something like that as a gift instead of the orchid. Flowers wilted.

"You're nice, Phoebe," he said. "But are you being too nice? I think so. I'm a dummy. I don't mind! Do I know who I am, anyway."

Phoebe smiled at him again. For the first time all night she wished that he would lean over and kiss her. There was a long moment while Duard thought about doing exactly this, but it passed, and then the two of them were left just standing there, the punch cups empty and the conversation exhausted.

"Let's go in the heart," Phoebe said, looking across the Great Hall to the exhibit's entrance.

"Wow," Duard said. "Cool. Can we get in there? I bet Mrs. Whatsherface will stop us."

"She isn't paying any attention," Phoebe said. She took Duard's hand and pulled him across the dance floor. "Look. She's busy with Stacy and Donna."

More couples were now crowding into the lap of Benjamin Franklin. There were eight or nine kids up there now, as well as Mr. Tuttle, the "hip" young biology teacher who let all the snakes and pigs in the biology lab run loose throughout the classroom because they were more free that way. Mr. Tuttle had a funny look on his face.

The Poison Squirrels were finishing up "There Is a Reason." Chim-chim sang:

There is a reason we sing in the quagmire
With cockles and skulls and the boxes of slime.
Sundays the basses with trombones in cases time
Middle-class waitresses practicing mime.

You picked a fine time to leave me, loose wheel,
Picking the daisies and dreams of the crazies
Are just pretty phrases for me.
You picked a fine time to leave me, loose wheel.
Being funny is no fun at sea.

"Gee," Duard said, standing at the entrance to the heart. "Sure looks dark in there."

"There are lights inside," Phoebe said.

"You've been in here before?" Duard said. "With someone else?" He looked crushed.

"Yeah," Phoebe said, distantly. "I've been in here before. But it was a long time ago." She looked at Duard, who seemed sad. "I was only like ten," she said. "I was with my 4-H club."

"Oh," Duard said, smiling again. "Then let's go."

"Okay," Phoebe said. "I'm with you, Duard."

She took his hand, and the two of them stepped forward into the darkness.

Back on the dance floor, Mrs. Hobson was now standing at the foot of the Benjamin Franklin National Memorial.

"I say get down from there this instant," she said, gesturing with a pencil. "Mr. Tuttle, you must assist me in the reestablishment of order."

"Ah, Shirley," Mr. Tuttle said, looking down at the headmistress. "Whyn't you go *get laid!* Ha ha ha. I tell ya, that's what you need, Shirley, is a good *pokin'!*" All the teenagers cheered. It was no wonder why Mr. Tuttle was so popular.

Demmie took off her guitar strap, leaned her Stratocaster against an amp. She rubbed her eyes with her fists, then looked at her watch.

Ah Jesus. She'd almost forgotten.

"Hey, Billings," she said. He looked over at her, and for a moment Demmie tried to picture him as a father, taking their child to the orthodontist and Cub Scouts. Billings wasn't the ideal husband, but you could probably do a lot worse. Was that a good enough reason to spend your life with someone, that there were other men more despicable than the one you married?

"What?" Billings said. "What?"

"Go get the dog, honey," Demmie said. "We have to find my father."

Wedley Harrison, somewhat tipsy, stumbled through the dark passages, the deafening heartbeat pounding in his ears. The curators of the Franklin Institute had paid close attention to detail. The walls of the chambers of the heart were damp and soft, moving slightly as the valves opened and closed. Membranous matter hung down from the ceiling between the chambers.

He walked through the right auricle, through a valve, into the right ventricle. This was a large, well-lit chamber. Someone had taken a Magic Marker, though, and left a graffito on the walls of the ventricle: CYCLONE 91. Next to this was a small heart with some initials in it. See that, Wedley thought. A little heart in a big heart.

Wedley walked up a set of blue stairs. A sign said: YOU ARE NOW IN THE PULMONARY ARTERY. EN ROUTE TO THE LUNGS.

Well, Wedley thought. What's not true in that?

He entered the lungs for oxygenation, then went down a set of stairs into the pulmonary veins. There was more graffiti on the soft, gushy walls. Wedley went through a small door and reentered the heart.

YOU ARE NOW ENTERING THE LEFT AURICLE.

The pulsing, which had grown softer while he was in the lungs, now grew loud again. A loudspeaker at the wall between the left auricle and ventricle suggested the opening and closing of the large valve there. Wedley looked around at the strange, circular chamber. All matter of guck was hanging down from the ceiling to make the chamber more realistic.

"Well," Wedley said. "This must be the place."

He heard a pair of voices and some footsteps coming down the stairway from the lungs, and Wedley moved toward the left ventricle to hide. It was entirely possible that Demmie still wanted to maintain some secrecy about this whole shameful business, and he would not deny her that.

When he first saw his daughter again, his heart leaped up for a moment. He thought, with wonder, how much she looked like Phoebe from this angle. But then Wedley realized that this was because it *was* Phoebe, arm in arm with Duard. They leaned against the wall at the entrance to the left auricle.

"Wow," Duard said. "Like, it's so grotesque!"

"Yeah," Phoebe said. "Isn't it gross?"

"It is," Duard said. "It's totally gross. I like it!"

They stood there for a moment, looking at the chamber.

"You know what, Duard," Phoebe said.

"What?" Duard said.

"I wanted to thank you for being a good friend," Phoebe said.

"Aw," Duard said.

"I mean it," Phoebe said. "Everybody else from Centralia just acts like I'm dead."

"Of course we're friends," Duard said. "Will we always be friends? I hope so. I wish Dwayne hadn't had to drive us in the goddamn cement mixer tonight. How do I feel? Stupid. If I had any brains I could drive a cement mixer by myself."

"You aren't stupid," Phoebe said. "You're kind."

"Aw," Duard said.

"Kiss me, would you, Duard? Please?"

"You want me to kiss you? You must. I mean, you asked."

"Duard," Phoebe said. "Shut up. Kiss me, okay? That's all."

Duard did not say anything. He put his hands on Phoebe's shoulders and leaned forward. Slowly he leaned over and kissed her. Phoebe made a soft sighing sound. Duard put his arms around her back.

Jesus, Wedley thought. Good god in heaven.

"There's something I want to give you," Duard said.

Oh no, Wedley thought. I don't want to see this.

"What is it, Duard?" Phoebe said.

"A present." He bent over and opened his violin case. He picked something up out of it, and presented it to Phoebe.

"Why, Duard," Phoebe said. "It's—it's that brain."

"Dominique gave it back," Duard explained. "Did she want it anymore? I want you to have it."

"Why, Duard," Phoebe said. "I don't know what to say."

Duard shrugged. He was blushing.

Phoebe reached out and took the brain in her hands. From all around them came the thumping of the giant heart.

"Do I love you, Phoebe?" Duard said.

Duard stood there in the entrance to the pulmonary artery, looking at his shoes. Phoebe held his brain. She was just about to lean forward and kiss him again when someone grabbed Duard from behind.

"Ugg," Duard said. A piece of cloth was pressed down over his face. Duard's knees crumpled, and he fell face forward into the soft membranes of the chamber.

Phoebe screamed. "Help! Somebody!"

Wedley, standing there in the entrance to the left ventricle, found himself suddenly frozen. He did not know what was happening.

"Pa," said a voice behind him. "What are you doing?"

He turned around, and there was his daughter Demmie. She did not look surprised to see him. To her left was a large bearded man wearing a Casey Jones hat and carrying a sack.

"Here's your dog," Billings said.

"Wuff," said Buddy.

"Help!" Phoebe cried again.

"Jesus," Demmie said. "What's going on? That's Phoebe! Whyn't you go save her, Pa? Hurry!"

But Phoebe was beyond saving at this point. Rusty pulled a bag over her head, then clubbed her with the handle of his gun. In a moment the girl had collapsed limply in his arms. Rusty lifted her up over one shoulder, then kneeled and picked up the brain with the other hand. He looked up at the left ventricle. Wedley and Billings and Demmie were running toward him. He turned around and fled up the stairs, back into the lungs.

"Stop him," Demmie shouted. "Billings. Go get him."

Demmie, Wedley, and Billings disappeared into the pulmonary artery.

Duard sat up, rubbing his head, hearing their footsteps receding into the lungs.

"Don't worry, Phoebe," Duard said, "I'm coming."

Duard, groggy and lovesick, stumbled toward the aorta.

Back in the pulmonary artery, Billings was having a hard time running. The fact that he was still hauling Buddy around in a bag slowed him down a great deal. Billings was also, unfortunately, in front of Demmie and Wedley, blocking their way on the narrow stairs that led back into the lungs. If there was anything true in the present situation, it was this: you couldn't get around Billings.

"Hurry up," Demmie said. "He's getting away."

"I'm going as fast as I can," Billings said. "I've got Buddy."

"Give Buddy to Wedley, goddammit," she said. "Hurry."

"Not until he gives us the fifty bucks," Billings said. "I'm not just giving Buddy away for free."

"Oh, Billings, just give it to him. Wedley will pay us. Won't you, Pa?"

"That wasn't the deal," Billings said, huffing and puffing. "We get the money first, then he gets the dog. For all we know he could just run off with the dog, never fork over the money. You think I'm going to let that happen? No way!"

"Is this who you've been hanging out with for eight years?" Wedley said. "This genius?"

"He's not a genius," Demmie said. "Don't call him that."

"Everybody calls me Billings," Billings said. He stopped at the top of the steps. "You want some gum?"

"Goddammit," Demmie said. "He's getting away!"

"Hey, he can't go that fast," Billings said. "Carrying her. She weighs a lot more than Buddy, I can tell you!"

"How do you know?" Demmie said. "How do you know how much she weighs? You lifted her?"

"I'm just saying," Billings said. "She's some fifteen-year-old girl. Buddy's a twenty-three-year-old dog. I'm just pointing out the difference. Don't get sore."

"I'm not sore," Demmie said.

"Yes you are," Billings said. "Jesus, Demmie. I'm just trying to help."

"Tell your boyfriend to shut up," Wedley said.

"He's not my boyfriend," Demmie said.

"Well whatever he is," Wedley said. They were running through the lungs. "What is he, anyway?"

From inside the bag, Buddy started barking again. He sounded upset.

"I don't know," Demmie muttered. "Maybe he is my boyfriend."

"You should be ashamed," Wedley said.

"I am," Demmie said. "You don't know the half of it."

★

Dwayne and Vicki stood at the top of the cement mixer, ready to jump in. Dwayne had stopped the drum from rotating entirely so that they could stand on top of the cylinder and open the hatch. Vicki looked down into the dark, damp chamber, full of wet cement.

"How long can we swim in it," Vicki whispered, "before it starts to harden? A long time, I hope." She reached behind her back to unhook her bra. For a moment she thought about Wedley. She wondered if her husband would ever want to swim with her in wet cement.

"Not very long," Dwayne said. "If we don't want it to harden we have to keep thrashing in it."

But at that moment a man came bursting out the front doors of the Franklin Institute. People were yelling and shouting after him. Dwayne recognized him: it was the same guy he had seen earlier, running up the steps. The man ran toward the street, rushed over to a Mazda Miata, and threw a large bundle down in the passenger seat. A pair of legs was sticking out of the top of the bundle. Another man, wearing an ascot, was waiting for him in the car and started up the engine.

Even as the Miata's engine turned over, three more people came running out of the institute. One of them was carrying a white linen sack. They were all pointing at the guy in the Miata, yelling. "Stop him," they said. One of the people shouting was Wedley. "Stop those guys."

"Uh-oh," Dwayne said. "Maybe we should—uh—"

"What?" Vicki said.

"Uh—get down. From the cement mixer. Something's—"

"Something's what, Dwayne?"

"Something's going on!"

Vicki stamped her foot angrily on the top of the cement mixer and started doing up the buttons on her jumpsuit again.

"There's always something going on, isn't there?" Vicki said, angrily.

The man in the Miata pulled out from the curb, tires squealing. Wedley and Demmie and Billings jumped into a green Falcon with the words THE POISON SQUIRRELS stenciled on the sides, and a moment later the Falcon was squealing around Logan Circle, in hot pursuit of the Miata.

From the front door of the museum, Duard exited suddenly, yelling and pointing and screaming. He seemed upset.

"Which way did they go?" Duard said. "Did I see them? No, of course not. I got lost! I thought I was going to walk around those lungs for like a week and a half!"

"What lungs?" Dwayne said.

"If you're looking for all the people that just came tearing out of here," Vicki said, "you're too late. They all went off around the circle. They're probably halfway to the art museum by now."

"We have to catch them. That guy. He's got Phoebe!"

"Phoebe?" Dwayne said. He looked at little Dwenda.

Duard nodded. "Phoebe," he said.

"Oh no," Dwayne said. "Something is happening." He looked at Vicki. "I told you."

Vicki sighed, furious. "All right," she said. "Let's go."

They all jumped back in the cab, Dwayne behind the wheel, Vicki in the middle, Duard on the far right with Dwenda in his lap. Dwayne started up the cement mixer and slowly pulled out into traffic.

"We'll never catch them in this thing," Vicki said.

"You don't know," Dwayne said. "Once it gets going, it's fast."

"Never," Dwenda said.

"Poor Phoebe," Duard said. His voice was trembling. "I'd just given her the brain. I'd just told her I love her."

"Jesus, Duard," Vicki said angrily. "Way to go."

✯

Phoebe's Uncle Pat, driving down the Benjamin Franklin Parkway with Isabelle, was trying to think of the right words to say.

After all, Isabelle could have just left him there, tied up to a hot radiator, until morning. It had been an act of great kindness for her to turn back, to cut off his binds with a plastic knife. She could have saved her work maybe, were it not for her pausing to help him. He wanted to tell her he understood.

"Thank you," he said, finally. "I appreciate what you did back there."

"What?" Isabelle said, looking out at the road. "What did I do?"

"I mean for saving me," Pat said.

"Yeah, well, I owe you I guess." Isabelle did not appear to be paying much attention. She was scanning the road for any signs of Barton Sumac.

"You mean," Pat said, " 'cause I put all that soy sauce in the gas tank? You owe me for that?"

"No," Isabelle said, still not looking at him.

Pat thought.

"Maybe you mean because I tried to stop the guy. 'Cause I got some Jimmy Stewart smashed on my head trying to save your stuff."

"Huh?" Isabelle said. "Nah."

Ahead of them was the entrance ramp to the expressway.

Pat thought some more, but came up empty. "Then I don't know. What do you owe me for?"

Isabelle squinted. " 'Cause I ran out on you," she said. "Last summer. When you got into that big mess. I left you to deal with it all alone."

Pat looked over at her. "You mean you're sorry?"

Isabelle nodded. "Yeah."

Pat blinked. He was not sure if this made him feel any better. His back was still a little hot from that radiator.

"Pat, look," Isabelle said. There was a red sports car in front of them. The car contained two men.

"That's him," she said. "The bastard. And look, he's got some accomplice. They must have ditched the other car."

A green Ford Falcon pulled up behind them, flashed its lights, and passed them. The people inside looked upset.

"Jesus," Pat said. "Look out."

The Miata put on a fresh burst of speed. A cement mixer was pulling up behind them, tailgating. It was practically on their rear bumper. The driver blew his air horn.

As they pulled out onto the expressway, the cement mixer behind them immediately passed Pat and Isabelle on the left. Ahead of them was the green Falcon, tearing up the fast lane, and the Miata, way out in front, blue smoke puffing from the tailpipe. The cement mixer was going almost seventy. The driver pulled on the air horn again, barreling down on everything in his way.

"Jesus, would you look at that," Pat said, shaking his head. "All the nuts are out on the road tonight!"

It was a quiet night in Centralia. Officer Calcagno sat in the patrol car, listening to the radio, thinking about his late wife, Elizabeth. On Route 61, leading up into town, most of the traffic had ceased for the evening. Anyone headed toward Centralia was already there for the night. The fire breakout near the top of the hill was particularly fierce this evening; thick mist and smoke puffed from the ground and drifted across the road. For some reason the fire seemed worst when it was cold.

From Officer Calcagno's position you could see the exact route of the underground fire by observing the places where the snow had melted. The dry, bare ground traced a pattern vaguely similar to that of the old mine shafts, hundreds of feet below ground. Since 1962 the fire had been moving through the coal seams, following the course of the old shafts.

Calcagno remembered laughing about the fire when he was first married, back in the mid-sixties. Both the fire and his marriage had started in some garbage dump near the Odd Fellows' Cemetery. He and Elizabeth had walked through the graveyard one day and stood at the far corner watching the smoke billow into the sky. There was no sense then that this burning thing would eventually sweep beneath the town and destroy them all. It was just a curiosity, and not an uncommon one at that. Mine fires happen in the anthracite region. There was no indication that there was anything extraordinary about the Centralia fire.

By 1982, the federal government had finally agreed to buy out the residents' homes. They came and boarded up the houses, places where people that Calcagno had known his entire life had lived. The government spray-painted big red numbers on the plywood sheets, numbers that indicated the order in which the homes would be razed. Now, ten years later, there wasn't much left, except for people like Wendy Walisko and maybe a few others.

They hadn't been thinking about the future on that clear summer day. Calcagno and Elizabeth stood in the graveyard, the smoke puffing from the nearby landfill, watching the blue jays and the grosbeaks flying overhead. A crow had landed on a cross-shaped stone.

"Boy what a day," Calcagno said out loud.

It had seemed romantic at the time. How odd that they could have been surrounded by all that death, and not to have seen it. The smoke billowing through the air was as sure a sign of their own end as the gravestones in front of them. But we were kids, Calcagno thought. A bottle of wine in a picnic basket. Blue jays and blackbirds. It was impossible to see in all of this anything other than their love, and their own future together.

When they got back to the house they sat on the front porch, talking late into the night. For some reason there was a canister of talcum powder on the porch and they wound up shaking the powder into each other's hair until it turned gray. "You see," Elizabeth said, laughing. "This is what we'll look like when we're old."

Officer Calcagno sat in his patrol car, looking out over the remains of Centralia. Pretty soon he would drive up to Buchanan for a doughnut maybe, talk to Cissy Baedecker at the Bess Eaton Donut Ranch. Cissy was beautiful, with great blue eyes and tangled hair. But she had been born in 1974, twelve years after the fire was already out of control.

From the far end of the valley, Calcagno saw a pair of headlights whirl into town around the Route 61 curve. It was a small sports car, easily doing over seventy miles an hour. This was odd. He started his engine. It looked like he was going to be writing out a ticket.

Before he even got the car into drive, however, another car screeched around the curve, in pursuit of the first one. Its bright lights stabbed through the drifting smoke.

Directly behind this one came a third, also speeding. Behind this came a huge cement mixer, swerving from one side of the road to the other. The four vehicles were all flashing their lights at each other and squealing their tires and blowing their horns.

"Aw, jeez," Calcagno said, putting on his hat. "Here comes trouble."

There was nothing worse than folks from out of town.

Emily Harrison was standing in the window of her younger daughter's old bedroom when the car pulled up.

She had been thinking about Phoebe, about Demmie, about the life she had once lived in this house before the fire came.

As it turned out, the greatest threat to Emily in the old house had not come from the Centralia mine fire but from her own ruthless memory. The place was falling apart, decaying, but it still held much of the same furniture that Emily and Wedley had bought when they first got married. There were some old clothes hanging in the closets, and some paint-by-numbers paintings of German shepherds and collies hanging on the walls. Emily had painted these herself, when she was pregnant with Demmie, back in 1966. The dogs had always made Phoebe cry when she was alone in a room with the paintings. *Mommy,* she used to say. *Their eyes follow me around.*

"Emily," said Rusty, bursting in the front door, carrying a large sack. A pair of legs stuck out the top of it. Rusty was accompanied by a large, arrogant-looking man with an ascot. "This here is Barton Sumac." He paused. "You know. The artist."

"I'm pleased to meet you, Mister Sumac," Emily said. "It's an honor."

"You heard of him?" Rusty said.

"No," Emily said.

"Me neither," Rusty said.

"Your boyfriend has graciously given me a lift in his car," Sumac said. "We are stopping here just long enough for him to deliver something to you." He pulled out a gun and squinted down at the barrel to make sure it was still loaded.

"Yeah, Emily," Rusty said. "You won't believe what I've brought you. I finally did it! Look!"

He turned over the bag and poured Phoebe onto the floor.

"Phoebe," Emily screamed. She ran down the stairs, stepping on Sumac's foot. "What have you done to her?" she yelled.

"I brought her to you," he said. "She's coming with us, to Nevada!" Rusty smiled. "God it felt great to put someone in a sack again. To think all these years I've been suppressing it, playing by society's bullshit *rules*. Man, I feel great, Emily, I feel like myself at last!"

"Oh you jerk," Emily said, rubbing her daughter's forehead. "What's wrong with you!"

"Nothing's wrong with me," Rusty said. "I'm just getting in

touch with my relatives. It's not my fault my ancestors liked to put people in bags!''

Phoebe made a soft whimpering sound.

"Wait a second," Rusty said. "I got to get the rest of the stuff."

Barton Sumac stood there, watching the mother and daughter embrace.

"Phoebe," Emily said, still holding her daughter's head in her lap. "Wake up, honey."

Several cars pulled up in front of the house. There was the sound of car doors opening and closing. Someone started shouting.

"Ma?" Phoebe said, sitting up, rubbing her head. "Where am I?"

"You're home again," Emily said. "I'm so sorry, honey."

"Home?" Phoebe said, looking around the strange parlor. She had a vague memory of having once lived in this place.

Rusty came into the house, holding another pair of linen sacks.

"Who's coming?" Sumac said to him. He pointed his gun at the front door. "Who is that?"

"Aw, no," Rusty said. "It's those people in the cement mixer. And some others. There's a whole slew of 'em."

"What do they want?" Sumac said. "Are these friends of yours?"

"Friends of mine," Rusty said, shaking his head. "Ha, funny."

The door burst open again, and Wedley, Demmie, and Billings rushed into the tiny room. Wedley looked around the place, at the interior of the house he had once lived in. There was a sneering man with an ascot, pointing a gun at him. A man with a shaved head, enormous muscles, and a multitude of tattoos stood at the bottom of a staircase holding some bags. His daughter Phoebe, her eyes puffy, her cheeks red, sat on the floor. She was being cradled in the arms of Emily, Wedley's ex-wife.

"Emily," he whispered. "Oh my god, Emily."

"Oh, Wedley," Emily said. "Oh, you can't see me, not like this. This is terrible."

"Ma," said Demmie. "Jesus, you're thin!"

"Hey, everybody," Billings said, dropping a bag on the floor. "I got Buddy!"

"Ooff," Buddy said. He raised his head, looking around at the house where he had once lived. Buddy wagged his tail, which made a hollow, snapping sound against the wooden floor. He liked it here.

"Buddy," Emily whispered. "You're still alive!"

"Hey, Ma," Demmie said, annoyed. "What about me? I'm still alive, too!"

"Oh my lord, Demmie," Emily said. "I wouldn't have recognized you!"

Uncle Pat and Isabelle Smuggs rushed into the room, which, including the two of them, now contained nine people and the dog. It was starting to get stuffy.

"All right, you bastard," Isabelle said, pointing at Barton Sumac. "I want all my guts back!" But even as she accused him, her voice died out. Sumac was holding a pistol, as was the man with the tattoos standing next to him.

"Gee," Sumac said. "Sure is getting crowded in here. Can somebody open a window?"

"Emily," said her brother. "It's me. Patrick."

"Patrick," Emily said, looking at him more closely, recognizing him. "Oh my god, what's happened to you?"

"Nothing," he said, shrugging. "This is what I look like."

"That's not true," said Isabelle. "A lot has happened to him. Most of it's my fault, too!"

"Well, isn't that interesting!" said Emily. "I'm Phoebe's mother. Pat's her uncle."

"I'm Isabelle Smuggs. It's a pleasure to meet you, ma'am."

"It's a pleasure to meet you, too, Isabelle," said Emily. She turned to Patrick. "Patrick, this girl is charming! Didn't I read somewhere you had married some nurse? I thought I saw her picture in the paper. You aren't her, are you, dear?"

"No, ma'am," Isabelle said.

A cop car pulled up in front of the house. The red beacons strobed through the windows.

"That's good," Emily said, her face darkening.

Dwayne, Vicki, and Duard ran into the room, which now contained twelve persons and Buddy. It was so crowded in the decaying parlor that everyone was practically standing on the shoes of someone else. Billings tried to move back a little bit and stumbled against a vase, which shattered onto the floor in fragments.

"Way to go, pal," Rusty said. "You know how much that vase was worth? A lot."

"Stop him," Duard said, pointing at Rusty. "He's got Phoebe!"

"Duh," said Demmie. "Jesus. Tell us something we don't already know!"

"I'm okay," Phoebe said, standing up. "See? I'm fine. Nobody has me."

"Hi, Phoebe," Duard said. "I'm sorry I gave you that brain."

"The brain?" Phoebe said. "What does the brain have to do with it?"

"Aw, no," Sumac said. "You mean some kid has had my brain all along?"

"It's *my* brain," Isabelle said. "I'm the one who made it!"

"All right," said Officer Calcagno, storming into the living room. He had to push everyone over a little just to fit in. "I'm handing out tickets like you wouldn't believe!"

Rusty pointed his gun at the policeman, but there were too many people in the way. If he had a little more room he could have got a sack down over somebody's head. Unable to shoot Calcagno, Rusty raised his tattooed arm and put the barrel of the gun next to Dwayne's temple instead.

"All right," Rusty yelled. His large earring swung back and forth. "One false move and this guy gets it."

"Dwayne!" Vicki screamed.

"Oh for god's sakes," Demmie said. "Shoot him. We barely know him!"

"I know him!" Vicki cried.

"You're not kidding," Phoebe said.

Barton Sumac, standing next to Demmie, raised his arm and held his gun next to her head as well.

"Tell you what," he said. "You let us out of here, or this one gets it, too."

"Why me?" she said. "I don't even know who you are!"

"You shut up, Sumac," said Rusty, still holding his gun next to Dwayne's head. "I'm the one murdering people, not you!"

Officer Calcagno drew his pistol. "All right, drop it, both of you, or I'll plug the two of yuz."

"Honestly," Emily said. "I've never seen so many people threatening to shoot each other in my entire life! I can't even keep track!"

"Ma," Demmie said. "He's serious."

"You better believe I'm serious," Sumac said. "You think this is all some big game?" He wrenched Demmie's arm behind her back. She cried out in pain.

"Billings," Demmie cried. "He's hurting me."

"I'm going to count three," Sumac said. "And then I want everyone to go up those stairs. Nice and quiet."

"I'm going to count three, too," Rusty said.

"I think just one person counting to three is enough, Rusty," Emily said. "Honestly, this is so confusing!"

"I'm counting to three also," said Officer Calcagno.

"Oh, not him too!" said Vicki.

"When I get to three I want you to drop your weapons."

From his sack on the floor, Buddy growled softly.

"Why should we drop our weapons?" Rusty said. "We've got hostages."

"Yeah," Demmie said, the barrel of Sumac's gun embedded in her temple. "He's got hostages!"

"Where's Dwenda?" Phoebe said, softly.

"She's out in the mixer," Duard said.

"You left that little girl out there?" Vicki said. "All alone?"

"Safer out there than in here," Wedley muttered.

"Yeah," Duard said. "Like a lot you care about Dwenda anyway."

"What's that supposed to mean?"

"One!" Sumac yelled.

"Ma," Demmie said. "He's serious."

"I can't believe some kid has had that brain all along," Isabelle said. "Hey, you, you know how much that brain is worth? Lots!"

"It's my brain, now," Phoebe said. "I told you he gave it to me as a present."

"He stole it, Phoebe!" Uncle Pat said. "You don't want to be accepting stolen merchandise!"

"I didn't steal it," Duard said. "I found it."

"Yeah, right in front of that old graveyard, too, I bet," Sumac said. "I threw it out the window last summer, right as I was driving by. I figured somebody would find it and get grossed out by it."

"Did I get grossed out by it?" Duard said softly. "Hell no. I *tasted* it."

"Two!" Rusty said.

"Hey, I'm the one counting," Sumac yelled.

"Nuh-uh," Rusty said.

"Yuh-huh."

"Nuh-uh."

"Jesus," Wedley shouted. "You can both count! What difference does it make?"

"I'm warning you," Calcagno said, pistol drawn. "You both drop it. Now. Or people are going to get hurt! You understand me? Injured!"

"Somebody do something!" Demmie cried out.

"No," Billings said softly. "What she means is, don't do anything."

"I know what I mean," Demmie shouted. "Don't tell me what I mean!"

"Three!" Calcagno shouted.

A gun went off. There was the loud sound of the pistol retort, followed by the *ping* of a bullet ricocheting around the room. Everyone screamed and yelled, covering themselves from what they assumed would be the forthcoming rain of bullets. Officer Calcagno dropped his pistol and started jumping up and down on one foot. "Goddamn stupid dog," he said, holding his leg. "Ow!"

Apparently Buddy had seized the opportunity to sink his teeth deep into Calcagno's calf. The officer, taken by surprise, had shot his gun into the ceiling. Now the gun was spinning around on the floor, unattended.

Phoebe Harrison reached forward and grabbed it.

"All right," Phoebe shouted. "Everyone get your hands up in the air!"

"Way to go, sweetheart!" Emily shouted.

"That's my girl," said Wedley.

"You too," Phoebe said, brandishing the pistol at her parents. "Especially you too."

"What are you doing, honey?" Wedley said.

"Shut up, Pa," she said. "Jesus."

"Darling?" Emily said. "Are you thinking about what you're doing?"

"Get your hands up, Ma! You too, Wedley!" Phoebe said. "Goddammit, I'm not kidding!"

Phoebe stamped on the floor in rage. She raised the gun over her head and pulled the trigger. There was another loud explosion. Plaster fell down out of the ceiling.

"I'm serious!" she said.

"I think we better get our hands up," Wedley said.

"Does that mean everyone," Billings said. "Or just your immediate family?"

"Everyone!" Phoebe shouted, and she shot the gun again. A picture fell off the wall.

"Look at yourselves!" Phoebe said. "What the hell is wrong with you! You think other families live like this? You think my friends at school have to wave a gun around in their parents' faces?"

"Those girls are not your friends," Wedley said. "They don't even know you!"

"Shut up," Phoebe yelled. "Everyone just shut up!"

"Darling," Wedley said. "I know you're just a little upset right now . . ."

"Upset," Phoebe said. "Like that's some big mystery? You want to know why I'm upset, I'll tell you."

She pointed the gun at Emily. "When I was six, *she* takes off. Why? 'Cause she wanted to be free, so she could walk around on some beach feeling sorry for horses!"

Phoebe moved her arm quickly so that the gun now pointed at Demmie. "Then I was eight, my *sister* took off. Why? So she could play in some stupid rock band that can't even tune its own instruments and hang out with this guy Billings who all he does is sit around and chew *Beech-Nut.*"

"It's true," Billings said. "I sure like gum."

Phoebe stamped her foot, then pointed the gun at Officer Calcagno. "When I was twelve, the town I was living in got torn down because some underground fire was wiping out the place, some fire the adults let burn for twenty years without ever thinking they should put it out!"

Phoebe swung her arm around again so that the pistol now was aimed at Vicki. "Okay. Then, when I was fourteen, my father marries *her.*"

"Oh boy," Vicki said. "Here it comes."

"This stupid dope who screws Dwayne behind my father's back, who burns my hair off and then lies about it!"

"I didn't do that on purpose," Vicki said.

"That's exactly my point," Phoebe said. "Jesus! Just for once, why doesn't somebody do something on purpose, something halfway decent and kind! Is it so impossible that just once someone would say they love me?"

"We love you, Phoebe!" everyone said quickly.

"Not *now*," Phoebe said, stamping on the floor. "Like maybe you should say you love me sometimes when I'm not holding a gun to everybody's head."

"I'm the one with a gun to their head," said Demmie.

"Me too," said Dwayne.

"You know what I want you all to do?" said Phoebe. "You know what I'd like to see all the adults do, just one time?"

"What's that, sweetheart?" Emily said.

"Dance," Phoebe said.

"Oh boy," said Dwayne. "I like to dance."

"That's not what she means," Vicki hissed.

"What does she mean?" Dwayne asked.

But Phoebe's meaning became clear in the next moment, when she started shooting at the floor of their house. The members of Phoebe's family began to dance up and down like the members of the Alvin Ailey troupe.

Officer Calcagno, who was not dancing, saw an opportunity. With one hand he reached up and turned out the lights.

In the darkness the silhouettes of many people moved through the small space and collided.

Calcagno decided that the best thing to do at this moment would be to run outside, get another gun, perhaps call in for reinforcements. It was a bit of a risk, but on the other hand he wasn't doing much good in here, besides offering an opportunity to get shot by accident.

The officer ran back out to his car. He turned on his radio and quickly called in to headquarters for help. The angry voice of Lieu-

tenant Stroke responded, as if Calcagno were in some manner responsible for the turn of events.

Calcagno got another gun, then slowly approached the place.
There was the sound of many people arguing with each other, more
guns going off. The dog had thrown back his head now and was howl-
ing.

"Oh, Jesus," Calcagno said. He really didn't want to go back inside, not with that dog in there. Last time it bit him.

Fortunately, it did not seem like it was going to be necessary to
enter the house. Many of the inhabitants were now pouring out the
front door and collapsing in the front yard. No one seemed to be
bleeding, at least not yet.

George Billings, his beard slightly singed, ran out into the front
yard, and looked back at the smoking house. "Demmie," he
moaned. "Demmie, sweetheart."

A moment later Dwayne and Duard stumbled through the doors.
Dwayne was carrying Vicki in his arms. He walked down the steps,
looked over at his own house next door, then back at the Harrisons'.

Sadly, Dwayne walked back toward his house. "Come on, Edith,"
he said to the woman in his arms, and carried her across the threshold. "It's time for you to stop falling."

More guns went off, followed by the sound of many people arguing and yelling. In the distance, sirens were approaching. Through
the smoke and the haze, Uncle Pat and Isabelle ran out the front
door and fell, coughing, into the grass.

Well gee, Calcagno thought. Now we're getting somewhere.

Dwenda, alone in the cement mixer, had watched the proceedings
from the dark of her own private world. As usual, her brothers had
gone off and abandoned her. They were clearly getting involved in
some big mess, which was what she expected. Still, it was dark out

here, and lonely. She wanted to go home, get out of this thing and get back to her room, but she was too far off the ground. Someone was going to have to help her down from the cabin. She was going to have to get somebody's attention.

The cement mixer was really not all that hard to get going. All that was necessary was to release the big long lever next to the driver's seat, just as Dwayne had instructed her. Soon the mixer was rolling down the hill. As it lumbered toward the house it picked up more and more momentum. This was fun. Dwenda reached up and pulled down on the air horn.

A skunk, alarmed by the sudden blast, fled from the shrubbery by the roadside and ran headlong toward the mixer's front tires.

"All right," said a voice from the house, stepping forward. "Excitement's over."

Barton Sumac walked forward, a gun held to Rusty's head. Rusty, in turn, was holding a gun against the sack that held all of Isabelle Smuggs's sculptures.

"You're going to let us get to our car," Sumac said. "And then you're going to let us drive away. You got that?"

"Officer," Isabelle cried. "They've got my whole life's work in there! Everything I've ever worked for!"

"One false move and I'll blow it all to bits," Rusty said.

"A second false move and I'll blow *him* to bits," said Sumac.

"Shoot him," said Billings. "A lot we care."

"You both drop it," said Calcagno. "This will never work."

"Of course it will work," said Sumac. "Just watch us go. You're going to shoot a man down in cold blood? Here? In Centralia?"

But at that moment a loud blast came from behind him, accompanied by the sound of something very heavy, lumbering closer.

Rusty Hawkins and Barton Sumac just stood there, watching her approach. At first she seemed to be barely moving. After ten or twenty feet, though, the mixer was picking up speed. By the time it jumped the curb, it was going thirty miles an hour, thundering down on top of them.

A little girl in a pink dress was sitting behind the wheel. There were ribbons in her hair. She was smiling and clapping her hands together and reaching up and blasting the air horn. She was bouncing up and down in the driver's seat, laughing and screaming, as the cement mixer, its drum spinning slowly, bore down on the Harrisons' house.

There was a single moment when the great grille of the mixer towered over the heads of Barton Sumac and Rusty Hawkins, while the two men still stood there, hoping they could escape. Then, dropping their guns, they turned and ran. The bag with the sculptures flew through the air.

The cement mixer crashed into the Harrisons' porch, but it did not stop there. It smashed through the living room, past the front steps, and halfway into the kitchen. When it finally came to rest, all that was visible from outside was its back end. Cement gushed down the chute. It glugged into a wet pile near the broken detritus of floor-boards, glass, and rafters.

Then there was silence.

Isabelle Smuggs was the first to recover. She went over to the bag that had flown, eager to recover what remained of her work.

Jesus, Isabelle thought. For once in my life I'm going to be given a second chance. Looking over at Patrick Flinch, she promised herself she would not blow it this time.

The sack moved slightly, and a dog's head popped out the top.

Buddy looked at her. He was shaking a little bit. "Wuff," he said. Brown goo dribbled from his eyes.

There were some soft moaning sounds from the debris under the front porch. Barton Sumac and Rusty Hawkins walked out of the smoke, their hands in the air. Calcagno slapped a pair of handcuffs on them.

Several more police cars drove up, and an angry-looking, red-faced man stormed out of one of them. "Calcagno," he said. "What have you done here?"

"I'm placing these two men under arrest," Calcagno said, shoving Sumac and Hawkins toward Lieutenant Stroke. "They've got records. Histories!"

"Go on, arrest us," Rusty said, looking regretfully back at the house. "She'll never love me anyway."

Other policemen rushed forward. An ambulance pulled up behind them. A man with an oxygen tank raced around clamping gas masks over people's faces.

Stroke clutched his heart. "How'd that cement mixer get in there?" he said, pointing toward the house. "Did you drive that in there, Calcagno?" he said. "Goddammit, that's no place for a cement mixer! You want to find a garage or something!"

"I didn't do it," Calcagno said. "This little girl did."

Dwenda, six years old, stood before the lieutenant, one finger in her mouth, sniffing back tears.

"Is that right, young lady?" Stroke said.

"I'm sorry," she said. "I didn't mean to do it."

"Hey," Duard said. "She said her own words!"

"Well of course she said her own words," Stroke said, looking at Duard. "Whose words would she say?"

But Duard just picked up his little sister and held her. "That was a very naughty thing you did," he said to her. "But I love you, Dwenda."

"I love you, too, Duard," Dwenda said.

"All right, all right," Stroke said. "Let's break it up. Anybody left? Anybody still unaccounted for?"

"The Harrisons," said Isabelle, petting the dog. Buddy whimpered.

"They're still in there," said Uncle Pat, shaking his head. "Oh no." He put his hand to his face.

"Don't worry," Isabelle said. "They'll be all right." She put her arm around him. "We'll all be all right."

"I don't know," Pat said, looking at the smoking house with the cement mixer smashed into it. "I don't know."

"Of course they'll be all right," Isabelle said. "You just have to have some faith."

The young woman reached up and kissed him. The two joined in an embrace.

Something in Isabelle's kiss reminded Patrick Flinch of Julie Zacks. There was something about it that filled him with a sense of inner joy. He remembered the sounds of summer nights on 113th Street, the air filled with fireworks and music. Bottles crashed on the street, and he fell out of bed, laughing. Will you love me forever, she had asked him, as a church burned in the distance. Not just while we're young, but forever?

Holding Isabelle Smuggs, feeling the soft crash of her kisses on his neck, Patrick knew that it would not be necessary to find her anymore, that it was not necessary to know why she had written him the letter that began *Dear Moron*. It was plain enough. He *was* a moron.

Patrick Flinch sniffed the air.

"Jesus, you smell that?" he said to Isabelle. The atmosphere had become acidic with an overwhelming skunklike stench.

"Of course," she said to him, and smiled. "What did you expect?" She reached up with one hand and again drew his face toward her own.

Officer Calcagno turned his back, looking away from the carnage out over the city. There in the distance was a cloud of smoke, rising from the mine fire. Even while all of this was going on, it was still burning, still spreading forward. He thought about his Elizabeth again, and that blue summer day long ago, when, as lovers, they had first seen the smoke rising into the air.

Oh sweetheart, he thought, watching the stars above Centralia. If only I had known. I would have put it out for you, if I could.

★

Smoke was still drifting through the kitchen of the Harrisons' house. For the first time in a long time the place seemed very quiet. From outside came the sound of cop cars starting up and driving away.

Phoebe sat up and dusted some of the fallen plaster off her skirt. Wedley stumbled through the doorway and sat down at the kitchen table.

"Man oh man," he said, holding his head. His tuxedo was burned and torn. "Does my head hurt!"

"Are you okay, Pa?" Phoebe said.

Wedley looked over at her. "Phoebe!" he cried. He hugged her. "I'm so glad you're okay."

"Where's Ma?" Phoebe said. "Where's Demmie?"

For an instant there was silence in the kitchen, and Wedley just sat there, holding on to his daughter. Oh no, Phoebe thought. Don't tell me they've disappeared. Not again.

Then, a weak voice said, "I'm here, Phoebe," and Emily got up from the corner. There was plaster in her hair. She moved slowly toward Wedley and Phoebe, and put her arms around them.

"I'm sorry," Phoebe said.

"Why are you sorry?" Emily said. "We're the idiots."

"Yes," Wedley said. "We are. Idiots."

"I know," Phoebe said. "But I shouldn't have grabbed that gun."

"God I'm tired," Demmie said, sitting down at the kitchen table. "I don't ever remember being this tired." Her hair seemed very gray to Phoebe.

"I don't know, Phoebe," Emily said. "Maybe there'd be a lot more families together in America celebrating traditional family values if only somebody took the time to try and murder them!"

"You know," Demmie said. "There's something in that!"

Phoebe brushed some plaster out of her hair and sat down between Wedley and Demmie. Emily hugged Wedley a bit longer, then sat down at the free end of the table.

The Harrisons sat there at the kitchen table, smoke still drifting through the air. It had been nine years since the last time all four of them had sat here in these chairs.

"Well," Emily said. "Who's hungry?" She stood up and went over to the refrigerator. "Maybe you'd all like a little snack. If I'd known you were all coming I would have made something."

"Maybe some cake," Demmie said. "Do we have any?"

"I'm sorry, honey," Emily said. "All we have is tea. There's chamomile!"

"Tea?" Demmie whined. "Is that it? Jeez, there's never anything to eat in this house!"

"Where's Duard?" Phoebe said. "Where's Billings? Where's everybody?"

"They're coming," Wedley said. "Any moment now, they'll all bust in here."

Emily turned on the burner beneath the teakettle. She got out some sweet-smelling tea and put it inside a porcelain teapot. The scent of chamomile filled the room.

For a while no one spoke, realizing the truth of what Wedley had said. In a minute or two the world would intrude upon them again, pulling them in many directions, pulling them away from Centralia, and each other. But for this instant, the four of them were together in the kitchen of their old house, steam rising from the kettle.

Phoebe looked at her father, at her mother, at her sister, and smiled. It was sort of like a family.

"Hey," Phoebe said. "I almost forgot. Where's Buddy?"

"There," Demmie said. "In the sack."

"Oh," said Wedley. "I almost forgot to pay you the ransom. Remind me, Demmie, I still have fifty dollars in my coat."

"Forget it, Pa," Demmie said. "I shouldn't have kidnapped him in the first place. Maybe we'll just call it even."

"Okay, sweetheart," Wedley said, taking Demmie's hand. "We'll call it even."

"Buddy," Emily said, as Phoebe pulled the sack over to the table. She remembered going to Whispering Winds Kennels out by the Centralia airfield, half a lifetime ago, picking out the puppy. The first night they owned him the dog had cried and cried. The next day they gave the dog an alarm clock, which was supposed to duplicate the sound of his mother's heart.

Buddy had chewed the clock to pieces, and swallowed the hands and gears.

"Oh, Buddy," she said. "C'mere boy."

Phoebe opened the sack. A moment later she was holding a guillotined, plaster of Paris head of Amelia Earhart by the hair. The eyes were little X's. Her tongue was sticking out, and purple.

"Boy oh boy," Emily said sadly. "He's really changed."

SPRING STARS

THE TWINS

You'd need a very clear night to trace the whole thing.

On the night of the spring equinox, Phoebe opened her eyes suddenly, stunned and irritated by an unexpected nightmare. *Jesus Christ,* she thought, getting out of bed. *I must be out of my goddamned mind.*

She went to her desk and got out a package of Tareytons, as well as a pack of matches and a candle. Then she turned, walked to the bedroom window, and raised the screen. In a single swinging motion Phoebe climbed out the window and onto the roof. Her mother's crystal swung on its chain.

It was a warm night for March, and the trees were full of life, peepers cheeping softly, crickets and cicadas chanting. Phoebe walked to the flat part of the roof and lay down on her back. Stars twinkled in the distant sky.

There, high overhead, were the Lion and the Virgin, signs of warm summer nights ahead. To the west was Perseus, sinking now with the other stars of winter, beyond the horizon. There they were, disappearing, and it wasn't even that late. At this hour, at this time of year, she thought, she was delicately balanced between the stars that were yet to come and all the ones now behind.

She lit a match and held it against the base of the candle until the wax melted and dripped onto the shingles. Phoebe pressed the candle into the hot wax. Then she lit the wick and watched the flame. The candlelight flickered in her face.

Voices traveled upward from the driveway. A couple was talking to each other.

"You want me to stay over again tonight, Demmie?" the man said. "I won't if you don't want me to."

"I want you to," Demmie said softly. "Please, Billings? I want for you to stay."

"All right," Billings said. "I don't want to go home anyway. It's lonely now since Buddy died." He paused, considering his sadness. "Sometimes, you know, I think I miss his whiskers most."

It was fun spying on them like this. Phoebe hoped the two of them would say something really disgusting to each other, but Demmie and Billings didn't cooperate. About the most disgusting thing they did was kiss, unless you counted talking about Buddy, which wasn't all that pleasant either, considering the way the dog had finally died. The vet they went to said that even though dalmatians were unpredictable no one had ever heard of one exploding before, at least not unless it went snorkeling. This was the first time anyone had had one that blew up on land.

Phoebe pulled out a cigarette, tapped the end down, then held it in the flickering flame. She took a few puffs, then blew a smoke ring into the air. It floated.

Billings and Demmie kissed for a long time out in the driveway. Phoebe could hear them making smacky sounds. From the stereo in the living room she heard her parents listening to an old song. *The Hendersons will dance and sing as Mister K flies through the ring.* The tune reminded her of Phartley Park, and all those kids screaming on the Sky Master.

Billings and Demmie walked toward the house.

So, Phoebe thought. Once again, the four of us are spending the night under the same roof. Me, Pa, Demmie, and Ma. Five if you counted Billings, which you really had to. It wasn't like he was just some gum-chewing homunculus. Vicki, of course, had cleared out. She had returned to Dwayne, and to Centralia.

A strange dank smell floated through the air, and Phoebe thought about her old dog. She felt sorry for Buddy, and understood exactly what Billings meant. Sometimes she missed his whiskers most, too.

She looked out into a part of the sky that she did not know, and exhaled. Somewhere up there was Hercules, and somewhere up there was the Charioteer. Uncle Pat's girlfriend, Isabelle, had not been able to make Phoebe see these the night she had explained the skies. This was about two weeks ago. Phoebe and Duard had gone up to Uncle Pat's house and lay out there on the cold ground, wrapped up in blankets, as Isabelle showed them all the constellations with a dim flashlight. Uncle Pat seemed better now since Isabelle had moved in. About the only thing that got on his nerves was this broken vacuum cleaner he had bought somewhere. Phoebe had asked about this when they were stargazing, but Uncle Pat just clutched his stomach and said he didn't want to talk about it. Isabelle ran her fingers through his hair and told him it was all right. It was just a vacuum cleaner, after all. The beam of the flashlight stabbed upward through the Milky Way and beyond.

To the east the stars suggested a pair of stick figures, two women holding hands, twins. One of them was whispering in the ear of the other. Life is long, she said. Life is sweet. Phoebe coughed into her fist.

She sat up and shook her head, feeling her hair in her face. Then she ground out the cigarette on the shingles of her father's house.

The cold wind gave her goose bumps on her legs. It was still a little too cold to be spending all night out here on the roof, imagining things. It was time to go inside, and go to bed.

She took one last look at the stars. In the distance she heard the approach of a freight train, passing through Valley Forge. Maybe the train she was hearing was hauling long dark cars, its hoppers full of anthracite. The train was headed to the east and south, toward the sea, away from Centralia. As she sat there on the roof of her father's house, she felt something ache beneath her misspelled tattoo. *I'm never going back there,* she thought suddenly. *I'm never going back there again.*

She bent over and blew out the candle. The curling smoke rose softly toward the heavens.

At about the same time, in Centralia, a car swept up the hill toward the edge of town. It approached and passed a mailbox covered with black balloons. Two young men stood nearby, dressed up like gladiators.

"Look at those two, Dominique," Elaine Voron said, pointing out the window at her classmates. "What a couple of like, *rejects!*"

"You got it, girl," Dominique said, stepping on the accelerator. "Good thing you aren't hanging around with *that* crowd anymore. Talk about uncool, I mean really. Gross me out raw!"

Elaine handed Dominique the bottle of Southern Comfort. "You want a little sip, Dominique?"

"A slug, sure," Dominique said. She took the bottle from her new friend and held it to her face. As the liquid poured down Dominique's throat there was a sound like *glug glug glug glug glug.*

Dominique and Elaine were wearing identical outfits this evening: tight blue-jean miniskirts, black ripped stockings, white T-shirts, and black leather gloves with little nuts and bolts on them. They had gotten them at Sears.

"So you figure out what kind of tat you're getting?" Dominique said. "Something juicy, anyways." She regretted the fact that Rusty's had closed. It was a much longer drive to the Den of Iniquity in Mt. Carmel.

"Yeah," Elaine said softly. A rubber band from her braces suddenly shot out of her mouth and bounced off the rearview mirror, then ricocheted back and hit Elaine in the forehead. She blinked. "Something juicy."

Dominique looked over at her. "You ever think about getting your whole chest done?" she said. "That's what I'd do if I was you. Have 'em do something that goes from your neck down to your belly button. That would make people remember."

"Yeah," Elaine said. "They sure would."

"In fact let's have them do that to yuz. Get a whole big mural done on your front. Like a big snake or some giant bats and shit. That's a great idea. You'll like looking like that. It'll be fun for you!"

"Yeah," Elaine said. "Fun." She put one hand on her head to feel her enormous hair. It felt kind of like an Easter basket.

"Well, goddamn," Dominique said. "You know, me and you, Elaine, we're like peas in a fuckin' pod, aren't we!"

"We're peas," Elaine said sadly. They would be at the tattoo parlor in less than five minutes. Elaine felt her heart thumping in her throat.

The car passed through the drifting smoke from the fire. The outbreak was particularly bad this evening. There was a dense bank of smoke, far thicker than fog, occluding the highway.

Suddenly the engine faltered. For a moment it recovered, and the Swinger lunged forward again. Then it stalled out once more, and did not revive. The car gently slowed, coughed, and died. It came to a halt at the edge of the Odd Fellows' Cemetery. Smoke curled around the windshield.

"Hey," Elaine said, squinting out the window to her right. Headstones were vaguely visible through the smoke. "I used to know somebody buried there."

"Goddamn that Duard," Dominique said, and coughed. "I should have known this thing was a piece of shit." Duard had sold her his old car shortly after Dominique got her license back from Grampa Stroehmann. The Swinger had cost her fifty dollars, plus she had to buy her own Crisco.

"Excuse me, girls," said a voice. A woman was standing next to the car holding a glass of milk. It wasn't exactly clear where she'd come from. Elaine figured she might have been sitting in the graveyard, talking to somebody. "You all need to use a phone or something?"

"Yeah maybe," Dominique said. "Fuckin' car just died on me."

"I hate that, when things die on you." She drank back a throatful of the glass of milk. "Mmmm," she said. "Milky." A creamy mustache stood upon her lip.

"It sure *looks* milky," Elaine commented.

"You want to use my phone, that's fine," the woman said. "My name's Wendy Walisko. I live near here."

Dominique was trying to get the car started again, but the Swinger would not respond. She coughed again. The car was filling with smoke from the mine fire.

"Come on," Wendy said, stretching her hand forward. "Let me help you."

Elaine looked at the woman fearfully. Something about her didn't seem convincing.

But then Elaine thought again. It was unkind to be suspicious of strangers, especially when they were trying to rescue you. Maybe this Wendy was someone who could show them things.

Elaine reached forward and clasped Wendy's hand.

There was a sharp, sudden spark of blue electricity. Elaine opened her mouth and screamed her head off.

"Yow!" Elaine said.

"Are you all right?" Wendy said.

"Sorry," Elaine said, letting go of Wendy's hand. "It's static electricity." She shrugged. "I get shocks from things."

"Well, for heaven's sakes," Wendy said. "I guess you do."

"It's true," said Dominique, getting out of the car. "Goddamn Elaine gets jolts from everything. Cheesecake, corn on the cob, bars of soap, you name it."

"It's a problem," Elaine said, slamming her car door. She followed Dominique and Wendy into the moving cloud of smoke. "The doctor says I'm not properly grounded."

"My house is just over this ridge," Wendy said.

"Goddamn piece of shit car," Dominique said.

"Yeah, well," Wendy said. "What's a car, really. Bucket a bolts, really." She spread her arms wide, her palms heavenward. "Is not life long? Is not life sweet?"

"Goddamn car," Dominique muttered to herself. "Piece a shit."

The smoke was all around them now. For a moment Wendy vanished from view. The air was rich with sulfur.

"Would you like some milk?" she said. Elaine couldn't quite see where the voice was coming from for a moment, then saw the hand holding the glass floating in front of her. As she drank the milk, she heard Wendy softly humming a tune.

"Mmm," Elaine said. "You know what? That's real milk refreshment!"

"Shut up," Dominique said.

"What's that you're humming?" Elaine said. They were practically through the bank of smoke now. Its outer edges were almost visible.

"Oh that," Wendy said. "It's nothing."

"It sounds familiar."

"Yeah, well. I call it the *Naked Music,* to tell you the truth," Wendy said. There was a long pause. "I bet you think that's nuts."

"No," Elaine said. "I don't think that's nuts. It's nice, really."

"It's kindly," Wendy said.

"Hey," Dominique said suddenly, listening to Wendy's song. Then more softly, she said it again: "Hey." A look of distant recognition spread across her face, as if something long forgotten had been returned to her. For a moment she stopped walking, stunned by this feeling of unexpected restoration.

"You'll like my house," Wendy said. "It's got stuff in it."

"I can't see anything," Elaine said.

"What did you say before?" Dominique said distantly. Wendy and Elaine were becoming vague figures in this thick sulfuric haze. "Life is long? Life is sweet?"

"That's it," Wendy said. By now she had vanished entirely. "That's it exactly."

"Where are we?" Elaine said. "We're lost!"

For a moment there was a gap of fresh air in the smoke, leaving them stunned and blinking in the soft light of the stars. Then, just as quickly, another arm of the cloud stretched forward and enveloped them.

Wendy's voice echoed gently through the smoke. She was laughing.

"You're not lost," she said.

AUTHOR'S NOTE

The town of Centralia in this novel, like its inhabitants, is fictional. Anyone wishing to learn more about the real Centralia may wish to read *Unseen Danger,* by David DeKok, or *Slow Burn,* by Renée Jacobs. Both of these excellent books are published by the University of Pennsylvania Press.

JAMES BOYLAN was born in 1958 and grew up in Newtown Square and Devon, Pennsylvania. He holds degrees from Wesleyan University and Johns Hopkins University. His first book, a collection of short stories, *Remind Me to Murder You Later,* was published in 1988, and was followed by a novel, *The Planets,* in 1991. Since 1988 he has been a professor of English at Colby College. He lives in Belgrade Lakes, Maine, with his wife, Deirdre, and his son, Zachary.

ABOUT THE TYPE

This book was set in Baskerville, a typeface that was designed by John Baskerville, an amateur printer and typefounder, and cut for him by John Handy in 1750. The type became popular again when the Lanston Monotype Corporation of London revived the classic Roman face in 1923. The Mergenthaler Linotype Company in England and the United States cut a version of Baskerville in 1931, making it one of the most widely used typefaces today.